CHOOSING ME

TONI KING

AMARO GROUP
PUBLISHING

www.AmaroGroupServices.com

CHOOSING ME
Copyright © 2024 TONI KING

Paperback ISBN: 978-1-961673-04-5

To those who have stood by me, believed in me, and offered support —My gratitude is endless.

And to you, the reader, who has navigated through your own challenges to find these words, this book is also for you. In sharing this journey, I hope you find a reflection of your resilience and the possibility of new beginnings.

Thank you for embracing this story. Together, let's dream big, for anything is truly possible.

Chapter 1

NADIA

So, let me tell you a little about myself and my circle. There are four of us. We grew up like sisters. There is Mel Cannon. Mel is short for Melissa. Then there's Eboni Edge, Terri Price, and myself, Nadia Stone. Mel and I grew up together. We were neighbors. Mel's mom was heavy on drugs, and it got worse as the years passed. So, at the age of ten, Mel and her brothers had to go live with her grandmother. Thank God her grandmother let her stay in the same school with the rest of us, and she could still spend the night at my house all the time. It felt like nothing had changed. When we graduated elementary school, we made sure we were able to go to the same middle school. We were all we had. We met Eboni in our 7th-grade year of middle school. She was a no-nonsense, feisty girl, and we loved it. The three of us automatically clicked. A few years later, in high school, we met Terri; she was also amazing and fit right in with our circle of sisters. At that point, we knew we were complete—the four stooges. We made a pact to never give up on each other. We would always be there for each other, no matter what was going on or what we were going through.

I grew up with both parents, two sisters, and two brothers. I am the baby. I had the chance to experience being an auntie before entering high school. I am spoiled, but not in a disgustingly bad way. I guess that's the benefit of being the baby, but at the same time, they are all overprotective of me. My parents always provided and made sure we never lacked. We didn't have it all, but it never felt that way, and they were always willing to help, give back, donate, whatever it took. If they didn't have it, we never knew. Our childhood was great, and I am forever grateful for the sacrifices they made for us.

I haven't been in a relationship for about three years. I have gone on a few dates, but nothing worth talking about—no big deal. I decided to take the time to invest in myself. The girls and I are always taking trips. Local or out of the country, you name it. We had a trip set to go to Bora Bora in a few weeks. Now, this trip has been in the making for a while. It's not every day you hear someone saying they're going to Bora Bora. We had to make sure everything was in order for this one. I've been really busy these past few months, and this "vacay" is more than needed.

Eboni just launched her new makeup line, and it's already flying off the shelves. Terri is a model, a very sexy one at that. Everything is going great for her as well. Mel is a well-known worldwide chef who can throw down in the kitchen. I am a writer, and I'm also a professional Interior designer. I remember, while growing up, my mom would always take me to the crafts stores. I used to hate it at first, but with time, I started to pay close attention. She would buy different fabrics and make curtains for the living room, bathroom, and kitchen. One day, I asked her if I could help, and she allowed me to design one room in the house. To my surprise, I had so much fun doing it. I could tell she was impressed. Everyone initially thought it was mommie who did it, but she quickly told them it was me. I received so many compliments. From that day, I knew I loved designing. Who would have thought that it would make such a significant impact on my life? To this day, I thank my mom because I got my decorating touch from her. I love my freedom, being free, coming and going as I please, and not having to answer to anyone is one of the best feelings ever. We're all entrepreneurs!

As I'm getting ready for this trip, I'm so excited and don't know what to pack. My phone rang, it was Mel. She asked, "What's up girly?"

"Nothing much, just trying to pack."

"So soon?"

"Yes, Mel, you know I'm not a procrastinator like you. I just can't."

Mel laughed and said, "Girl, I know; you should come and pack for me too."

"You know I will."

We both giggled.

"Have you heard from Eb and Riri?" I asked,

"Yeah, they told me they wanted us to meet this Friday evening to try out this new restaurant that opened a few weeks ago and get a few drinks. Plus, we have to celebrate Eb's launch. Eb said it's been a while since we hung out."

"Oh my god, really? You guys were just over here like three days ago. Well, I guess that's long." She laughed. "Why didn't they call me?"

"Because I called Terri, and they were together, I told them I would call you. So, stop being a crybaby and get in the shower. You can finish packing tomorrow. I'll be there in about an hour."

"We really need to find you a man, a one-night stand or something, Damn it! So, is this what this night is about?"

"Of course not, Nadia, but I'm sure you have some needs that your dildo; what do you call him? Tristan can't fulfill."

"Hahaha, very funny, Mel."

"Go find a sexy dress; I'll be there soon. Eb said she would come a little early to do your makeup. I'll bring my keys."

All I could do was shake my head. Nothing surprises me with these ladies anymore. I love them like my blood sisters. I went ahead and did as I was told. I put on the radio; Beyonce was playing, *yes, you guessed it,* Single Ladies. Turning the volume up where I could hear it through the water, I jumped in the shower. The water felt so good dripping down my body. It had been a long day of running around trying to tie loose ends before our trip in a week and a half. We were going to be gone for a week. I didn't want to come back and have to go straight to work; no one should have to.

In the shower, my thoughts began to drift. As the water began rolling down my body, I closed my eyes. I imagined my man joining me, kissing me on my neck and whispering what he would do to me while making his way to my nipples. Before I could get the moan out, I heard Eb and Mel enter the house. They were a little loud. Who am I kidding, they were very loud, caught up in their conversations, and just laughing.

Mel said, "Nad, we're here. We decided to come here and get ready if that's okay with you. Terri is on her way."

Now they know that I wouldn't have a problem, and if I

did, what difference would it make at this point? I yelled back that I was in the shower, and it was cool with me.

I have a four-bedroom house, so they all had a designated space to get comfortable. We all had our areas at each other's house, yet we always ended up in one space.

After my shower, I came out in my robe. Both Mel and Eboni were lying comfortably on my bed, laughing and talking about our trip. One thing I can say about these ladies is that they are beyond confident. I ask myself sometimes, how do I fit in with them? Mel has thick, black, bouncy hair that reaches the middle of her back. She is 5 feet 4 inches, very sexy, and has a flat stomach and a B-cup. You can imagine what she looks like in her clothes. Eb is a beautiful chocolate woman; her hair is short and funky to match her no-nonsense, feisty attitude. She, too, has a very sexy sex appeal. She is 5 feet 9 inches, a slim C-cup with a nice round booty to match. You just want to squeeze it. Terri, well, as we already know, Terri is a model. She is 6 feet 3 inches, no joke, and she kills it every time she puts those heels on. Her hair is shoulder-length; she doesn't care for long hair. It doesn't get far past her shoulders before she's chopping it again. She is an A-cup, which in my opinion works well for her profession, and she has hips and a nice booty.

Now, I'm 5 feet 6 inches with thick, curly hair. I'm a double D with a flat stomach that I bust my ass to get and keep especially when your bestie is a chef. I have a nice booty with hips to match; maybe that's where the food is going. I can't forget my dimples, my best feature if you ask me.

They make fun of me, saying I'm not girly enough, always telling me that if I decide to invest in my girliness, I can stop the crowd. I am girly, just not as much as they would like. If you compare me to them, I may not be girly at all. I love them, though; they keep me on my toes. Before I knew it, they were in my closet, finding me something to wear tonight, totally disregarding what I originally picked out and it didn't stop there, they began picking out what they thought I should take to Bora Bora.

"You need to show more skin," Eb said. Just then, I heard Terri come in.

"Goodnight, ladies," Terri greeted.

"Hey Terri, so, what are the plans?" I asked.

Terri replied, "Well, first, I need y'all to get in the shower so we can get the ball rolling." Mel entered my shower, Eb entered the guest bathroom, and Terri waited for the first available bathroom. We sat there and caught up.

Terri said, "This big fashion show is coming up, and I will be a part of it. It's in a little over a month, and I want you guys to be there. I just left my agent's office. That's why I'm running a little late."

I exclaimed, "Oh my god, Riri, this is amazing. I'm so happy for you. You know we're always down to support you. Where is it?"

Terri had a nervous smirk on her face.

I asked again, "Riri, where is it?"

"ITALY!"

I started screaming with excitement, and I startled Mel in the shower.

Mel asked, "Is everything okay out there? What's with all the noise?"

I replied, "We're going to Italy!"

Mel started screaming as well and ran out of the shower.

I told her, "Riri is going to be part of a big fashion show in a little over a month."

Mel said, "Congratulations, Riri, I know you can make

anything happen. Please, get the exact dates so we can get our tickets and hotel."

Excitedly, Terri said, "Okay. Also, are you done with the shower?"

Mel replied, "Oh yeah, sorry."

When Eboni came out of the shower, we told her the great news. It was about 7:30 p.m., and everyone was getting dressed. Eb just got done with my makeup. I swear, she is a master at what she does. The ladies looked stunning. Mel had on a sexy red dress that was a little over her knees, Eboni had on a black backless dress that hugged every curve on her body, and Terri had on a leopard dress that screamed confidence; not everyone can pull leopard off. I wore a little black dress that stopped over my knees and had a deep v-cut. You couldn't tell us we weren't fly! We were excited; we hadn't dressed to go out in a while. We always hung out, but nights like this weren't as often as they used to be, especially with our busy schedules. We took a couple of selfies and group selfies and exited the house. Eb decided that she was going to drive.

We hopped into her 2019 BMW and began our girl's night. Music was blasting as we drove down to this beautiful restaurant. This was the first stop; reservations were already made. We pulled up and valet parked then we walked our grown and sexy asses into the restaurant. We ate, and laughed, the dinner vibes were amazing, and the food was great.

Mel said, "Terri, I know this really nice lounge/ club we can go to; maybe Nadia can find someone to clear her mind for a few days."

We all laughed.

I asked, "Why are you guys always picking on me?"

Eboni answered, "We love you, but three years is a long time not to release, explode, scream, and moan."

I replied, "Ummm, well, occasionally, I release my stress, and I can put it back in the drawer. I don't have to worry about where he is and who he's doing."

Mel said, "Like I was saying, no one wants to hear about Tristan. I'm talking about some real dick. Dick that will make you arch your back. Nad, you can't keep going through your life like this."

I replied, "I'm starting to wonder if this is a dick intervention."

"Let's go out and have a good time and promise us that if someone shows interest in you, you won't be quick to shut them down."

I replied, "Fine, I'll try."

All the ladies at the same time, "Man, we already know what that means."

We all laughed.

We pulled up to the club that Terri recommended. It was nice, the vibes were nice, *boy oh boy, there were some fine, fine men in there; maybe one of them may get lucky,* I thought. We made it to a table, started with two bottles, and vibed to the sounds of Rihanna. We took our first drink and then Terri drifted off into the crowd. She became temporarily out of sight. While moving to the music, a guy came to me and asked for a dance, and I agreed. My girls smirked, and I heard Mel say, "Maybe that will be the lucky dick she gets to ride tonight." We walked into the crowd. We danced; he said his name was Brandon. Without missing a beat, Brandon pulled himself closer to me, and I felt his man parts rubbing on my ass. It had been a long time since I felt the hard stiffness of a man. I was getting a little turned on. I looked over to our table, and no one was there. Looking around, I saw Mel in the crowd having a good time, dancing with a guy who seemed like he couldn't get enough of her. Eb was walking from the bar back to the table with a drink that a guy just bought for her. I finished dancing with Brandon and returned to the table to get a drink. Eboni and I gazed through the crowd and saw Terri still turning up; she loves having a good time. Suddenly, I heard Eb say, "That guy you were dancing with, he's coming over."

I exclaimed, "For what!"

Eb replied, giggling, "He's fine though, just put it on him once, do it for you, hell, do it for us; you don't have to see him again."

She was right. He was indeed very handsome, well-dressed, and earlier on, his dick felt wonderful through his pants. Unconsciously, I started wondering what it would feel like inside me; but I quickly shrugged it off. I swear these ladies are rubbing off on me. Then I heard his voice say,

"Hey Nadia, I don't want to seem pushy, but just in case I don't see you before I leave, I just wanted to know if we could exchange numbers?"

I gave him my number, and we spoke for a few minutes; then, Eb and I returned to the dance floor and danced some more. This night turned out to be absolutely amazing; what wouldn't I do for my sisters? Terri finally made her way back to us in the crowd; I saw Mel coming from the bathroom to join us.

Eb had her share of relationships, so at this point; she just wanted to live with no commitment. Mel had her boyfriend, Jeff. They had been on and off for as long as I can remember, but they loved each other. Terri, she's just living and enjoying life and of course, there's me.

It was Friday night, so there was no need to rush home; we drank and danced like there was no tomorrow. I woke up Saturday morning on the couch in the living room, starving!

Everyone was still sleeping. I ordered breakfast, extra tea, and coffee. We had a busy day ahead of us.

We were looking forward to our trip to Bora Bora. We had some things planned out for when we got there, including relaxing—a much-needed relaxation.

Chapter 2

I sat there while they were sleeping and wondered where I had gone wrong. I know you're wondering why I've been single for so long; Well, let me tell you.

I started dating this guy two weeks into my first semester of college. We hit it off right away. He had one child, and I honestly didn't want to go any further once he told me, but I'm not judgmental, plus I really liked him. As time passed, we got closer, and my family loved him. He brought his son around, and everything, I must say, was going great, outside of the fact that the mother of his son had her imaginary problem with me. She would send messages to try to start problems. She even tried to turn his son against him. You name it, she tried it. It became so annoying and frustrating that I thought about leaving him. I had a lot going on already with school. My goal was to make sure I could work for myself and get my degree. No one was going to get in the way of that.

Andre proposed to me two years into our relationship, and of course, I said yes. I loved this man. I loved everything about him. Our sex life was everything. His touch alone could make me have an orgasm, the way he sucked my nipples, Jesus! I swear the first time he sucked my toes, my spirit left my body, and the way he made love to my womanhood with his mouth, Lord have mercy! We made love anywhere and anytime we had the chance. It wasn't just about sex, I really felt like we were connected. Time passed, and we were getting ready to plan the wedding. I was so, so, so excited; my girls were just as excited as we planned and picked a location. My dreams were finally coming true. Here it was: I had the man of my dreams, three of the best friends a girl could ask for, and I was graduating soon. Then it happened. Three weeks until the big day, my life was turned upside down. I received a phone call from a friend, "There's something I need you to see." Check your phone. Hearing my phone going off, I was nervous, gasping for air as I opened the messages. It was pictures of my husband to be on a date with the mother of his son. I tried not to overthink it. Maybe they were discussing their child. After all, they have to communicate, but those thoughts went out the window once message after message started pouring in with their conversations, pictures with them on dates, you name it. He had been cheating on me with her for some time, let's say over a year.

My friend said, "I'm so sorry to throw all of this on you, Nadia, but you're a good woman, and I know your big day is coming up, but you have the right to know."

"Thank you, thank you so much." Was all I could muster up at that moment.

I was angry, livid, but more so, hurt. How could he do this to me? He claimed he couldn't stand her, yet alone like her, or want to have anything to do with her, and here he was in a fucking relationship with her, going on dates to basketball games, concerts, and fucking her while he was with me. Why didn't he leave? He could have just left! I was full of rage; I felt angry, he had me looking like a fool, and this bitch thinking she had something over me. Not too long after, Eboni stopped by, and I told her everything. I couldn't hide it; she could clearly see that I had been crying. She was ready to fight, she was angry, but we had to be mindful because we had a lot going on. We were angry because this bitch knew me. It's not like she was some random woman who didn't know left from right and just had to go with what she was being told. That's who you call a desperate, no-class jezebel, harlot hoe. If I didn't care about our future, all I had to do was give EB the okay, and she would be at that bitch's house, NOW! Once Eb calmed down, she called Mel and Terri three-way and told them. I couldn't stop crying; I couldn't understand why. My heart was gone. Then I came up with a plan. Dre came home that night.

"Hey, baby."

"Hey, Dre, I replied

How was your day?" He asked.

"Full of surprises.

Good surprises, I hope.

"Only if you knew Andre."

"What was that babe?" He asked.

"I guess you can say it was." I replied, "Oh, okay, good. Andre, is there anything I need to know before our big day?"

"No, babe, you already know how much I love you and how happy, thankful, and grateful I am that you are in my life, and I can't wait to make you my wife. Mrs. Nadia Bell, doesn't that sound great? Mr. & Mrs. Bell."

"Yeah, it does," I replied.

He asked, "What's wrong, baby? You don't sound like yourself; as a matter of fact, you look like you've been crying."

"I'm fine, baby, just don't feel good, plus it's been a long day."

It took everything in me to keep my cool because I wanted to snap and finish it with a punch in his mouth.

I said, "I've been thinking and decided that since there are three weeks left until the wedding, we shouldn't sleep with each other anymore; it will be fun; you know, save something for the honeymoon."

"Are you serious, Nad? I wanted to put it on you tonight!"

I replied, "I bet you did!"

I couldn't help but laugh at that one.

I told him, "You will be okay. Before you know it, I'll be Mrs. Bell, and you can rock my world."

He walked up to me from behind and tried to whisper in my ear. He knew how sensitive I was to his touch. I almost gave in, but it was too late for him. He would have had me rushing to take my clothes off any other time just by doing that.

"I'm really tired." I said, "I'm just going to take a shower and go to bed."

The next day, Mel called me. I told her, "Girl, it's okay, Mel, I got this. Go ahead and plan the bachelorette party, and make sure we have an amazing time. I'm going to need it."

Mel said, "I'm so sorry, Nadia."

I interrupted, "Don't be; it's just another life lesson that, unfortunately, I have to experience."

Everything was set for the wedding. I couldn't cancel it; people had already paid for their tickets from different places, states, countries, and hotels. The hall and dresses had been paid for. We couldn't disappoint the people. The two weeks leading to the day of the wedding were so hard; to make it worse, Dre had been extra clingy and wouldn't leave me alone. I had to drown myself in school, work, and the wedding to keep myself busy so I wouldn't lose it. One time, I caught myself rolling up to this bitch's house and sitting in the parking lot. I had to remind myself that she wasn't worth it.

The week of the wedding came. It felt like the longest three weeks ever. I ensured everything was in place as I continued praying for God to give me all the strength He could dish out. Three nights before the bachelor and bachelorette party, Dre left his phone open on the bed, and she happened to text him, "I miss you; I haven't seen you in two weeks. I know it will be hard for you to sneak away, but even if it's for one day out of the week, that's fine; just stop ignoring me; I need you. I'll give you a key to come and go as you please. I know how to play the role; talk to me, please. Andre, please call me." I sighed in disgust reading that shit. I had never seen anyone so desperate in my life.

Mel gave me the best bachelorette party any woman could ask for. It was different, and she knew just what I needed. So many people made it. Those strippers looked finger-licking good and were willing to do whatever you requested. We drank until we couldn't drink anymore, but honestly, I didn't drink that much; they didn't know that, even though I had all rights to. Plus, someone had to ensure we made it to the wedding in one piece.

* * *

On the wedding Day, I was nervous, angry, and had all kinds of emotions running through my body. I felt nauseous walking down the aisle, the sight of him there was enough to make me turn around and head straight back to my house; but people were present, smiling, and taking pictures. So I took a deep breath and willed my legs to move towards Andre, who was at the altar, looking as handsome as ever. He smiled at me. He was tall and handsome. When we first met, he had a fade, but he had let his hair grow, so now it was braided. I loved his beard, and he always said it was my beard because my fingers were in it every chance I got. The tears started rolling; he looked so happy up there. *I thought he loved me, so why did he put me in this situation? Maybe I was making a mistake with what I was about to do. Maybe I should just run out now. Nope, I have to do it.* It felt like forever before I could make it up to him. I made it. The priest started talking, and Dre wanted to say his vows first. Perfect. Dre was saying all that good stuff that I would have believed once upon a time. His words and the passion in his voice almost made me fall for it and forget my plan. The tears came down uncontrollably, and I started to feel sick. I drank the night before, but not that much. When it was my turn to say my vows, I started to feel sorry for him; he was gazing into my eyes. He was happy; at least someone was. Still holding hands, I said, "Dre, you know I love you with everything in me."

He smiled and nodded his head.

I continued, "You promised never to hurt me, and you know how the saying goes, dating is just a preview and practice for what you will have in your marriage, so doing good in dating should mean you will have a better marriage, right?"

He said, "Baby, you know I will never hurt you; you are my world, and there has never been anyone like you all my life." The timing couldn't have been better.

"Dre, I gave you all these years of my life and this is what you did to me?"

Right then, Mel played the video.

I continued, "You shattered my heart and one thing I know is the pieces can never go back into place. I would ask you why, but it doesn't matter anymore."

Dre was shocked! He couldn't move as the video showed the texts up to the other night, the emails, and the pictures. Everything was big enough, and there was a clear view.

I continued, "You played me for her; you hurt me for her. There is nothing you can say to justify this, but I hope she was worth it. Now you can be with her."

He stared at me; I could hear the shocking gasps, sighs, and whispers of everyone around us.

"Let me explain, Nadia," he said, grabbing my arm to pull me closer.

"Andre, there is nothing you can do or say to explain this long-ass affair you had going on. Please, let me go. I'll send your things to your mom's or whoever's house they need to go to. It was amazing, and I really did love you, which you already know."

He stood there, tears rolling down his face, as I ran off.

He cried, "Nadia, please, Nadia."

The only thing I remember hearing was someone saying to call the ambulance. I had passed out. I was rushed to the hospital; my blood pressure increased from dealing with everything. The doctor came into my room, asked me a few questions, and told me I was pregnant. "Pregnant?" I asked.

The doctor replied, "Yes, Nadia, so please take it easy once you leave here."

I replied, "Will do."

I was still trying to register everything she said. Almost all my close family and friends, even Andre, came to the hospital. You can see that he cared, and he was concerned. The ladies wouldn't let him come into the room.

I could hear his voice, "Mel, is she okay?"

"No, Dre, she isn't, but you should know that she's pregnant."

He was happy and overwhelmed with joy.

Mel said, "This should have been news we would celebrate after your honeymoon, Dre, you really fucked up a good thing."

He replied, "I know, Mel, I know.

* * *

After I was released from the hospital, everything hit me again, I felt so sad. Terri took me home. Eb and Mel returned to the reception hall with the rest of the family to make sure that the guests were having a good time, to apologize on my behalf, and to help my parents out.

At home, I didn't even shower. I took my dress off and crawled into bed. Terri made me some tea, she lay in bed with me, and we cried until I fell asleep. When I woke up, Riri had left. She did leave a note saying, "I didn't want to wake you, Nad; I'll be back later. I went to help out at the reception." I looked at my phone: over 100 missed calls and text messages from my mom, dad, nieces, nephews, cousins, sisters and brothers, Dre's family, and of course, Dre. I didn't want to be bothered, so I turned off my phone and cried. I cried, cried until I fell back to sleep. I woke up the next afternoon not in the mood to do anything. I was tired and drained. I lay there just staring at the ceiling; my phone was still turned off. I heard someone come into the house. I was a little nervous at first because Dre still had keys. It was Eb and Terri. Thank God because I didn't have the strength to deal with him. I heard them talking while walking to my room. They walked in, smiled, and just lay on my bed with me. Mel brought some food. I said, "I'm not hungry." They began screaming at me, "It's been twenty-four hours; we know you haven't eaten anything other than drinking the tea since Terri left. You need to eat! Plus, you have our niece or nephew in there; you will eat." I felt sad again. They said, "Nadia, you need to turn your phone on."

I asked, "Why? There's no need to; I don't want to talk to anyone. I just want to lay here until I'm ready. I need to get Dre's stuff out of here, too. I can smell him. Maybe tomorrow I'll pack his stuff; I think I want to move; I can't be here."

Terri said, "Remember the doctor said you need to relax, no stressing."

I replied, "I know, Terri, but that's easier said than done."

Mel went back and brought me some soup. To make them happy, I ate a little bit and drank some juice. Mel also brought me some prenatal pills. We laid on the bed, and they watched a movie while I cried myself to sleep.

"Get up, Nadia," Mel said. I didn't even realize I slept until the next day.

"Get in the shower!"

"What time is it?"

"9:20 a.m. We're taking you out of this house! I know you don't want to, but we will not let you lay here like this, not even today," Eboni said.

My eyes began to water for many different reasons, one was because of these three ladies. What would I have done without them? I got in the shower; it had been like three days since water last touched my skin. I made the water as hot as my body could take, letting it hit me from my head down to my toes. I washed my hair, cried, and let it all out in the shower. So much was running through my mind; sleeping was the best thing, except the first night when Dre came into my dreams. In the dream everything was so right, it was like nothing ever happened; we celebrated our pregnancy.

"Nadia, are you okay in there? It's been about forty-five

minutes; I know it's been a few days, but I have to check." Terri's question broke through my thoughts. I smiled through the tears, Terri knew how to make me smile, and I was happy she interrupted those thoughts. Everything happening was so much harder than I thought it would be. "I'm coming out now."

When I came out of the bathroom, Terri had a nice little summer dress on the bed. I slipped it on and sipped on some mint tea Eb had made, it was my favorite. Mel had started packing Andre's things and I was really grateful to her that I wouldn't have to deal with that emotional battle. Standing in front of my mirror, I looked at myself. Fully seeing who I am and all that I am supposed to be. I let my hair down today and let my curls take control. I allowed it to flow in the wind. I didn't leave my hair down often but today, anything went. I grabbed my phone from the dresser. Someone had to have charged it, the battery was full. We hopped into Terri's car and took a drive to the beach. Usually, when any of us was down, we would go to the beach, wet our feet, sometimes we talked, sometimes we were silent. So that's what we did. Being there, surrounded by the most precious people in my life, I couldn't hold it in, and I cried, we cried. After some moments, I turned my phone on and saw I had almost one hundred texts from Andre. I missed him; I was only human, but this was one thing I couldn't tolerate. I decided to call him back. I was pregnant with his child, though I knew it would take some time before I could really face him.

"Hey baby, how are you feeling? I've been worried about you." Dre said once he answered the phone. *Is he serious?*

"Why were you calling me? What do you want?"

He replied, "Do you really think I wasn't going to? I just wanted to make sure that you and our baby were okay."

"You know what, Dre! I'm not okay, which you already know, but I will be. So stop acting like you care because you don't. Once I have all your stuff together, you will be notified."

"Nadia, I'm so sorry. I was…"

"Stop!" I hung up before he could finish his sentence. I couldn't put myself through this again right now. I hate him for this. We hung out at the beach for a little longer and then went to Eboni's house, so I didn't have to go home. Having a different scenery helped. Eb had a beautiful three-bedroom house. Her personality was all over it. She had a thing for art. It made sense as she was a makeup artist. There were some beautiful pieces on her wall. In her backyard, she had a pool with an attached Jacuzzi. We sat in the living room while she showed us some of her ideas for the line she wanted to bring out. The colors were amazing. We went to the backyard, where they drank some Amaretto, and I had a glass of iced tea. We laughed a little then I dozed off on the lounge chair. Sleeping was my best friend right now. I woke up to a harsh pain in my stomach. I screamed. That's how bad it was.

Mel jumped up, "Nadia, are you okay?" She tried to help me get up, but I couldn't. Terri got on the other side, and they carried me to the car. "You are bleeding," Eboni said. I was feeling lightheaded, and my heart was racing. I knew I was going to lose my baby. I was crying.

Terri said, "Just hold on, Nad, we're going to get you to the hospital. Don't cry." Once in the car, Terri drove like a mad woman and ran a few lights, but she got us there in one piece. I was rushed into the emergency room where I was told I had lost my baby. I was almost two months pregnant. I was going to go to the doctor next week, but my baby didn't make it because of all the stress and my blood pressure which hadn't gone down well enough. I was heartbroken all over again. I had to stay overnight at the hospital; they didn't want to leave me, but I told them to go. I asked Mel to please get Dre's things out of my house and if she could do so before I got home. She told me she would get her brother to help her and get it done the next day. I didn't want to involve them in all this, but I felt a little better with them than calling my brothers. I told them that I loved them and would see them the next day. Once they left, I cried. I was surprised I still had tears left. My heart was broken twice. I couldn't sleep. Every time I closed my eyes, I got a vision of them together, the messages, the thought of Dre satisfying her the way he did me, or even better, then coming home to me like he did nothing wrong. I became angry again. My nurse entered my room and said, "You need to relax, or you will be here longer than you want. You're a nice girl. You're young, don't make this your final stop."

I was released the following morning. Mel picked me up, and she brought me a change of clothes because my dress was ruined. We returned to my house, and she stayed with me for a few hours.

"Mel, you did an amazing job."

"Thank you."

"I would have never known a guy stayed here." The house did look like I was its only occupant, there were no signs that someone had lived there with me.

"I got your back, always. I have to go prep some food. I have a catering job tomorrow. Once I'm done, I'll be back. I made you some food; please make sure to eat, you need the strength."

"Well, since you made it, I guess I have no choice."

We laughed and hugged. She said, "I spoke to your mom. She will be stopping by later today with your sisters, and of course, you know Eb and Terri will be in and out. By the way, I told Dre what happened, and he cried. He really cried to the point that Brian had to walk away. I did go off on him, maybe a little more than I should have, but he took it all in. I told him not to contact you again and that he should call me if he needs to know anything because he has done too much damage, and you need your space. He wanted me to let you know that he loves you, and he's truly sorry and knows that won't heal your heart, but he's sorry."

"Thank you, Mel, I love you."

"Love you more."

* * *

"Nad, Nad, Nadia! Are you okay?" I looked up and saw Eb standing there looking at me. My face was wet from crying, I hurriedly wiped my face with my hands hoping she hadn't seen it yet. I think I was too late. She asked, "Are you okay?"

"Yep, I'm fine," I said. Trying to switch the subject, "I ordered breakfast. Is everyone still sleeping?"

Eb replied, "Terri went to pee; she woke me up while trying to rush to the bathroom. Mel is still sleeping."

"Okay, well, let's wake her up; we need to eat and get our day started."

"Okay, I'll wake her," Eb said. "Have you eaten yet?"

I answered, "Nope. I was waiting for you guys to wake up."

Eb woke Mel up, "Good morning, everyone."

"Hey, sleepyhead. There's breakfast, coffee, and tea in the kitchen; eat. I'm about to take a shower."

I'm so happy that Eboni snapped me out of that. It's a place in my life I never want to revisit. Sometimes, we are better understood when our story is told. I saw Andre a few months later; he tried to speak, but my heart wasn't ready. Then we ran into each other again. We exchanged words, nothing much; his feelings were still there, but mine were tucked away. I heard Mel go into the other shower, and as I came out, Terri went in. I found some sweatpants and a cami. I love wearing no bra, but these Double Ds don't give me that option sometimes, so I take advantage of the opportunity when possible. I have the biggest boobs out of us all, so I get a little jealous occasionally. Eb was the last to get in the shower. While they were getting ready, I ate breakfast and drank my mint tea. We went to pick up a few more items for our trip. Eboni even brought two boxes of condoms; she said she was going to make memories. We all laughed at her. She was too much, but we knew she was serious. We went to Dick's Sporting Goods to get our wetsuits. Snorkeling was a must. We had a few things planned: Jet skiing, ATV riding, Hiking, Snorkeling, and a day or two to relax. Knowing us, we may add a few more things to the list just because this trip is about celebrating life and accomplishments. We worked hard to get where we were, and it was time we enjoyed it.

"Hey, Eboni, Terri, Melissa,"

Mel screamed out, laughing, "Oh my God! Nad called us by our full names."

Eb replied, "I know, right? What did we do?

"Oh oh," Riri said.

They thought it was hilarious. I asked, "Did you guys pack your stuff?" They burst out laughing at the same time. "Well, of course not."

I replied, "Okay, I don't want to hear that y'all forgot anything."

Riri replied, "We're going to go home after we're finished and get it done, I promise."

I said, "Okay, Riri, if you say so. You're just going to throw the whole closet in the suitcase."

"You too," Mel said.

I told her, "Yeah, but the difference is, I'm almost done. Once I put in what we brought and add a few more things, I'm done. I'm going to have a relaxing Sunday."

Eb mocked me, "I'm going to have a relaxing Sunday." We laughed. We store-hopped a little longer and grabbed some ice cream. Then we went back to my house. We hung out for a while before they left. I put on my favorite Whitney Houston CD to get me in the mood to finish packing. I love me some Whitney. Once I was done, I put the two suitcases and my carry-on in the living room. That wasn't too far in case I had to add more things. I cleaned up a little, lit some candles, and went to take a bath. I made the water a little hotter than usual because by the time I get in there, the temperature will be just right, and lit some candles around the tub, which set the mood. I sat in the tub and began to relax. I closed my eyes and allowed the music to take over. Joe's 'All the Places' was now playing. I began to caress my breast; it had been so long since I had been touched and felt the heat of someone's body on mine. I slowly moved my hands to my womanhood and played with my clit. As I rubbed my hands up and down, it felt so good. I had Tristan waiting for me. I usually caught myself thinking about Dre at times like this. He was the last person I had been with sexually. I slowly inserted Tristan while he vibrated inside me. Continuing to caress my clit, I started to moan, and my juices erupted all over him. Tristan always got the job done but for the first time I wasn't satisfied, I wanted and needed more. I hope I meet someone in Bora Bora, even if it's a one-night stand. I miss the feeling of a real dick inside me being caressed by my walls, someone to hold on to while he makes me cum and beg him not to stop. I got out of the bath feeling refreshed and washed off in the shower. I got a glass of wine and lay naked while watching a movie.

The day was finally here. Mel and Eb had spent the night. Terri came this morning. We're taking an Uber to the airport. Parking was one less thing we would have to worry about. We had to be there by 9:45 a.m. The flight was at12:45 p.m. When we get to Bora Bora, it would be about 5:30 p.m. We will be going back in time. We made it to the airport at 9:50 a.m. because we ran into some traffic; thank God it wasn't bad. We all had two suitcases plus our carry on, so we still had to get on the line.

Chapter 3

MEL

I remember meeting Nadia like it was yesterday. Maybe when she was five years old. We were next-door neighbors. Nadia was always nice to me. We went from being really cool to being inseparable. We told people we were sisters; that's just how it felt. The slumber parties were always the best. I loved being at her house; it was my second home. My mom was a heavy drug user and didn't care what my siblings and I were doing. I have three older brothers; I am the baby of the bunch. Nadia is the sister I never had. She also has two older brothers and two older sisters. So, when we were all together, it was so much fun. I'm a few months older than Nad. So, she's the baby sister. When we thought things were getting better with our mom, she took a turn for the worse; she returned to drug use and used more than before. Our dad was in and out of our lives and wasn't much help. It then got so bad with my mom that the day I never wanted to happen happened. We had to go live with our grandmother. She didn't live in the area. I was hurt, angry, upset, everything all in one because now, I wouldn't be able to see my sister every day. I might have to change schools, and my life will change because my mom was selfish. The day we were leaving, Nadia and I hugged each other so tight and cried; we didn't know when we would see each other again and didn't want to be apart. Luckily, Grandma left us all at our schools; she said she didn't want to put us through the transition of having to start over because she knew it could be rough sometimes, and we had enough going on with our mother. She also spoke to Nadia's mom, who agreed I could still spend nights and go to school from her house when needed. I was so happy. When I was there, I still saw my mom, but she was so caught up in her drug life that we didn't exist to her. Sometimes, she acted like she didn't know who we were when we tried to talk to her. That hurt so much. Nadia and her mom don't know what they did for me. I could never show my full gratitude to them. My life could've been different. Nad and I were like glue. No one could come between us, and believe me, people have tried. There wasn't anything that we didn't share with each other. In middle school, we met Eboni. She fit in like we knew her forever. By the time I got to my senior year of high school, my mom had enough of the drug life and decided to put herself in rehab. I was happy for her. I was glad she was ready to see life instead of watching it go by. I was still back and forth between Grandma's house and Nad's house. Her mom always said I was her daughter and never treated me any differently. We all got the same treatment, and when we did something wrong, we got the discipline that suited us. I remember her mom once said that if it were the other way around, she would want to know that her children were also treated well. Even my brothers had spent many nights and were shown the same love. Nadia's mom is the best; I see where she gets it. It was all love. Terri came along when we were in high school. It was amazing. I went from having one amazing sister to adding two more to the list. We've been together ever since. I started to feel the pressure a little during my senior year of high school. I wasn't sure what I wanted to do. I knew I loved to cook. Between my grandma and Nadia's mom, they showed me how to throw down, plus I added my own twist. My grandma always told me I could make a life out of cooking. I used to laugh at her; I thought she was doing what grandmas were supposed to do. One day, the ladies suggested I attend culinary school and see how far it would take me. I smiled and thought about Grandma. I must say, it was some good advice. I couldn't wait to share the news with my grandma. Right after high school, I got on it. I didn't waste any time. I went straight to culinary school. I kicked ass! I loved it. I was so good that the chefs recommended or sent me when they had big jobs, even for celebrities, or knew another chef who needed assistance. I never turned anything down. I knew my goals, and I would work hard until I didn't have too anymore. It got to the point that I was being requested; I couldn't believe it. That's when I knew I made it. They knew my name. I put my all into what I did; my name and reputation were attached. I remember going to a famous person's house. I'm not going to say who, but I was excited, and I kept my cool. Before I left, they asked for my number to do private services for different events they had coming up. I was told that if my food was as good as my personality, I had the power to take over. That meant a lot to me. I couldn't do anything but thank God and the people that believed in me and pushed me. Hard work pays off.

Jeff and I have been on and off, let's say since we graduated high school. We loved each other, but sometimes I feel like he isn't ready. Jeff is also a chef; his food is to die for, so I understand his schedule is just as busy as mine. Jeff is 6ft of fine chocolate, with the sexiest hazel eyes you can find. He is muscular and always told me he had to keep fit because he cooks and doesn't want to lose himself in his food or mine. He has a low fade; he switches up the type of style when he's in the mood. A few months ago, he had a mohawk. I love his free-spirited personality. That's my Jeff.

We were so excited to start planning for Nad's big day.

Nad asked, "Hey, girly, how are you?" Nad always has a little nickname for us.

"I'm good sissy, what's up?" I replied.

"Nothing much, just checking on you. We need to plan our next girl's night and get together."

"Okay, well, I'm meeting up with Jeff tonight, so we can do it tomorrow if everyone is free."

She responded, "I'm free; I'll check with Riri and Eb and see if they have any plans."

"I'll do it because Eb called me earlier, and I told her I would call her back."

"Okay, so you and Jeff are meeting up, huh? Go ahead and put it on him good tonight!"

"And you know this."

Nadia finished with, "Mannnnnn." We started laughing. She loves Chris Tucker.

She said, "Well let me know what they say; I'm down either way."

I replied, "Okay, I'm going to call her now. Cool, love ya, talk to you soon, love you too."

I called Eb, "Hey Eb, sorry about earlier; I was a little tied up and couldn't talk."

Eb replied, "I mean were you like literally tied up because that makes a difference." I expected nothing different from her. "No girl, I wish I was though, but we never know what may happen later. Are you free for girls' night tomorrow?"

"Hell yeah, that's what I called you about. It's been a while."

I swear I love her energy.

She asked, "How have you been? I know it's only been a week, but a lot can change or happen in that time."

"I'm great, Eb, how are you?

She answered, "Great as well."

"That's awesome. I look forward to seeing you guys tomorrow."

She asked, "Are you going to let Terri know?"

I replied, "I sure will. Once I find the meeting spot, I'll let everyone know. Love ya."

"Love you too."

I called Nadia back, as I promised, to let her know we were on for tomorrow. I told her to figure out the meet-up place and time and let us know. I got waxed earlier today. I love how soft and smooth my body feels. I jumped in the shower. I have to make sure my lady parts are all fresh. I love steaming hot water; it dripped from my head and rolled down my nipples. I wanted to start the party early. I rubbed my hands across my clit, caressing it like Jeff was on his knees and about to capture every drop of my juice in his mouth. I was moaning; the sensation was hitting me. I got on my knees; I felt like I was about to release. I let out a soft moan of satisfaction, getting more excited by the thought of being with Jeff. As I began to soap my body, my phone rang; it was my baby.

I answered, "Hey, Jeff."

He replied, "Hey baby, what's up?"

I asked, "We're still on for tonight, right?"

He answered, "Of course we are."

I asked, "Do you want me to come to you, or will you come over?"

He replied, "You can come over."

"I have a surprise for you.

You know I love surprises."

He responded, "I know, babe."

I said, "Okay, well, I'm getting out of the shower. I should be there in about forty-five minutes."

He replied, "Okay, see you soon."

I wanted to have a little fun tonight. I packed an overnight bag; even though I had clothes at his house, I never knew what I wanted to put on, plus I knew I wouldn't be coming back home tonight. I threw some toys in there, went into the back of my closet, and found my black trench coat. I put my hair in a bun, grabbed a pair of heels, and put my coat on. I turned off the lights, and I was on my way. Jeff doesn't live that far from me; I would say thirty- thirty-five minutes maximum. The drive was smooth. It's 8:30, and I was jamming to Erykah Badu. When I pulled up to Jeff's house, I parked in the driveway. There weren't many lights on in the house, which is no surprise. You were never sure if he was home. I grabbed my bag, fixed my lipstick, and walked to the front door. I could smell the aroma of the food and candles he was burning. I have a key but don't really use it because he leaves the door unlocked whenever I'm coming. Why? I don't know. I remember one time I did that; he was mad at me, said it wasn't safe, and that's why he had a key.

To my surprise, before I could open the door, he did. He was holding a glass of wine in his hand. He gave it to me, took my bag, placed it on the floor, and pulled me in for a hot, wet kiss. I almost dropped my glass. He always turns me on, always!

"Good night to you too," he smiled. We walked into the kitchen. He had cooked some sautéed potatoes, shrimp, and steak. His cooking was amazing. He taught me a few tricks as well. As he walked past me, I couldn't help but lick my lips. He had no shirt on, just boxers that showed how firm his ass was and the print of all that good dick. Jeff served our food, and we sat, talked for a long time, and drank more wine. I love our relationship; we can talk about anything, our conversations can jump to anything, and we would be comfortable. I got up and walked over to him, and we started kissing. He let out a slight moan that instantly turned me on, all the time. I opened my coat and let it drop to the floor while keeping my shoes on. He looked me up and down. I got to my knees and grabbed his trophy, slowly putting it in and out of my mouth. He moaned, slowly rubbing his balls as I sucked up and down. He gently tugged my hair. I was more turned on now!

As I'm sucking on his trophy, I began to play with myself; I could taste his precum in my mouth. He grabbed me, picked me up, and took me to the bedroom filled with candles. He slowly put me down on the bed and nibbled on my nipples, making his way to my candy box, as he inserts his tongue in and out, caressing my clit. I couldn't hold it back; he was taking in my entire flavor. I moaned out of control; he flipped me over, inserted his trophy into his prize, and stroked it slowly from the back, leaning forward to play with my nipples while nibbling on my ear. I was throwing it back, and he was catching it. He's keeping up, I felt drops of his sweat on my back, and just like that, we were done.

I woke up to Nad's message, "Hey ladies, we will meet up at Terri's house around 4 p.m. We will go to a restaurant at the beach and watch a movie."

It was about 9 a.m., so I made breakfast for Jeff and me. He had a few errands to run, so he left me at his house. I called Nad to see what she was up to. "Hey, Nad."

She replied, "Hey, sissy, what's going on?"

"I'm going to come to your house earlier, and we can drive

to Terri's house together. Jeff had some things to do; he left about an hour ago, and I don't want to be here by myself."

She replied, "Okay, well, come whenever you're ready; I'm still lying down, but I know what I'm going to wear."

I told her, "Girl, I hope it's something revealing!"

"No, just some jeans and a nice shirt with a pair of sandals."

I responded, "That's what I'm going to wear too! I'll be there in forty-five minutes. I'm going to take a shower."

I pulled up to Nad's house; I remembered I had a few people to do a catering event for and may need help. *I will ask Nadia if she can help.* I used my key to get in even though I tried not to use it much since she started dating Andre. I knew he wasn't there, so it was okay today. "I'm here," I yelled once I walked into the house so she wouldn't be startled. Nadia responded, "I'm in my room catching up on Power."

I said, "Okay, I'm going to get something to drink; I'll be there."

"Hey, Sista from another mista," she said, and we giggled.

One thing I love about our circle is that we are truly young at heart. We're big kids, always finding a reason to laugh and enjoy the moment.

"You look very refreshed Mel."

I replied, "Yes, Jeff worked me last night, and I slept like a baby."

She responded, "I bet you did."

"Nadia, before I forget, I may need a favor."

"Anything, what's up?"

"I have five catering jobs, and I wanted to know if you could help."

She said, "Well, you know I can't cook like you, right?"

"Girl, please, I just want you to help me prepare, and if you can, make like three two-layer cakes, maybe a pistachio, carrot cake, and a chocolate cake, you know when it comes down to baking you are the shit, I always wondered why you didn't push to start your own business in that area."

"I thought about it but it would take up too much time with everything else I have going on. I love it and don't mind doing it from time to time."

"I understand Nad. I'm going to be slicing it, so it should be enough. If I do need more, I'll let you know."

She replied, "No problem, I got you. So, when do we need this done?"

"The first event is in about a week and a half. This is a new client, and they came highly recommended, so I want to get in and show out."

"If you need me to be at the event, you know I will be there; I can put on that button-down shirt and black slacks and cater for you.

I told her, "I know you will. Thank you."

Nadia got up to get dressed, and I finalized my dates to get things started. Since Andre proposed a few weeks ago, Nad has had a different type of glow and happiness to her. I would do anything to keep that smile on her face.

Nadia said, "I'm ready. Let's head over to Terri's house before they start calling us and going off."

I laughed, "I know."

Nadia decided to drive while I finished up my work. Eboni pulled up at the same time we did to Terri's house. We hugged and made our way to the door. Terri has a very nice yet simple house. She doesn't like to clutter and loves mirrors; I'm not surprised. Her house has three bedrooms with lots of windows, it was very airy. "Terri, we're here."

"I'm still getting dressed," she said. Nad and Eb walked to the backyard; there was a little tiki bar and some lounge chairs back there. I was right behind them. Ten minutes later, Terri came out to tell us she was ready. We finished up our drink and jumped into Nad's car. We got to the restaurant Ocean2000 at 3:35 pm; our table was outside where we could enjoy the nice breezy weather. We talked, laughed, and caught up on the little things. We talked about the wedding, the date, and what needed to be finalized. At the movies, we had a ball. Watching Black Panther was amazing; we were like four big kids. Chadwick and all the cast members did their Thang. I'm telling you everyone walked in there feeling one way and came out another. It was beautiful seeing the culture represented. Once the movie was done, we went straight back to Terri's house. We didn't stay long because Andre was coming over in a few hours, and I promised Jeff I'd rock him back to sleep tonight.

Once we got to Nadia's house, I hung around for about thirty minutes and then headed home. Jeff was coming over tonight. I got home to my comfy three-bedroom, two-bathroom home. I love my house; I knew I had to have it when I first saw it. It's open and airy, with a two-car garage, but the kitchen sealed the deal. It was big! I had enough counter space to prepare my food, with a deep double sink. I had a kitchen window, which is a must and a plus. Every kitchen should have that natural light. I added my special touch to complete what I needed my kitchen to look like. I went and took a shower while I waited for Jeff to get here. I didn't even know when he got in. I just happened to be tossing around when I felt his body. I looked up, and he was sleeping. He had to be tired and came in late. I reached over and kissed him and went back to sleep. I woke up to the smell of breakfast in the air. That's his way of making up for coming over so late. I loved to eat, especially his cooking; it didn't matter what he made. My stomach started to growl, so I put my robe on and went to the kitchen. "Good morning, sleeping beauty."

I replied, "Morning, babe." And I kissed him.

He apologized, "I'm sorry about last night; everything ran later than expected."

I replied, "At least you still came. What time did you get in?"

"At about 2 a.m., you were out like a baby, and I didn't want to wake you. I'm happy to see you."

I replied, "I'm always happy to see you."

I swear he knew just what to say, and we kissed again. "I made scrambled eggs, strawberry waffles, and bacon," he said, "I also made you your favorite French vanilla cappuccino, and there is a smoothie in the fridge for later. Oh, I almost forgot, there's a salad for you and a bowl of mixed fruits. I don't want to hear you say, I don't make you anything healthy."

I replied, "Damn baby, what time did you get up to make all this?"

"Not too early; you know this is our thing. Once we get in the kitchen, it's easy breezy."

I laughed, "That's true; I was going to make you breakfast."

He said, "I know; that's why I made sure to get up before you." We laughed, and he continued, "So what do you have planned today?"

"Nothing, really. Later, I might swing by Nadia's house so we can make any final changes and adjustments for the wedding."

He replied, "Wow! They are not playing about this wedding."

I told him, "Nad is okay with waiting, but Dre said by the end of the year he wants her to be his wife, and he said she deserves a wedding, or he would have taken her to the courthouse right away."

"Hmmmm."

"Why are you 'hmmmming', Jeff?"

He answered, "No reason. Just let Nad know if anyone is walking with you at that wedding; it will be me!"

I laughed, "Of course, but she's doing it a little differently. I am the maid of honor, but she didn't want Eb and Terri to feel left out, so we're all going to be the maids of honor; isn't that cool?"

He replied, "That's nice of her; she really does love you guys."

I answered, "Yes, she does. That's my sister."

We went to take a shower and started our day.

I asked him, "What are your plans today, Jeff?"

"Not much; I have a big event next week. I'm going to buy some stuff, possibly prep and season what needs to be seasoned, and put them in the deep freezer, and that's it. So don't be surprised if you come home and I'm here."

I replied smiling, "I would love to walk in the door, and you are here."

He smiled, kissed me, and we went our separate ways.

Andre was a little older than her. He had a son. He made her happy, though. If she's happy, I'm happy. The night he proposed, we were all excited, like he was asking us. Well, in so many ways, he was. I always felt a way about his son's mother. She just gave me that sick feeling; trust me, how I felt wasn't a secret. I hid nothing from Nadia. She brought too much drama; every time you turned around, this bitch was trying to start something, some problem; she wanted to feel important. Only God saved her from getting her ass beat, and it seemed like his family always entertained the bullshit, like they were scared to put this bitch in her rightful place. In the beginning, Nadia had doubts about him because he had a child, but he loves my sister, and she loves him, so it is what it is. It was three weeks before the big day when Nad got the worst news of her life. I felt a rage take over me; I was right! How could he do that to her? He could have left! When Eb called me, she had to calm me down; everyone knew how angry I could get, and it was worse because it was about my sister. My anger became hurt. I cried; I cried for her. For the first time, I wasn't sure what to do. I took a deep breath, and I called her. I could hear the hurt in her voice; she cried, and I let her. After some time, she put her big girl panties on and told me to continue with everything. The wedding was still on. "What! Are you crazy? He doesn't deserve you."

"Please, I know what I'm doing; I will fill you in later," she said. I was worried because Nadia could get a little crazy if pushed. I threw the best bachelorette party you can throw, one to go down in the history books. The wedding day was here. Jeff looked so delicious in his suit, and I just wanted to rip it off with my teeth. When I get the chance, I need to talk to Jeff. We need to figure out what's going on between us.

I was given specific orders to follow from Nadia. We all played our parts. She looked stunning! But I could see the hurt. I felt all kinds of emotions, and it wasn't even me. Once she started saying her vows, I got into place. Once I got the cue, I started playing the video. I felt bad for both of them, but he deserved the embarrassment that he got. He didn't care when hurting her, so he got what he deserved. Everything just happened so fast and went downhill from there. Right after everything happened, she had to go to the hospital, found out she was pregnant, lost the baby, and went into a mini depression; it was spiraling out of control. We had to come together and snap her out of it. We understood, so we gave her space and time, and she started coming around. Through it all, she still handled the situation better than many. Andre tried to reach out to her a lot of times since I dropped his things off. He was trying to explain and beg her to give him another chance. She didn't want to be bothered. After about a year and a half, she went on a few dates, but her guard was so high that no one had a chance. I felt like she didn't put forth the effort, which was fine. When the time is right, it will happen. Nad just went headfirst with work and even started working out more. Then, she helped me out when she was free. Talk about just staying busy. We still had our girls' nights and trips. I love my girls.

Jeff and I were becoming closer than we were before. Which is crazy because I didn't think we could be any closer. About nine months ago, we separated for about seven or eight months. I told him that I was tired of being like this. I knew I had his heart but didn't feel like I did. He said he didn't know if he was ready to settle down, but he was not fucking anyone. He did admit to going on a few dates, but again, nothing sexual. I told him I didn't want to feel like I was his last resort so when he knows what he wants he can find me and hope another man doesn't find me first and appreciated what he had. He was mad, ughh, he was just as sexy mad, but I stood my ground. He said I was being unfair. We've been together since high school. He cheated on me once, right after high school. It broke my heart, but I forgave him. We did get back together, but it has been off and on since then; I guess I had trust issues under it all. When we separated this last time, I did go on some dates, nothing sexual though; my heart always seemed to direct me back to Jeff. This time, I was tired; tired of feeling as though I wasn't good enough for him. That's why I made this move. Show him who was the boss. He still calls me. Six months into our separation, he called me like he always did. "You call me more now than when we were together."

He replied, "That's not true." I laughed. We spoke about the trip coming up.

He asked, "Where are you going again?"

"Bora Bora."

He responded, "Nice, you deserve it."

I replied, "I know!"

We saw each other a few times, and as hard as it was, I didn't sleep with him.

I said, "Hold on, Jeff, I have another call coming in." I continued, "I'm back."

He replied, "Sorry about that, babe."

I replied, "Please, don't call me that; we're not together."

He said, "Babe, I want to see you tonight."

I responded, "I think we are seeing each other too much for people who are separated, don't you think?"

He replied, "Mel! Hell no!"

I told him, "Well, I can't see you tonight; I have a date."

He exclaimed, "A date!" I could hear his emotions changing in his tone. Even though we knew we were dating other people, we never said it to each other.

I continued, "Yes, a date!"

He asked, "So, you can't cancel your date for me?"

"No, do I ask you to cancel your dates for me?"

He replied, "So, is this dude more important?"

"No, but he can be!"

I knew I had struck a nerve; he never liked the idea of anyone possibly getting close to me.

I asked, "Hello, are you there?"

He replied, "Yeah, I got to go."

I asked, "So soon Jeff? Okay, talk to you later."

I had a date and was going to go out and have a great time. I met up with Anthony later that night at the improv. This was my second date with him. I wasn't comfortable enough to have him pick me up or ride with him. We had a really nice time. He's a real gentleman, a sweet guy. The night was nice. He walked me to my car and even opened the door for me. I was about to get into my car when he reached over and kissed me. I was shocked, but I kissed him back, and he smiled. He said, "I enjoyed my night; I had a great time with you again. I hope to see you again sooner than later." On my way home, so many thoughts were going through my mind. *This guy seems to be nice, but he's not my Jeff. Ugh, this feeling sucks. Snap out of it, Melissa. Get your mind right.* I pulled up to my house, and it looked so lonely. I walked into the house and started laughing about one of the jokes the comedian had said. I took a shower and lay down. Anthony had texted me to find out if I had made it home safely. I texted back, letting him know I did, and thanked him for a nice night. It was still early, so I checked some emails and started watching reruns of 'Martin' until I fell asleep.

Nad called me early the next morning, which made me wonder what time she got up. She is a true early bird. It doesn't matter what time she sleeps; she can get up on time, poor us. I already knew why she was calling; she loved Jeff. I met him through her, but I was always her main concern.

Nadia asked, "Why are you still sleeping?"

I replied, "No, good morning?" She laughed. I continued, "You're the only one that gets up at the crack of dawn."

"Whatever! How was it?"

"It was really nice."

She said, "Yayayaya, that's good to hear."

I said, "He kissed me".

She replied, "Oh shit! Really? What did you do?"

"Hell, I kissed him back. What else was I supposed to do? His lips were nice and soft, too. He's a really nice guy, but…"

"But what, Mel?"

I answered, "He's not my Jeff!"

She said, "I know it's hard; I know you love Jeff. Take your time; there's no need to rush. If you want to go on a few dates, that's fine, but take your time. Give him a certain amount of time to get it right; if that time expires and he doesn't have it together, do what you have to do."

I responded, "You're right. Talking about Jeff, I pissed him off yesterday."

She asked, "How?"

"Long story short, he wanted me to cancel my date to be with him. I told him no; he then tried to guilt trip me by asking if Anthony was more important than him. I told him he could be."

She exclaimed, "Oh, fucking shit! You told him that?"

"I sure did."

She said, "You know you fucked him up with that one."

I responded, "Yeah, he kinda deserved it."

She replied, "Well, I'm glad you had a good time; that's all I care about. On another note, in a few more weeks, we will be on our way to having so much fun in the sun. It's unbelievable."

I replied, "Yeah, I can't wait; it is so needed. We do a lot of stuff, but we have never had any real away time in a while. We have to make this trip worth it. We really do."

"What's your plan for today, Mel?"

I replied, "Oh no."

She asked, "What?"

I answered, "I have an event coming up, and it's with Jeff!"

She said, "This is going to be interesting, Mel."

I replied, "I can do it, Nad. Once I stay focused, he won't get me weak. I haven't seen him in a few weeks, so that should help."

She responded, "No, it won't." I can always count on Nadia to keep it real. I continued, "Okay, it won't be easy, but I got this, I do. I'm going to put on my big girl panties, for him to take it off." I heard Nadia mumble. I continued, "Like I said, I will put my big girl panties on, go in there, do my job, and get out."

She said, "You know I'm here for you, any support I can offer."

I replied, "I know, Nad, thank you. I'm just going to stay home today; I need to wash, finish reading my emails, and clean up a bit. I'll come over tomorrow, and we will do something or I can cook and tell Terri and Eb to come over if you want."

She responded, "Now, Mel, you know I can't say no to that; it sounds like a plan."

I said, "I'm going to see what I have, and if I need anything else, I'll go to Walmart."

She replied, "Love you, Mel, I'll see you later."

I replied, "Love you too."

I forgot that my laptop had died. I plugged it in and messaged Eb and Riri about tomorrow. Eb said she would be a little late and would bring the wine. When we were done talking, I laid back down, but I needed to get up. So, I got up, went to my refrigerator, found something to cook tomorrow, and took it out; thank God it was already seasoned. I always season my meat and put it away. Thank God for bad habits. I put on Michael Jackson, and I started my adventure. I did need some potatoes, so I had to go to Walmart anyway. I started in my room and cleaned the bathroom. I haven't cleaned in almost two weeks. I've been really busy. Thank God it's just me, so it's really not dirty. I finally made my way to the kitchen. That seems to always be the end spot for me. Before I mopped, I prepared everything for tomorrow's dinner. Whew, I was finally done but then realized I was starving; While cleaning, I neglected to eat. I took a shower, washed my hair, and felt so relaxed; I wrapped my hair up in this pretty little hair towel that I couldn't resist buying from Bed Bath and Beyond. I made a salad, with craisins, and crotons with some eggs because it was quick and easy. That was my lunch with a bottle of water. It was delicious. I love it when my house smells 'Febreze fresh.' Laying on the couch, I found a movie and just relaxed. It was almost 2 p.m., and I had no plans; I was good. Once I returned from Walmart, I put everything away, prepped the potatoes, took my clothes off, found my robe, and headed back to my couch. While out, I picked up some Chinese food: General Tso chicken, Shrimp Fried Rice, and some Crab Rangoon.

It's 6:30 p.m., and I'm still full from the salad I ate earlier. I almost dropped my laptop with the news I just received via email. I couldn't wait to share it with the ladies over dinner tomorrow.

Tired was an understatement; I fell asleep at about 3:30 a.m. watching TV, flipping back and forth between shows, and now here it is 10:30 a.m., and I'm awake. While stretching, I grabbed my phone and saw a good morning text from Anthony and another guy I went on a date with about two months ago. Anthony wanted to know if I was free tomorrow to meet for coffee. I really didn't want to, but why not? I told him I should be free and I would confirm later. He was okay with that. I was still tired. Thank God I did everything yesterday. The food was in the oven, so I went and showered. The ladies should be on their way soon. It was 6:30 p.m. I got out of the shower to Nadia's voice calling me, "Mel, where are you?"

I replied, "I'm in my room." I heard Terri saying that it smelled delicious in here. I replied, "Thank you. Everything should be done in about thirty-forty-five minutes."

"I brought a bottle of wine and champagne," Terri said. She continued, "I know we probably won't drink it, but just in case. Eb told me she was bringing a bottle, too. Well, it will be here whenever we need a drink." When I came out to join them, they were in the living room and kicked back, just talking. We always had something to talk about. "What's on the menu," Nadia asked.

I replied, "Baked lamb, Loaded potatoes, Asparagus, Jasmine rice, and of course salad. I made a small pan of shrimp just in case you want it for the salad."

"You spoil us," Riri said.

Nadia said, "She sure does. I brought some cheesecake for dessert, but if you add anything else to that menu, Mel, we will be spending the night."

I replied, "Nadia, stop acting like you're saying the impossible." We laughed.

I asked, "Hold on, did you make that cheesecake, Nad?"

She replied, "No, I didn't know I was supposed to."

I responded, "What do you mean? You know we love your cakes."

She said, "Sorry, I owe you guys."

"So, my mom called today. We got back in contact after she got out of rehab. In the beginning, it was hard; we were not where I would like us to be, but we're working on it."

Terri said, "That's good; in time, it will get better."

I replied, "Thanks, Terri, that means a lot. We speak a little more now. She sends random texts saying that she loves me and is very proud of the woman I became."

Eboni finally made it. It was now 7:30 p.m.

Eboni apologized, "Hey guys, sorry I'm late."

I replied, "We're glad you made it; now let's eat. Terri, can we start with the champagne? I'm going to get the glasses. I only want a little. I'm taking a break from drinking until we leave." Nadia grabbed the salad. Eboni poured champagne into the glasses, giving me just enough to make a toast.

I said, "I have some news to share with you; I've been holding it all day."

They looked nervous. "Are you pregnant?" Nadia blurted out.

I replied, "No! I received an email inviting me to appear as a guest star on a cooking show!"

They screamed! They jumped up and down and almost spilled the champagne; they bum-rushed me with hugs. I almost cried from all their joy and excitement.

"I'm so proud of you, yes girl, congratulations; we knew you could do it. You better get on the show and let them know who Chef Mel is."

I replied, "Thank you so much, ladies. It was hard holding this all day. Cheers to us, cheers to success."

"Cheers to you. When do you go?" Nad asked.

I answered, "Two weeks after we get back."

She replied, "That's what's up! I am proud of you, sis."

I said, "Y'all are going to make me cry."

Eb replied, "That's okay. It's tears of joy, good tears."

I said, "You're right, Eb." We ate and talked like we always do. "This lamb is amazing, Mel." The great thing about these ladies is that they will let me know when it's good, bad, or in between. I'm always happy to be around my girls. A piece of me wanted to share this news with Jeff.

. . .

It's been a week and a half since I heard from Jeff. We are going to Bora Bora in four days. I heard my phone going off and ran to pick it up. It was Jeff, my heart skipped a beat.

I answered, "Hello."

He replied, "Hey babe."

I giggled, "How are you, Jeff?"

He replied, "Not too good."

I asked, "Why? What's wrong? Is everything okay?"

He responded, "Mel, I miss you so much. I thought I could do this, but I can't. Even when you asked what was wrong, I heard the love and concern in your heart. I'm so sorry, Melissa."

He doesn't call me Melissa often, so I knew he was serious.

He continued, "I'm not asking you to forgive me, but I need to be a part of your life. I can't stop thinking about you. I try to act tough, and that's not proving anything. I realized that the last time we spoke. I love you, baby, and no one has ever made me feel like you do. You complete me, and I don't want to go another day not talking to you, seeing you, touching you. Please, can we start over? I promise you, I'll be all you need and more. I'm not just saying this; please give me the chance to prove it to you."

I was speechless; I had been waiting to hear those words from him for so long that I was scared now that I finally got it. I began to cry.

He asked, "Mel, are you there?"

I replied, "Yes, I am."

He said, "Please don't cry."

I responded, "Baby, I love you more than I can explain. Hearing those words gave me nothing but joy."

He said, "Yes, I want to make it work; I want you! You're all I ever wanted. Nothing makes me happier."

I said, "I'm so happy to hear that I am still in your heart."

He said, "Mel."

I responded, "Yes?"

He asked, "What are you doing?"

I replied, "Just got out of the shower, laying down and getting ready to watch some TV.

He said, "Can you walk to the window in the front of the house?" I was a little nervous as I took baby steps towards the window.

When I looked out the window, Jeff was standing there with two dozen red roses.

He said, "I love you, Meli, and I didn't want to wait any longer. It was now or never. I didn't want to lose you."

I dropped the phone with tears streaming down my face and ran to the door. He was crying, too, and I jumped in his arms; it felt great being held in his arms again. I kissed him the way you kiss someone when you miss them. It had been seven months. The longest we had ever been apart. My towel was falling while he was holding me. He carried me inside, I held him tight, and I could feel every beat his heart made.

I said, "I love you."

He replied, "Love you more."

He took me straight to the bedroom and laid me gently on the bed. The way he kissed me was different; his scent was amazing. He started to massage my body, and his touch was driving me crazy. I didn't know how far I would make it. Turning me over to massage my back, he started kissing my neck, making his way down the middle of my back. I felt his tongue stroking up and down, and he rubbed my butt while gently kissing my back. I couldn't control my moans. The kisses made their way to my waist, down to my butt; he showed equal love to each side. I felt his tongue slowly slide down my candy box, up and down, up and down. I opened my legs slightly so there was just enough room. He slid his tongue inside my candy box and kissed it. He licked it and sucked it like he missed it; he whispered, "I'm not stopping until you cum; I want to taste all of you," he flipped me over and started sucking on my nipples. Oh my god, I tried fighting the urge to cum, but his touch was everything. I tried to get a hold of his trophy to express how much I missed him, but he stopped me. "No, baby, I just want you to lay there and let me take care of you tonight." Fuck! That turned me on a little more; he was really trying. He made his way back to my candy box and dived right in while my legs struggled to stay straight up. While enjoying my flavor of love, he slowly put his fingers in. "Ohhhh baby, I'm cumming," I muttered, and he moaned more, "Yes, baby, cum for me." Whatever didn't come out on its own was sucked out. He gently placed his trophy inside of me. My eyes rolled back; every stroke was slow and gentle. Tonight was different. Tonight, Jeff showed me he loved me, and I felt it.

It felt different and amazing waking up in Jeff's arms. This was the best sleep I had in a long time. I still had my guard up, but I loved him and was willing to see if he was finally ready. I opened my eyes to Jeff looking at me, smiling.

He said, "Good morning, babe."

I replied, "Good morning." He reached over and kissed me.

He said, "You are all I ever need and want. What are your plans for today?"

I answered, "No plans for today. We have girls' night tonight; you know we leave for our trip on Monday, so to make it easier, we're all spending the night at Nadia's house. How about you?

He replied, "I have a party tonight, busy all weekend, but I want to spend as much time with you until you leave."

I responded, "We can make that happen."

We spent the whole day together, we caught up on things, and I told him about the good news; he was so happy and told me he knew I could make anything happen. We made love about two more times, got something to eat, and fell asleep. This day was priceless. We didn't want to leave each other, but he had to go make that money; if he didn't, I would have canceled my plans. We kissed, and I watched him walk to his car.

Girls' night started with dinner. I wanted to wait before I told them that Jeff and I had gotten back together. During dinner, he sent me cute little messages that had me blushing. After eating, we went to this club. The vibes were on point. We danced, drank, and had an amazing time. I danced with this guy I met there; this night was all about having a good time, and that's all it was going to be. The guy kept on trying to feel me but I had to cut it short because my baby and I were back together again, so there was no way I was going to let him touch me in a way that would make him think I was agreeing to his advances. I wasn't trying to send mixed signals. He was all over me and I was so happy when his friends called him for a drink. I don't know when or what time we got back to Nadia's house. I just remember Eb waking me up and Nadia telling me to eat so we could start our day. While waiting to get in the shower, I called Jeff. He answered on the first ring.

He replied, "Hey babe, good morning."

I said, "That was quick."

He replied, "I was waiting for your call."

I said, "Sorry, I just woke up about fifteen minutes ago and I'm about to get in the shower. I needed to hear your voice."

"I was getting worried. I'm on my way to the brunch and

covering the wedding. Once I'm done, I'll call you, and we will meet up."

I responded, "Okay, have a great day. Love you."

He replied, "Love you more."

The girls and I did some shopping; and got whatever extra items we needed and didn't need. I am a procrastinator, and I wait until the last minute and then run around like a crazy woman. I am working on it; baby steps. So, I have to go home and pack. The good thing is I know what I'm taking; I just have to put it in my suitcase. Once we got back to Nad's house, I told them I had some news to share. "So, what is it?" Terri said. I laughed, "I just want to let y'all know about my night on Thursday." Nad looked at me and smiled. For some reason, I felt she already knew but was waiting for me to say something.

"What Happened?" Eb said.

Giggling, I replied, "On Thursday night, Jeff and I got back together." They screamed. I think we scream for everything. "I knew it; you were glowing more than normal," Nadia said. I smiled at her. I told them everything. "Smart man" was the words of Eboni.

Terri said, "I'm so glad that he finally came to his senses. I'm so happy. Y'all are meant for each other. I think he realized that if he waited any longer, someone else would make you moan."

I exclaimed, "Terri, what!" She couldn't stop laughing,

Terri continued, "I'm just kidding, but you know it's true. On a serious note, he wouldn't want to know someone else was making you smile and happier than he did, if possible."

I made it back home but still had a lot of stuff to do and I was feeling hungry. I should've grabbed something to eat on my way home. It was 7 o'clock now. Jeff hadn't called yet, so he was probably still working. I put some Michael Jackson on to keep me motivated while I packed. I loved to dance. I was singing away and touching up on my moonwalk. One suitcase was done quickly. Whew, look at that, I killed two birds with one stone. I burned some calories and packed one suitcase. Go me! I went to take a shower, got a bottle of water, and started on suitcase number two. I moved on from Michael and put on some Jill Scott. I felt like switching up the vibes. Plus, I didn't want to get sweaty from dancing again. Music definitely helps you complete things so much quicker. To my surprise, it didn't take long for me to finish it. My stomach started growling, so I went to the kitchen to see what I had.

I screamed, "Oh shit, you scared me, Jeff!"

Laughing, he replied, "Sorry baby, I called to tell you I was on my way and ask if you wanted something to eat, but you didn't answer. I figured this was what you were doing, so I got some food anyway. I've been here for about ten minutes listening to you sing and having a good time."

I laughed, "I didn't even think to look at my phone. I figured you were still working. So how was it?"

He replied, "It was good; the scenery was beautiful. I think I just made some new clients."

I replied, "That's great. I'm so happy for you."

We ate. While he was in the shower, I finished packing my carry-on and found what I was wearing for the long flight. We lay down and watched a movie until we fell asleep. I got up and made breakfast. I wasn't really hungry because we ate late. I made omelets and French toast; Jeff loved French toast and a glass of orange juice. I'm so happy I don't have to do my hair. I had it twisted about a week ago. I didn't want my head to hurt from it being tight, and then, I wouldn't enjoy myself.

Jeff said, "I'm going to miss you, baby."

I replied, "It's only a week plus; you can call me. You better be ready for me when I get back."

He replied, "I'm always ready for you. Make sure to take lots of pictures."

He had canceled all his plans for the day, so I didn't make it to Nad's house until about nine p.m.

While waiting for our flight to board, we ordered some drinks. Terri and I sat together. I had the window seat, which Terri was okay with because she wanted to stretch her legs. I was able to enjoy the view. Once the flight took off, maybe ten minutes in, I was out! I woke up about four hours into the flight. I played some games on my phone to help the time pass. I don't even remember falling back to sleep. When we landed, I was so happy to be finally off that plane. The air smelled different. Once in our bungalows, we hung out until we fell asleep.

The past three days here have been so relaxing. Jeff calls me every day. Today is one of the days we've been so excited for; we were snorkeling. We had our wetsuits, cameras, and everything. It looked like we did this every weekend. The thought of swimming next to a black-tip shark gave me a rush. It's an experience that everyone should have, if possible. The water is beautiful, warm, and clean. We were on the water for maybe three hours out of a four-hour tour, but who's counting? There were two instructors and they were amazing. You could tell they loved what they did. And that, of course, makes it more fun. They provided food, snacks, and drinks, holding us out until we were done. I didn't think I would have been able to do this, but I am so happy I could push my fears aside and live. I can't wait to see all the underwater pictures.

Chapter 4

EBONI

I grew up in Brooklyn, New York City. My parents decided to move to South Florida when I was in the 7th grade of junior high school. I wasn't happy at all. I was hoping they would leave me with my auntie but neither one of my parents were having that. I have one sister and three brothers. I am the second youngest. So basically, child number four. Growing up, my mom always taught us to be respectful but never afraid to stand up for ourselves, speak how we feel, and never tolerate nonsense. Growing up with three older brothers taught me how to be tough. The area that we moved to in Florida was really nice. My parents had purchased a nice four-bedroom house. My oldest brother had his room, my other two brothers shared, and my sister and I shared. Starting school was, of course, nerve-racking for me: a new state, new people. Two weeks passed, and I met Nadia and Melissa in one of my classes. We had a group project due and were assigned to work together. They introduced themselves to me and welcomed me to hang with them. They were too nice to be true. I was hesitant, but I put my guard down after some time, and I'm so glad I did. They were the best friends anyone could ask for.

I've always been the girly type from a little girl. I love to do my nails, hair, and makeup. Every chance I had, I was in my mom's makeup, having the time of my life. Mel and Nadia let me practice on them when we had sleepovers or hung out. As I grew, my mom started buying me my own makeup and I started mixing and creating my own colors with what I had. People would ask me, where I got my makeup from, or say that they never saw these color, etc and I would let them know I created it. Mel, Nadia, and I also went to the same high school; that's where we met Terri. She is tall, you couldn't miss her in the crowd, but she was confident, and it showed. It's amazing how we all clicked like we knew each other from birth. While our senior year was approaching, we were trying to figure out what we wanted to do and what direction we were going. I knew I loved makeup but didn't want to be an average makeup artist. I wanted to go further. Once we left high school, I attended school to improve my craft. I loved it. I loved seeing how people felt when my job was complete—such a confidence booster. I knew in my heart that I didn't want to stop there. I started doing more research. I wanted to start my line, and that's what I pushed for.

My personality is very strong; so, a lot of guys usually don't want to stay with me. I can say it's frustrating sometimes because I felt like I could have really had something with some of these guys. At the same time, maybe not. I wasn't made for the weak and I didn't fall for the nonsense. Don't get me wrong, I did have relationships, but their favorite line was: "You're too strong, you're too independent." Like, who the fuck says that? So, after my last relationship, I just had friends, and whenever I was in the mood to get fucked, I would give them a call. One of my "friends" has been trying to be more than that; he told me he wasn't scared of my strength. He finds it sexy. He's fine as hell, too, but I don't know if I'm ready for a full commitment anymore. His name is Dante. He is an up-and-coming model. I met him while going to an event to support Terri. Did I say he was FINE! 6 feet 3 of fineness? Slim and muscular. If you gave him the chance, he would live in the gym. He takes pride in his appearance, as he should. He has a low brush cut with smooth caramel skin. We've been messing around; that is my nice way of saying that we've been fucking, going on four and a half years, but we never put a title on each other. He dated other people, and so did I. He has brought up the topic of becoming more serious, but I always brushed it off and found a way to change the subject. I really do like him, and whenever I find myself wanting, needing, or possibly falling in love with him, I pulled away. I'll find so many reasons, stupid reasons. Like, he could have anyone; why would he want me? I mean, I can really understand why he likes me; I can't blame him, but why? Or I'll think he'll be like the others and run once they realize I am strong or feel like he can't deal with me. So, I just left it as it is.

With time, everything started to fall into place with my makeup life. I remember when Dante and I went on a couple of dates back in the beginning of our "fuckship." He always brought me candles and the scents would always be different. I know that seems weird, but I loved it. That showed me that he listened. I had told him that I stock up on candles because after I clean, I love to light them to make everything complete. One night, we went to dinner and a movie, it was simple. We went earlier than usual, so the night was still young, and we agreed to head back to my house. We talked and had some drinks. The mood was right. I wanted to get a little more comfortable. I told him to "make himself at home," and he did just that. I went into the shower; I didn't want to keep him waiting too long. I got in and the water, it felt good on my body. My shower head made you feel every drop of water that came from it. I had a long day. I thought I heard a noise, but I brushed it off. Dante had come into the bathroom. I didn't know until I felt a kiss on my neck. He was gentle, his whole demeanor was gentle. He rubbed my shoulders, slowly kissing me down the middle of my back. Then he turned me around and sucked on my breast gently as the water rolled off his head. We moaned together. Before I could move, he picked me up, put me against the wall, and slowly entered my pussy. I wanted to resist, but I couldn't. He held on tightly with every stroke. I felt every inch of him. Feelings I never felt, ever! Hitting spots I didn't know existed. I didn't want him to stop. He didn't disappoint me at all. This was our first time, and the way he gave it to me, I knew we would have many more times ahead of us.

Dante wasn't my "man" but he was around enough where he ended up being apart of Nad's wedding so he witnessed all that drama. I'm telling you if she gave me the okay, Andre and his raggedy baby mom's ass would be beat. I remember when she told me what happened; I automatically wished I could take her pain away. She's a tough one, though, because that stunt she pulled at the wedding took a lot of balls, but she did it. Ever since then, she just refused to talk or commit to anyone. She went on a few dates but didn't bother to give them another chance or make any effort to go past the first date, and it's not like guys didn't try to talk to her. She's gorgeous but refuses to allow anyone to get close to her. I understand, even though our reasons may be different.

Every year, we take trips near, far, and wherever may come to mind. The next trip on our list is Bora Bora, and I'm so excited. We over deserve it. I can't wait to see whose son is going to distract me.

As it was getting closer to our trip, my makeup line finally launched. I'm so ecstatic that words can't explain my happiness and humility. This has been a long time coming—more reason for us to celebrate.

We met up at Nadia's house. We've been trying to help her find somebody's son to take her mind off things. I got there early so I could do her makeup, and we were all going to get ready there.

"So, are you guys excited about Bora Bora?" Mel asked.

I replied, "Yes, yes, yes. I can't believe it's time already."

"We're going to have so much fun," Mel said.

I said, "I wish you would be a little more revealing sometimes, Nad. It will be okay."

Nad replied, "Look at my breasts, compared to you guys; it's not that simple."

Terri was the last to show up, and she came with amazing news. We will be going to Italy to support her in the big fashion show she will be taking part in. Doing Nad's makeup was so much fun. I kept it simple. She looked amazing.

"Go look at yourself," I said.

She replied, "Eb, this is amazing. You can't really tell that I even have anything on."

I replied, "Exactly, thank you, and anytime, Nad."

I was driving tonight. We had to break in my new 2019 BMW. This car is amazing. We valet parked at the restaurant, ate, laughed, and had a good time. This guy tried to talk to Nad on our way out of the restaurant. She told him, "No habla English." We laughed so hard. "Nad, you didn't have to do him like that," I said. That was just an example of her shutting people down. As we pulled into the club, we noticed it was crowded. I was ready to dance. I was letting this music be my high. I had my eye on this guy since I walked into the building, it didn't look like he was on a date, or with a woman, so it was a free game. Once we got our table and some bottles, I was getting ready to make my move, and another guy stopped me and asked me to dance. Why not? While dancing, I kept a close eye on my prize. He was looking at me too. Our eyes remained locked on each other. The song was finally over. My dance partner offered to buy me a drink, and I politely took it and returned to my table. I sat there looking through the crowd as I was getting ready to blend in. The guy who had been dancing with Nad was coming. I told her, and without thinking, she said, "For what?"

I replied, "He's fine, though; get his number, put it on him, and move on with your life." I finally made my way into the crowd. I found him. We danced to a few songs, and he brought me a drink. I took it but didn't need it. We made our way to a corner of the club that was pretty dark and wasn't in everyone's view. As we danced, I felt his dick rise. It got me excited. It was big! I slowly grind on him. "I've been watching you since you came in the door," he said. While slowly putting his hand up my dress and moving my panties to the side, he asked, "You got a man?" I replied, "It's a little too late to be asking, don't you think?" He smiled. He started playing with my clit like it was an instrument, not missing a beat. He inserted his fingers, going up and down to the beat of the slow song that was playing. Up and down, licking his fingers and putting it back in. We were on our own cloud. This was so daring. It was a rush. I love it when a man knows what he's doing. Picking up speed, he made me cum! I turned around, thanked him for his services, and joined my girls on the dance floor. He seemed shocked that I walked away from him. I felt him looking at me. As much as I would like to know how that dick felt because he did wonders with his hands, I had to pass. We danced and had an amazing time. We knew how to have a good time no matter what we did.

Once back at home, we all passed out in the living room. The only reason I woke up so soon the next morning was because Terri almost tripped over me while rushing to the bathroom. I got up and saw Nadia sitting by the window. It looked like she was somewhere else. I stood right next to her and called her name a few times, but there was no response. I called her one more time, and she finally looked at me. I could see that she was crying. She tried to wipe her face, but I already saw what she wanted to hide. I already knew what it was, but I would never try to help her relive it. I ate my breakfast and drank my coffee. I love coffee. There's no special time of the day for it to me. Two more days until party time. We hit the streets to see what else we can get. I honestly believe we got way more than what we needed. But it's better to be safe than sorry. You know your girl had to stack up on those condoms. After all, I'm going to have all kinds of fun.

Once I got home, I played Biggie Smalls to help me get through everything I needed to do. I had to finish it all tonight because I had a noon hair appointment to get my hair braided tomorrow morning. It's the best thing to do. That way, I can get up and go. I'm on vacation to have fun and I'm not trying to worry about combing my hair. I had already packed some of my stuff, so I added most of the things we bought today. Everything wasn't for the trip that we got. Hey, we love to shop. I put my iPad in my carry-on, packed my makeup; I can't forget that, and I packed a few sneakers in there too. It only took me about two hours to get it all done. I need to pat myself on the back. I outdid myself this time. I put all the bags in the living room. I was going to drop it off at Nad's house tomorrow after I got my hair done. I took a shower and lay down until I fell asleep. I woke up at 9:30 a.m. I hadn't slept this late in a long time. I had a few missed calls. I got in the shower, made my coffee, and returned calls as I dressed. I was coming out with a lip gloss line and had to give feedback on it. I also spoke to my mom. She makes it her mission to speak to me every Sunday. We talked on other days of the week, but Sunday was a must. Today is a sweatpants and a T-shirt type of day. It's Sunday, I'm relaxed, and I have too much to get done. I left at about 11 a.m. I may not be one to wake up early, definitely not an early bird but I don't like to rush; leaving early works for me. On this beautiful Sunday morning, there wasn't any traffic. I made it to the hairdresser at 11:25 a.m. Earlier than I expected. Thank God she didn't have anyone, even though I'm the first appointment anyway; I'm sure other people think like me. Once I went in, she got straight to work. I was out of there by 12:30 p.m. She's really quick, plus I wasn't getting anything that was time-consuming.

I called Nadia once I got in the car. "Are you home?"

She replied, "You know I am."

I'm trying not to leave if I don't have to."

I replied, "I know that's right."

"What are you doing to your hair?" I asked.

"I was going to get it braided, but I don't want to be bothered. I'll deal with my hair. I packed some of my hair products; it will be okay."

I replied, "If you change your mind, let me know. I can call my stylist."

She responded, "Okay."

I said, "I'm just leaving there now. I'm going to come over. What do you have to eat?"

She replied, "I was just trying to figure that out. I have some shrimp. I can make some shrimp Alfredo with some garlic bread."

"Yes! I said, that sounds great. I'm on my way."

When I made it to her house, it smelled delicious. The food was almost done. The noodles were boiling, and the garlic bread was fresh out of the oven.

"Good afternoon, Nadia." I said,

She replied, "Hey, hun, your hair looks nice. She did an awesome job, as always."

I replied, "Thank you.""Did you bring all of your stuff with you?" She asked.

"Yes, I sure did."

"I hope you didn't forget anything." She said with slight sarcasm.

I responded, "Ha, I think I'm over-packed; there's enough stuff in here that we can share clothes. So that's not bad. And can you believe that I still have space! Go me, go me, go me."

She replied, "Job well done, Eb. Job well done."

My stomach growled.

"Eboni, was that your stomach? She asked.

Yes, Nadia.

"You weren't kidding when you said you were starving." I took my shoes off and got comfortable; before I could blink twice, I heard Nad say "Come eat." We ate and made a few phone calls. Dante had called me as well. I told him I wouldn't be here for about a week, so we could meet when I returned. Nad was also closing up some loose ends, saying she's not doing any kind of work while on vacation unless she has to. I felt the same way. I had a few things I had to finish up that may run into tomorrow, and then it will be fun in the sun.

I woke up to Nadia and Terri talking. I guess I had fallen

asleep at some point. Terri asked Nadia when she would be performing again. She hadn't performed her poetry in a while. Nad is an awesome poet. She brings the crowd to life. You see a different side of her when she recites.

Nadia replied, "I'm setting up to start back in three weeks when we get back."

I said, "Yes, that's what I'm talking about." Terri looked over at me when she heard my voice. "Hey, sleepy head," she said and then she continued, "Thank you for your input; Nadia really needs to hear that."

"When did you get here, Riri?"

She replied, "Like fifteen minutes ago. You were sleeping like a baby, drooling and all. I'm about to eat some of this food. I wonder if it will put me to sleep too, she laughed.

What time is it?"

"4:45 p.m." Riri said.

I asked, "Is Mel coming over?"

"Yeah, but she's hanging out with Jeff, so she said she will be here later, and she would just spend the night.

I'm thinking about spending the night, too, Nad. I'm already here."

"Sorry, guys," Terri said. "I have to eat and run. I have to do a few things with my mom, so I'll have to come early in the morning."

I didn't need anything from my house. So, I was good. When Mel got here, she brought a salmon salad. Delicious. When I say she knows what she's doing, you can taste her confidence. We relaxed for the rest of the night. I was watching movies to avoid getting too much sleep. We had a long flight ahead of us.

Thank God I stayed the night. I was able to sleep for an additional hour and a half. We got up at 7 a.m. and started getting ready. We were taking an Uber, which was less hassle. Terri arrived at 8:15 a.m., and we had our coffee and got ready to go. The Uber came at 9 a.m. We're flying with United Airlines. Flying into (Bob airport) we checked in, got our tickets, and were on our way. Nad and I sat together. I didn't get much sleep because I wanted to finish what I had to do. Once I make it to Bora Bora, work will not be on my agenda. Nad kept me company for a few hours, and then she was out like a baby. This trip came at the right time. Life is a reason to celebrate. I'm so happy that these three ladies are part of my celebration and most importantly a part of my journey. Hopefully, we will soon have four great men/ spouses to add to the team. Four hours into the flight, I finally knocked out everything and went straight to sleep. It was a sight when we were getting ready to land from the sky. Being able to have this view from the top is breathtaking. This Island is beautiful, and I don't feel like that's a good explanation for this beauty.

Our first day was spent at the beach, it was fun and very relaxing. It was a good way to start things off. Nad saw a guy that actually caught her attention. Can you believe it! You could hear the excitement in her voice. We were stunned; we never thought the day would come. We had already started to believe she would convert into a full-time Nun.

It was ATV time. That's what was on our agenda. It was going to be a three to four-hour tour, and we were ready. We had our hats, glasses, sunscreen, t-shirts, and sneakers. Don't get it twisted; we're girly but can quickly switch it up in a heartbeat. We packed lots of water. There was no need to pass out from dehydration. We carried one backpack and will take turns carrying it if needed. Once we made it to the meet-up locations, the instructor reviewed all the instructions. He was kind of cute, but not my type. I would still fuck him, though, I laughed at my inner thoughts. I really have to do better. I was a little hoe, but I was trying to do better; but honestly, there was nothing wrong with just having thoughts! I was not acting on them. While waiting, we hooked up our GoPro Hero 7 black camera. We believe in capturing memories; to top it off, it'll all be from different views. The only thing I remember hearing was, "Let's go!" Man, this machine is powerful! We saw the island from a different view. Beautiful, beautiful, beautiful. We went up and down, got dirty, and saw the volcanoes from a distance. We had an awesome time, not just us, but the people there too. You could hear the laughter and see the smiles; after all, that's what this trip is all about. We were burnt out once we got back.

"I want a drink and then go lie down," Nadia said.

"Me too," Mel responded.

Terri said, "I do, too, but we also need to eat."

"That's right, Terri. We need to eat. How could we forget about the food," Nadia said. We laughed. We went to get some food and some drinks to take back to our room. One of the guys in the group riding with us was in here. He looked good. Not so much of my type, but I didn't quite come here for my type, did I? He kept looking at me and smiling. I didn't really feel like socializing because I was sweaty and dirty. Screw it; he knows why, we were in the same place. I excused myself and walked over to him.

"Like what you see?" Yes, I am confident enough to start a conversation this way.

He replied, "Yes, I do."

I smiled, "What's your name?"

"Carlos."

I said, "Hey, I'm Eboni."

I asked, "So, are you here by yourself?"

"No, I'm here with a group of friends."

"Is any one of them your girl?"

He exclaimed, "Wow! You're very straightforward, a get-to-the-point type of woman."

"Yes, I am. I don't have time to play games. So, is any of them your girl?" Laughing, he replied, "Who told you there were any girls here?"

I answered, "I know there are girls here; I saw you guys earlier."

He said, "Well, to answer your question, No."

I said, "Cool, that wasn't so hard was it?."

He asked, "So how about you? Who are you here with?"

"I'm here with my girls."

He asked, "Okay, so Eboni, what are you about to get into?"

"Not sure yet."

"I would like to hang out with you if that's possible."

"Carlos, anything is possible. How long are you here for?"

He answered, "Two more days. Work calls."

"Let's exchange numbers. We can probably meet later today or tomorrow." I said. I left him waiting for his food. Nadia was calling me to let me know they were ready. I know we had plans to come back out but our bodies was telling us something different.

Snorkeling was on the agenda for tomorrow. Something new to all of us. We got back to the room, showered, and ate our food. I dozed off. Maybe about two hours later I woke up to my phone vibrating by my leg. The number was unknown; who could this be? I wondered. "Hello," I said, trying to clear my throat.

"Hi, Eboni."

"Who's this?"

"Carlos."

"Oh, hey, Carlos. I thought I saved your number. I'm sorry."

"Did I wake you?"

"Yeah, I fell asleep; I didn't even know I did."

He laughed. "Are you coming out tonight? Maybe we can grab a drink."

I asked, "What time is it?"

"8:15 p.m."

I said, "Okay, let me get dressed, and we can meet by the bar on the beach."

I was still a little tired; Nadia and Terri were up.

I said, "Ladies, I'm running out for a little while to meet Carlos."

"Who is Carlos," Nadia asked.

"The guy I was talking to in the restaurant earlier."

"Oh, weren't you just sleeping?" She asked.

"Yes, but he just called me." They shook their heads. I put on the blue sleeveless body-con dress I ordered from Fashion Nova with some gold sandals. I grabbed my purse, put some condoms in it, and left. The air was fresh. I walked to the bar, taking in the night view, then Carlos came right after I did.

"Hey gorgeous," I heard him say.

I replied, "Hi." We walked over to an available table and ordered some drinks.

I asked, "So, Carlos, where are you from?"

"I live in Cali."

I answered, "Nice. I plan on coming out to Cali soon."

"Hopefully, sooner than later, so you can stop by to see me." He said with a smirk. I smiled; he was trying to throw some game, so I'll play along.

I asked, "Are you inviting me?"

"Yeah, whenever you're ready, let me know."

I replied, "I might just take you up on that offer."

So, what brings you to this beautiful island of Bora Bora? I asked.

"My best friend. We're here celebrating his birthday."

Okay, that's a good enough reason to be here.

We laughed.

Before we knew it, we were on our third drink. He reached over and kissed me. I kissed him back and began rubbing on his dick; I had to see what I was getting myself into. It was thick, not too long, but I would be able to work with it. He was hard! He kissed me on my neck.

"Let's go back to my room." He said. As we made it back to his room, it was quiet and dark. There wasn't anyone here, so I didn't know if he shared it with his friends or if he had his own room. I didn't care, though. He took me back to where the bedroom was. Lifting my dress, he bent me over, took his fingers, and started playing with my clit from the back. "Ummm, nice and wet," he said before licking his fingers. I got the condom out of my purse that was still hanging across my shoulders. "Here, put this on."

He replied, "Damn, you came prepared."

"Always! now put it on!" Taking the condom from me, he put it on. Still bent over, he slowly pushed his hard dick into my pussy.

"Ahhh!" was the first sound that came out his mouth; he started off going slow and then picked up his speed. I was throwing it back at him, and he was holding my waist tight. He was keeping up, turning me around; he took off my dress, my girls were free, and he sucked on one of my breasts and then the next. Lying on his back, dick still up and ready to feel me again, I climbed on the bed. With my ass facing him; I slowly sat on his dick and started going up and down; it felt so good, I had to direct him a little to my liking, but it was still good marching to the beat of my drum. "Oh shit, reducir la velocidad allí mismo voy a cum," him speaking to me in Spanish turned me on. I was stroking him slowly, and he picked me up and laid me on the bed with my legs straight up; he dove back in. "Oh, Dios Mio." He laid on me for a few minutes and started to kiss me. He could kiss; he got a few extra points for that.

I asked, "Can I get a towel to take a quick shower?"

He replied, "Yes, of course." I didn't stay long in the shower.

He asked, "Are you leaving so soon?"

"Yeah, I have an early and busy day tomorrow, so I should get some rest."

He asked, "Can I see you again?"

"Well, I can try to see you before you leave."

He replied, "I'm not just talking about here, senorita. I'm talking about once we all get back home."

I said, "Well, you live in Cali; we are in two different states. I can't promise how soon we will see each other again."

He said, "I know. We can talk on the phone, and maybe I can come see you."

I replied, "We will see what happens."

He pulled me close to him; he had just a towel on and began to kiss me. There was something about his kiss that I couldn't resist; before I could blink my eyes, again, he picked me up, placed my back against the wall, and his towel was on the ground. He began to fuck me, this time better than the first; I guess he had to prove something to me. I held on to him tightly, and he didn't slow down. Why did I let him kiss me again? I should have just left. I let him take the lead, and he walked to the couch, where he placed me on the arm of the chair; he took one of my legs and placed it on his shoulder. Oh,

I was feeling all of him. "Talk to me, Papi," I said. "Tu coño es tan bueno," he slowed down and stared at me for a second. He picked up the pace. I was throwing it back at him while I was rubbing my nipples and making my way to my clit. Was he trying to make me fall for him? I began to moan, and he did, too. I whispered I was going to cum, and he held me close. My body felt light. I'll give it to him; he handled me right. I got myself together to leave once again; smiling at me, he said, "I look forward to seeing you again; we will figure something out." He walked me to the door, "Eboni, this was fun. I hope you don't play hard to get."

I replied, Carlos, "yes." He answered.

Tuve un gran tiempo."

He smiled, "I didn't know you spoke Spanish."

I smiled, "*Buenas Noches.*"

He replied, "Good night, gorgeous."

By the time I got back to the room. They all were sleeping. I changed my clothes and joined them. I did see Carlos again the night before he left. We didn't sleep together. He took me out to dinner, and we had a nice nonsexual time. He was a really fun and intelligent guy. I found out that he was a middle school English teacher; he had been teaching for five years. He was born in Panama but has been living in America since he was four. We spoke a little more about his family and up bringing. It's beautiful to meet people from different ethnicities. He said that he wants to see me the next time he has a long weekend and is willing to take the trip. I told him we would talk about it and see where things go.

Chapter 5

TERRI

For as long as I have known myself, I've been tall. My dad played basketball for years. He played since high school; that's how he met my mom. She also played basketball in high school, and I heard she was one of the top players. She wanted to pursue into professional WNBA, but at the end of her junior year in high school, she became pregnant with my older brothers. She was a little disappointed because that meant she had to put her dreams on the back burner. My dad was worried but excited. That made him push more for his career and to become successful. My mom was the love of his life, and he didn't want to let her down. He went hard. He was already in college when my mom became pregnant, and my mom did what she had to do. She stayed focused and went to school until she was ready to have the twins. I don't even want to imagine how she felt having not one but two babies at the same time at seventeen. She wasn't going to be eighteen until May. Mom always said that she couldn't have done it without the support of her parents, my amazing grandparents. Daddy's parents were also very involved and supportive. I couldn't have asked for better grandparents. They did a great job raising them. The twins were born in February. She stayed home for a few weeks; and then she went back to school. she was determined to get her education and graduate. My dad kicked ass in college. An NBA team picked him up. Dad and Mom were still going strong. Two years later, she had another son; Then I arrived three years later. They were super excited to have me. I was the first girl: Daddy's princess and Mommy's twin. We had a pretty good life.

I've always enjoyed school; I was an honor roll student for most of my high school years. And I played basketball just like my parents did. I even started back in middle school. I loved it and I continued to play throughout high school. I felt the pressure when I went for tryouts to get on the girls basketball team. I kept telling myself, *You can't let mom and dad down.* After all, look at who my parents are. I became so obsessed that all I did was practice. I was tired but kept pushing and when the day came for tryouts, I'm not going to lie, I messed up. It wasn't bad but it was bad to me. Thank God they already knew my potential and brought me back for the second rounds of tryouts. Of course I made them not regret any decisions when it came down to me. I played with the team for the full four years of high school, experiencing two championship wins but by my senior year in my heart, I knew I didn't want to continue basketball as a career. Believe it or not, I am a girly girl. Growing up, mommy had me in modeling. I did so many different things. I loved it. Now and then, I still did it. I always got calls, but my education came first. That's one thing I learned from my mom. Never put anything or anyone in front of your education. I admired her for that. Even though having us hindered her dreams, it never stopped her from being the best mom she could be, and that's why she pushed us all so hard.

All of us are tall. I'm the shortest of the bunch. My twin brothers are 6 feet 4 inches, my brother after them is 6 feet 5 inches, and I'm 6 feet 3 inches. My mom and I are the same height. When I started high school, I wanted to go to a different high school, not the school that I was zoned too. A few of my middle school friends ended up at the same school I went to. I have always been a social butterfly; meeting and getting to know people was easy for me. I met my three forever sisters there. We met one day at one of my basketball games. They were always there, talk about school spirit. They had it. After the game, while I was walking around, they stopped me, telling me that I played a good game. Mel was like, "Can I ask you a question?" I said sure. "Have you done modeling before? I could have sworn I saw you on a few bulletins, even a few commercials."

I replied, "Yeah, I have. I love it; I still do it from time to time when I have free time and as long as it doesn't affect my schoolwork." Mel turned around and said to Nadia, "I told you! I told you!" We all started laughing. I didn't notice that we were talking for thirty minutes. We exchanged numbers, and from that day, we've been forever sisters. By my senior year of high school, I finally told my mom that I wanted to go back to modeling full-time. If I wanted to continue basketball, I would have gotten a full scholarship to college, but that was not what my heart truly desired. My mom was always a big supporter; her main concern was that I didn't make the same mistakes she did. She didn't have to worry; I didn't want any children any time soon. Plus, I think I like girls; well, let me rephrase I'm bisexual, I think. I realized this during my sophomore year of high school. A group of my friends and I went to the beach. I remember seeing this girl, and I thought everything about her was fine: Her face, ass, everything. I didn't think anything of it because I'm very comfortable with myself and didn't see anything wrong with admiring someone of the same sex. Then I noticed that girls started hitting on me a lot.

It was my senior year of high school; I recall going to a college party with my brothers, some of their friends, and some of mine. My brothers love hanging out with me; they always say that I'm the life of the party. Plus, they feel like they are supposed to always watch over me. It's like I had four dads. We drank a little, danced, and everyone was having a good time. Then this girl at the party came over to where we were and started dancing and hanging out in our area. She had to be about 5 feet 9 inches, very shapely, beautiful chocolate complexion. She was very attractive. She then came up to me and started talking casually. She seemed nice; while talking, she reached over and started kissing me. That was weird but I was drinking, so she caught me off guard; before I could resist, I found myself kissing her back. My heart was racing; this was the first time I ever kissed a girl. I never acted on those feelings before; I thought it was just a phase. She pulled herself closer to me as she stuck her tongue in my mouth. She took my hand and placed it under her shirt so that I could feel her breast, and without thinking, I began to rub her nipples. I couldn't believe it; I felt myself getting wet and turned on. At that moment, her friend came over, and she was smiling; the way she was looking, I thought she was going to make a move, too. She was just watching. *Did they plan this? Were they watching me since I had been here?* All these thoughts were running through my head at the moment. She gave me her number and asked me to call her.

"My name is Bree, I would love to get to know you better," she smiled. I knew what that meant. I was still shocked. *What made her think that I would be interested in "women"* She was bold and brave to do that, I thought. I never acted on the feelings I had, and I didn't say anything to anyone. But from that day, in my mind I knew I was more than just attracted to women. I did call Bree; we actually became friends, but nothing more ever came out of it. She did try, but I didn't bulge. To me it was just a moment. Nothing more, nothing less.

We were weeks from graduating; I had so much going on. My mom had modeling work lined up for me, starting two weeks after graduation. Her friend played a part in a big fashion show, and I had the opportunity to be a part of it. I didn't really have time to date. I hung out with the ladies and my family. One day, I decided to let them know that I was bisexual. Only Mel was brave enough to voice her opinion. Three months into modeling, I met a young lady named Vanessa; she was also modeling as well. We had a few jobs together and we became friends. She was beautiful inside and out and always made me laugh. She reminded me of me. A year into our friendship, I realized that I was falling for her. We began to hang out more and more by ourselves. I tried to control my emotions; I didn't want to ruin such a great friendship. Vanessa is shorter than me. She's 6 feet, and definitely thicker than I am, with a size D cup breast. I think I'm drawn to breasts because I don't really have any. She was just beautiful to me. One evening, after I came back from doing a photoshoot, Vanessa called me.

"Hi Terri, what are you up to? I'm headed home. My parents are away for their anniversary, so I was going to be home alone. I just wanted to relax.

I wanted to know if we could meet up to grab something to eat. We haven't hung out in a while."

I replied, "No problem."

We met at outback steakhouse. I was starving; I didn't eat

all day. Vanessa made it there before I did; she got the table and ordered our drinks. She got me a strawberry daiquiri with an extra shot. "Terri, you look tired."

I replied, "I am. I've been at this shoot all day, but you look good."

"Thanks, Terri."

"So, how have things been? I haven't seen you in a few weeks." I asked.

"It's been good. I have a job set up in a few weeks in NYC."

"That's great, Vanessa; let me know how it goes."

She replied, "You know I will."

It was still early when we finished up, so we just went back to my house.

We decided to watch a movie. It had been a long day for me so while I took a shower Vanessa found a movie to watch. She also got herself a glass of wine. She chose 'Coming to America.' I love that movie; nothing like a good laugh. Laying there, I began to wonder, *"We're here by ourselves, she's laying in my bed and I'm still a virgin."* I don't know why these thoughts were happening now, but I liked Vanessa, though, and I knew she liked me. I remember when I told the girls that I was bisexual, they weren't judgmental at all, but I remember Mel saying to me, "You can like what you like, but why would you want to lose your virginity to a dildo?" I was kinda mad at her; I felt some type of way. How dare she judge me? I know she wasn't, and she was right. Maybe I was looking into it too deeply. I mean, you only live once; you can only lose your virginity once, you might as well lose it to a real dick to get the true feeling; plus, it's not like I'm not attracted to men. I like them too. But if we're being honest, I feel safer with girls because I don't want to make the same mistakes my mom made, especially being the only girl. I didn't want to be the disappointment.

There was a guy named Tyler who had been trying to talk to me. I had been brushing him off for as long as I could remember. I think I'm going to call him. I heard Vanessa laughing in the background of my thoughts. I looked over at her. She looked good; her long legs were curled up next to me. She could be about 130 pounds; most of it was ass and breast. She was really cute. She had on some tights and a crop top. Showing her stomach. Who could blame her? There was nothing there.

"You're quiet over there. Are you okay?" She asked.I replied, "Yes, I'm okay. I'm a little tired."

"I can help you get up," she mumbled.

I asked, "What was that?"

Laughing, she replied, "Nothing, but if you want, I can leave so you can get some rest."

I replied, "I have all night to sleep. You're fine." I tried to focus on the movie, but so many thoughts were running around my head. She ran her hands across my legs while laughing, and then she moved in a little closer, but still focused on the movie. I dozed off, waking up to Vanessa touching my face softly; she gave me a peck on my lips. I opened my eyes; she was smiling. Her eyes were dreamy. She leaned back in and started kissing me. She was hard to resist. I was battling within myself on what to do. Vanessa is four years older than me, so I'm sure she has the experience. She knew that I was a virgin. So, it's obvious that she had the upper hand. I kissed her back. She was making all the right moves. As we were kissing, she started to rub my nipples. I only had on a sports bra and some boy shorts. All these different sensations were happening all at once. I didn't know what to do. This was new to me. I moaned while trying to go with the flow. I didn't want to make the moment seem awkward, so I started to rub her back. Nessa kissed me like someone who knew what she wants, and she wanted me. The kisses came down to my neck. It stopped. I could see that she was smiling, looking at me, and taking it all in. "Are you okay?" she asked while biting her bottom lip with a slight smirk. I nodded my head; I couldn't even answer. My heart was racing. I didn't know what was going to happen. She sat on top of me and gently took off my sports bra. Her lips were placed on top of my nipples. I didn't have breasts; they were small. I had the type that you could wear anything without a bra. While slowly caressing my nipples with her tongue, the other nipple had the attention of her hand. Then she switched. I couldn't believe this was happening as I heard my heart pounding through my chest. I touched her breasts; they were perfect. I began rubbing her nipples. She moaned; the sound of her voice, the soft purrs of her moans, turned me on. She kissed me more this time. It was more intense. We exchanged tongues with our kisses. She stroked it with her mouth. Wow! This woman was amazing. When I tried to show some affection by touching her, she stopped me. She took my hand and started to suck on my fingers. She brought my hand to her breast and allowed me to rub her nipples. I could tell she liked that. She started kissing around my stomach. She moved down to my navel and stuck her tongue in and out of it. My toes curled. She got up and took my boy shorts off; I had no underwear on. Oh shit, oh shit. She climbed back on the bed and paid attention to my breasts again. All of a sudden, I heard Mel in my head, "Why would you want to lose your virginity to a dildo?" I tried to tune it out, but I couldn't. I started to feel angry. Why was this happening right now? I could really beat Mel's ass. Vanessa was making her way to my girl box. I stopped her.

"Nessa, I really want to, but I can't. I don't want to lose my virginity this way." She placed her fingers on my lips, smiled, and said, "Shhhhh, I understand." She gave me a deep kiss and then whispered in my ear, "Let me take care of you tonight." Before I could say anything, I felt my legs being opened. The warmth of her tongue stroked my girl box, moving slowly, and every glide of her tongue made me shiver. I couldn't believe how good this felt. Is this what I've been missing? With her tongue, she played with my clit; going in and out of my hole and catching every drip of my liquid as it came out. She was a multitasker; she never, not one time lifted her face from my girl box; she just raised her hands and started caressing my nipples. That was it for me. I couldn't hold it back anymore. As the moans slipped out uncontrollably, I was cumming. It felt amazing. I had played with myself many times before, but it never felt like this. I didn't think I was going to survive; I did. She kept on licking for a few more minutes. I couldn't take it. She must have felt sorry for me when she stopped. I was drained. I didn't know what to do next. She got up and smiled at me. "Terri, that was delicious," she said and kissed me. I have a chair in the corner of my room. Nessa walked over and sat there. "I want you to look at me," she said. Licking her fingers, she ran her hands across her breasts, then down to her girl box. Inserting two of her fingers, pulling it out, and then licking it. She was playing with herself. One hand on her clit, the other playing with her breast. She was into it. She was moaning while looking at me and softly saying my name. "Terri, ohhh, Terri." I felt like I was a part of her moment. "Yes, Terri, right there, baby," she was turning me on again. She pulled out the dildo from the bag that was next to the chair and sucked it. Did she plan this? Because I don't want to believe she walks around with a dildo in her bag all the time. She moved her tongue around the tip and down the side as if it were real. After sucking it for a few minutes, while still fingering herself, she slowly pushed it in. One hand holding on to the chair, the other holding on to the pleasure maker. "Oh, yes, Terri," she said while picking up the speed. "You like what you see?"

I replied, "Yes," and I licked my lips. I couldn't wait to experience what it felt like to have a dick in me. She made it look good. I just didn't want my first time to be this way. Her moans became louder, "Terri, I'm cumming," and she did. She spent the night. I surely wasn't disappointed with my first sexual experience.

Vanessa, at this point, wanted to be more than friends. She stepped back because she wanted me to have the male pleasure as well. "Why don't you talk to Tyler," she told me. She was so eager for me to be with a guy so that way she could really have all of me. I understood where she was coming from, but I started to feel like she was becoming pushy.

On the flight to Bora Bora, Mel sat with me. I had always imagined being there and how beautiful it would be, but my imagination did no justice. It was like a different world. Then, to top it off, I was with three of my favorite people. What more could I ask for? We've been through our fair share of things, but I wouldn't change it for the world. While on this very lengthy flight, I took the time to reminisce about my life.

Thinking back to when I lost my virginity. A few weeks after the sexual encounter with Vanessa, she wanted more. I really liked her, but I wasn't ready at the moment. Plus, with our careers going at the pace it was, we hardly had time to see each other. On one of our girls' nights, I ran into Tyler. I have known Tyler forever, and he has always liked me. We hadn't seen each other in a few months, but he just happened to be at this house party that I went to. Tyler is 6 feet 4 inches and has a medium build. He has a small gap in his teeth, but he looks so cute with it. His gap is a part of his image. He had long dreads. The way he was dressed at this party had all of my attention. He has swag, always did. He had on some jeans that fit well with a button-down shirt, tight enough to show his biceps and he wore it with some loafers. "What's up sexy Terri, looking good as usual," he said.

"Thank you, Tyler," we hugged.

I asked, "How are you?"

"Good, now that I see you," he said with a smirk. You could tell that the chemistry was there. I just never gave in, but he is a good man.

I asked, "Where is Nicole?"

He answered, "We're not together anymore; we only dated a few months, and it just didn't work out."

I said, "Sorry to hear that."

"I'm not; all she did was occupy my time while waiting on you. You know you're the one that I want. You're just giving me a hard time." He said while touching my arm.

I blushed, "You know I like girls Tyler."

He said, "Ha! What does that have to do with me? Give me a chance; I'm guaranteed to change your mind."

I asked, "Are you sure about that? I'm dating someone now." *Why did I just say that?*

He insisted, "It seems to me like you didn't hear me clearly. Do I need to repeat myself?"

I answered, "No, Tyler."

I did like Tyler and his confidence.

He said, "Damn, Terri, the way you just said 'No, Tyler,' you sound so sexy, say it again."

I said, "Stop it."

He laughed and I continued, "Okay, okay. Well, what are

you doing next weekend?" Shocked by my question, he hesitated but was quick on his feet.

"Going out with you."

I laughed, "Cool. So, I'll see you on Saturday."

He asked, "So, what's up with the person you're dating?"

I said, "Call me Tyler." I left him there smiling. As I walked away, I could feel him watching me. The ladies were dancing and enjoying the music. There's nothing like a good house party.

"I saw you over there, Riri; you better let Tyler put that dick on you." I don't even have to say who told me that. If Mel doesn't mess with me, it wouldn't be right. I did have plans for him to put it on me. He just didn't know it. My curiosity had me going insane, especially since I hadn't been touched since that night with Vanessa.

I spent the day with my parents today. I'm still living with them. I'm saving up to buy a house and this is the smartest way to make it happen. It's not like I have to rush. Even though I still live there, I haven't seen them lately. I've been busy living life and so are they. It's Sunday. So, we just made it a family day. Everyone happened to be free today, which doesn't happen often, so it worked out well. My oldest brothers had moved out; they were doing well for themselves. The first twin and my brother right before me played basketball. The other twin played football. I was happy to be around them at the same time. The oldest twin had a baby a month ago. I was finally an auntie and couldn't wait to hold him, spoil him, and do what aunties do best. My daddy loves to cook. He pulled out the grill and got to work. This day was so much fun. We played basketball against each other, and my mom and I had to show the guys we still had it. I remember seeing Mommie and Daddy playing against each other one on one, and she had him on his toes. I secretly recorded them. One day I'll show it to them.

I have a few auditions for this week. I'm excited. I'm going to be trying to do something different. I hope I get it. I like to stay busy. I'm giving myself two years maximum to buy my house. Daddy said he would help me, but I want to show him that his princess can hold her own, even though, if it was up to them, I'd stay here forever. I want my own space where I can have company as I please, and not feel like I have to restrict myself. Regardless of what, they are my parents, and I will respect their house. Mel is the first of us to get her house. We were so happy for her. She closed about two weeks ago. She was adamant on breaking the cycle. She started working as soon as she hit the legal age, and she started working with a catering company and saved her money. She was scared because buying a house was a big step, especially so young but she had the support from all of our parents and her grandmother.

I couldn't believe it was Friday already. We were having movie night tonight at Eb's house. I wondered what movie she had in store for us. She was always switching it up on us. I had a pretty relaxed day today. While waiting to get ready to go to Eboni's house, Tyler called me.

"What's going on, slim? What are you doing?" he asked.

"Relaxing. About to get ready to go to Eboni's house later."

He asked, "Are we still on for tomorrow?"

I answered, "Are we? What's tomorrow?"

"Why do you play with me like this, Terri?"

I replied, "Because you let me. All jokes aside. Yes, we're still on. What are we doing, if you don't mind me asking? I just want to know how to dress."

He answered, "Dress comfortably, okay."

I asked, "What time?"

He replied, "About 2:30."

I said, "That's early."

He answered, "I know. I want to have as much time with you as possible. I've been waiting for this day for a very long time. I have a few things planned. Do you want me to pick you up, or do you want to come meet me at my house?"

I replied, "I'll just come to your house. It will be easier."

"Cool, I'll see you then."

I was here announcing my presence as I rushed into Eb's house. Mel was already here. Nadia was on her way. I brought popcorn, juice, and water. Mel brought her famous dip and nachos. "What are we watching tonight? Ladies," Eboni answered, "Tonight is throwback night. So, we're going to be watching a throwback movie."

"Ughhh," Mel and I said. Eb laughed. Eb and Nadia took movie night to another level sometimes. The thing about Eb is she didn't have a favorite genre of movies, so we don't usually know what we were about to walk into. "Tonight is going to be creepy, scary lights off, drum roll, we're watching Freddy Kruger! Elm Street, oh shit!" I said sarcastically. Eb laughed again.

"Where is Nadia? I can't believe she's missing all these dramatics," Mel said.

"She said she was on her way," Eb said. Mel continued, "Maybe she ran into traffic. I'm giving her ten minutes before I start calling her." Nadia walked in the door five minutes after that. "Sorry, I'm late. I left my phone at home. Had to go back and get it."

Eb said, "We started to get worried."

Nadia replied, Aww I knew y'all loved me."

As we were preparing to watch 'Freddy Kruger,' I spilled the beans.

"So, guess what?" I asked excitingly.

"What's up?" Nadia said playfully. I could always count on her to go along with my crazy excitement. Nadia is a goofball by nature. We all complete each other. Out of the four of us, I can say confidently that Mel and Eb are the most serious. Don't get me wrong if it's a situation where Nadia and I needs to be serious we can definitely handle our business, but they have us beat.

I said, "I have a date with Tyler tomorrow afternoon."

"Make sure you're shaved up," Mel said. Without cracking a smile.

"I know you're going to give him some. You better give him some Terri."

Nadia said, "He's been chasing you for as long as forever, and he isn't afraid to admit that he likes you and you like him too. All y'all doing is playing around with each other. So, stop playing."

I replied, "That's true, but I don't want to give it up on the first night."

"Who's going to judge you? If that's what you want to do, do it! And you don't have to give it up on the first date, but if it happens, it happens. Plus, what if he's not good?" Eboni said.

"She doesn't have anyone to compare it to," Mel responded.

We laughed. I swear she knew just what to say.

That was a low blow, Mel.

"Terri, you know it's all out of love but it's true. You have nothing to compare his dick to."

Nadia said, "Listen, Terri, go out, have a good time, and let him bring you over to our side."

I replied, Thanks, Nad. I'll let y'all know. Let's get this movie over with. We will see what happens tomorrow."

I didn't care for scary movies. It wouldn't be my first

choice, but I couldn't complain. We all played movies that one of us could care less about.

I got an early start today. I went and got a full body wax. My wax lady is the bomb. I left with my skin nice and smooth, like a baby's bottom. I'm still tired from last night. It's 10 a.m., and I'm going to go take a nap. Once I got up, it was 12:45 p.m. I found a nice summer dress. It wasn't tight. It was a flowing type of dress with some Michael Kors sandals. That was easier than I thought. Tyler did say to be comfy. Which I am. I just didn't want to show up in sweatpants. I'll take my chances. I plugged in my phone, played some Mary J. Blige, and jumped in the shower.

Chapter 6

JASON

I was forced to go on this trip with Tiffany. She knows I'm a sucker. She was caught cheating on me again and begged for forgiveness. I told her that it was over but she kept pushing. She went ahead without letting me know and purchased tickets for us to go to Bora Bora. I'm not going to front; I wasn't going. Call me grimey but I only agreed to go on this trip because it was free, and really, it's Bora Bora. But Tiff and I were over. And I was putting an end to this whole charade once we returned.

We were set to go in two weeks. She made it so that we were going to be there for a week. Oh, I can just see it now. Tiffany and I have been together for almost four years. It was great at first. We met through mutual friends. She's a hairstylist. She was fun to be around. I love the fact that she was able to make her schedule; that was a plus, especially since I'm the type who likes to get up and go. My boys said that I spoiled her too quickly, so she took me for a sucker. I'm starting to believe that she really did take me for some type of a fool. I grew up in a single-parent home with three brothers and two sisters. I saw what my mom had to go through, yet she always found the time to love us and made sure we knew how to treat each other and people. She always told us to treat people how we want to be treated. Also, never play with anyone's heart. If you know that you don't like them, don't plan on going further with them; leave them alone, or at least be honest. Most importantly, in a relationship, never allow anyone to get you mad to the point where you put your hands on them. My sisters were drilled just as much as me and my brothers were. Mom made it clear that there was no special treatment. Women can be just as bad as men. I'm thankful that my mom showed me how to love. She had a huge part to play in the type of man I am today. My dad was in the picture. He did come around but didn't play the role he was supposed to since he and my mom separated. My oldest brother had a different father. His dad was in his life and did what he had to do for him. I promised never to be like my dad when I had children. I remember hearing my mom crying many nights after she and my dad separated. He had left her for another woman, who eventually left him for someone else. Karma, I tell you. Mom didn't know we knew. She started to lose herself. After all, she did have four children with this man and was left to carry the burden alone. After a few years, she found herself and started dating, and then she came to realize that my dad leaving was the best thing that ever happened to her. I remember her telling me one time, "Sometimes, you have to lose it all to find it all."

After high school, I got a full football scholarship to college. What a blessing that was. In my sophomore year of college, I was drafted by the NFL. Again, another blessing. The first thing I bought with that money was a house for my mom. I told her she wasn't paying any more rent, and at this point, if she wanted to retire, she could. She was set for life. I was still dating my girlfriend I met when I started college. We dated for three years but broke up because she became insecure with my status and people knowing me. She couldn't handle what came with the title. I thought I would have a future with her. I tried to tell her that before I cheated on her, I'd leave, but in her mind, I was already doing wrong. I came to realize that, indeed, it had nothing to do with me, but it was her battle, so I stopped trying. A year later, I bought my house, and my career was going great. It felt great to have people who knew who I was and looked up to me, especially the children. I gave back to the community; I knew how it was to struggle. I even opened a few sports camps. In my career I made it to two Super Bowls. The last year I played, I got injured; thank God it wasn't bad to the extent that I would have needed to make life changes. I could have continued to play, but my contract was going to be up, so I decided to change my path and become a sports agent. I love that just as much as being on that field. Life was great.

I've been a sports agent for five years. I also invested in a few properties and opened up a convenience store for my mom —something she could have for herself. I believe you should always have something to fall back on.

I was happy when I met Tiff. I had been single for eleven months. I haven't had many relationships because I was always in long-term relationships. I did date a little in between, but I was focused on my new career choice. As I said, things were great between us until I caught her cheating on me in the first year of our relationship. She gave me the worst excuse in the world. She told me that I was always tied up and busy making money, and most of all, she wasn't sure where this relationship was going. I gave her everything, including my time. So, I knew that wasn't the issue. I told her to leave; shocked, she told me she was wrong, that she wasn't thinking, and all that shit that didn't make sense, but I loved her. I was even thinking about proposing to her on her birthday, but I'm glad I found out before I did. Nonetheless, I did give her another chance; sitting here now, I realize that, too, was a mistake. Two and a half years later, I tried to speak about us starting a family, she said, "I don't want any children. I don't want to share you with anyone else." I must say that was a turn-off. I really wanted a family. Why not? She wouldn't give me a straight answer. I had the money, the house. We were stable and we were happy, well so I thought. I left it alone for now. Hopefully, if I were to bring it up again, she would have a change of heart. I do whatever I can to make sure she's happy: Date nights, Spontaneous trips, gifts, and most importantly, my time. I even told her she didn't have to work if she didn't want to. When I love, I love hard, and it shows.

I'm 6 feet 4 inches and muscular. I had dreads, but I cut it last year. I was ready for a different look. When I bought my house, I added a gym. I didn't want to have any excuses as to why I couldn't work out or stay in shape. Working out became part of my everyday routine. Mike, Chris, and Eric would come over, and we would work out for hours. Those guys are my best friends. They've been down since day one. We grew up together. I know a lot of people, but my circle is very, very small.

Now, we're getting ready to board this plane. Tiffany seems to be the only one who's excited. But hey, I'm just reminding myself it's a free vacation where I can kick back and relax. For the first time, I was being treated to something; I was going to enjoy every piece of it. You would think that alone would have me excited, but I'm not. Tiffany was talking to me but for some reason, I couldn't hear her. There were these four ladies who were too excited about something, I'm guessing it was the trip. I wish I could share their joy, walk over, and join them.

"Baby, don't you hear me talking to you? They're calling for our seats; we have to board," Tiffany said.

"Sorry, I was just thinking about something," I replied but honestly, I couldn't get one of those ladies' voices out of my head. I tried to turn to see if I could figure out who she was, but I had no luck. As we boarded the plane, I prepared myself to take this long flight. I knew in my heart it was the end of us. Even my boys felt that I would forgive Tiffany. To be honest, I was tired. I'm a good man and I'm going to enjoy this trip for what it is and go from there. I put our carry-on in the overhead basket while Tiff sat in the middle seat, and I sat in the aisle seat. I watched everyone board the plane: couples, friends, even a few solo people. Tiffany tried to have a small talk; I tried to engage her just for the sake of it. Then, the group of ladies that I heard laughing and talking earlier boarded the plane. I was talking to Tiffany, so I didn't see them again! But when I heard her voice again, for some reason, it made me excited. It showed a little because Tiff got excited, thinking it was for her. I had to find the woman with that voice.

The flight was ready for takeoff. We were two hours into our very long flight. Luckily, no one was sitting next to us. The flight was almost full, give or take, a few seats. We had our pillows and throw blankets. I got comfortable and dozed off. I was awakened by my dick being rubbed up and down. Tiffany and I haven't been intimate since I found out she cheated on me over a month ago. She continued to stroke my dick. I opened my eyes to see her staring at me. I wanted to tell her to stop, but it felt so good. My eyes began to scan my surroundings. It was pretty dark on the flight. The people across us were sleeping. I felt something wet. I looked down, and she was stroking my dick with her mouth. Oh my God! I started to release light moans. I couldn't help it. It felt so good. Tiffany had a way of manipulating my dick with her mouth. I tried to keep my composure. She began to go faster, reaching down to play with my balls in the heat of the moment. I couldn't hold back anymore; I put my pillow in front of my face, I gave her what she wanted, I came in her mouth, and now I was breathing heavily; she looked up at me, smiled, and wiped her mouth. I got up and went to the bathroom. My heart was still racing. The release felt good and the rush from the possibility that someone would see us made it exciting but now I was wondering if she thought that meant we were good. I washed my face and fixed my pants; I'll worry about that later. I walked back to my seat. It looked like more than half the flight was sleeping. Tiff was watching the movie that they were playing, and I went back to sleep.

Once we landed, we had to board another flight that would take us over to Bora Bora Island. This flight was less than an hour. That wasn't bad. Once we landed, again, the view of this Island was beautiful. It looked so peaceful. The weather was just as refreshing. We were able to get transportation to our bungalow. I was officially jet-lagged. I just wanted to lie down for a few hours where I could stretch my legs. It was late afternoon. We grabbed a bite to eat and once we settled in, I went right to sleep.

I woke up to the sun shining through the windows. I couldn't wait to get my day started. There were so many different things to do, yet sitting here and just staring out at the ocean was also a great time pleaser. Tiffany was still sleeping; she looked so comfortable lying there, and I didn't want to bother her. I wanted to go take a stroll on the beach, get my feet wet a little, and scan the area.

It was almost 10 a.m. There were a lot of people out here already. They weren't wasting any time. I didn't blame them. The weather was beautiful, not too hot, it was comfortable, and the wind complimented it. As I walked, I recognized a few people from my flight. Everyone seemed so alive. This feeling, the scene, and the energy are all worth having to deal with Tiffany for another week. There were a few cabanas that people sat in to hide from the sun. As I got closer to one of them, my eyes saw someone, and my heart, for some reason, skipped a beat. Guesstimating, she was about 5 feet 6 inches with nice curly natural hair, she had some color in it, and her breast in that bathing suit made you just want to touch them, then suck them but her smile had me in a trance; I had to snap out of it. I hope she didn't notice me staring. As I passed by, she looked at me, smiled again, and said, "Hi, how are you?" At that moment, I was stuck in my tracks. It was her! That was the sweet voice I heard in the airport that had me zoned out. I said Hi back, smiled, and tried to get out of there before I made a fool of myself. She was beautiful. There was a slight shyness about her, and it made her more beautiful. I noticed by the way she spoke. I hung out at the beach for another hour before heading back to the bungalow. I walked in the door; it looked like Tiff was just waking up. "Morning baby, where were you?" *Is she really calling me baby? Does she really think because she sucked my dick extremely well on the plane that, we are cool?* This last deception did it for me. I loved everything about Tiff. I used to admire her free-spirited nature and the way she didn't seem to carry a care in the world. She didn't let things get to her like other people did. She wasn't tied down to time like the rest of us. She slept late and was unapologetic about it. Being a hairdresser afforded her the luxury to just be. But all these attributes that I once loved about her have become a major annoyance. I don't see her like I once did. Sleeping late was a habit I couldn't stand but tolerated. She was just a late starter. You would think that because we were in a different country, a beautiful one at that, she would want to get up early and explore, see, live, and not just sleep most of the day away. We went to bed pretty early, so there was no excuse. I replied, "I just went out to the beach to stretch my legs. It's beautiful out there."

She replied, "Oh, okay. What time is it?"

"It's 11:30 a.m

Maybe you should get up so we can get something to eat and get the day started."

She said, "I know what we can get started." I acted like I didn't hear anything she said.

I asked, "What do you have on the itinerary for today?"

Rolling her eyes, she replied, "We're going ATV riding today at 1 p.m. Then we can probably go for a swim and have lunch, depending on what time we get back."

I replied, "Sounds good. I'm going to start getting ready."

At this time, it was hot out. We made it to the ATV location. I was so ready for this. I hadn't ridden one of these in years. I had my face mask, scarf, and sneakers. Ready to get dirty. Tiff, for some reason, wanted to be cute. She put on makeup and a nice brand-new t-shirt with some light blue jean shorts. I asked her why she was dressing up. "I have to look good at all times," she replied.

I asked, "You do know where and what we're going to do, right?"

She said, "Yeah. I sure do."

. . .

Poor Tiff was already sweating. I could see she was starting to get frustrated, and we hadn't even started yet. The child in me wanted to say, "I told you so," but I was going to be nice. "Are you okay?" I asked.

"Yeah, I'm good." She replied.

I asked, "Do you want some water? I had grabbed a few bottles before we left."

She replied, "Sure, thank you."

The instructor was going over the do's and the don'ts while giving us a little history of the country. For some reason, I thought I heard her voice again, the voice from the airport, the same voice from the beach. I started looking around, but she wasn't here.

Tiff asked, "What's wrong? Are you okay?"

I replied, "Yeah, I'm good."

I didn't want to believe I was hearing things. I just couldn't get her off my mind, and we hadn't had a conversation yet. What if I don't even like her? Impossible, what if she's crazy? Nah, I don't think so. All I kept saying to myself was I had to see her again.

Finally, we got on the ATVs, man this machine was amazing. We went up, down, over bumps, dirt kicking up this way, that way. I loved it. I had to snap a few pictures for the memory book. My boys would love this. We will definitely have to do this one weekend. We rode for three hours. Stopping along the way to take pictures and to get a better view of the areas we were riding through. Fun, fun, fun. We had a fun group of people with us. Everyone got along well, which made the ride more enjoyable. Felt like a big group of friends. At the end, we all took a group picture. On our way back to our room, Tiff and I stopped to get some ice cream and some pizza from Mitira Pizza.

. . .

We got in at about 6:45, and I jumped straight in the shower. Talk about feeling refreshed. That shower was everything at this vey moment. I grabbed a slice of pizza and walked out onto the balcony to take in the view. We were literally in the water. I could see the fish under us. The water was clear. I was hoping to be able to see the sunset from this view, but I missed it. Maybe I could catch it before we leave. I went back in for another slice of pizza and a bottle of water. It tasted really good. Tiff was just getting out of the shower. She looked good. I loved her, but I knew I was done. She joined me on the balcony with her pizza and some wine. We spoke a little, but most of the time, we sat in silence, staring out at the ocean. The wind was cool. All of a sudden, the airport lady ran across my mind. Why didn't I talk to her? Ask her for her name or just say something. I kept playing the scene at the beach back in my head. I could beat myself up. I felt hands rubbing on my legs, making its way up to my dick and pulling it out of my basketball shorts. Her tongue made circles around the head, and I was at attention. She began to stroke and suck like she knew it was her last time. I moaned as a light wind blew. She was in control. She began to pick up speed and then slowed down. In my heart, I didn't want to have sex with her, but I'm a man. I placed my hand on her head to help with the strokes. I was okay with just cumming in her mouth, but since this was going to be the last time, we might as well go out with a bang. The good thing is we used condoms when we fucked. She didn't want any children. She tried birth control twice, but the side effects made her gain weight and lose her hair. So, she got off. We didn't use condoms for a while after she was off the birth control, and then we had a pregnancy scare. So, condoms it was, all the time.

Then, once I knew she cheated on me, condoms were okay in my book. When I felt the urge to cum, I moved her head, laid her back on the lounge chair, and sucked on her breast. We didn't kiss; she wanted to, but kissing meant something to me; it was intimate, especially during sex and it just wasn't there. When I was sucking on her breast, I began fingering her pussy, and caressing her clit. She began moaning out of control. I grabbed the condom and slid it on while still sucking on her breast.

"Take it off, I'm ready Jason." I heard her, but I kept it on. I penetrated my dick into her pussy; she began to shake. I fucked her good, with a little anger and hurt. She began to scream my name. Her moans let me know she was cumming. "I love you," she said once we were done, leaving her with no response, I went and took a quick shower while reevaluating my life. I knew I shouldn't have slept with her. That was a big mistake. I should have left things how it was. All of a sudden, she came into the shower with me. Fuck! She came in, touching me. I just gave it to her again. It was quick. I didn't cum; she did, though. I had to let her know that we were done. I didn't want to ruin the trip. We had only been here for two days, with five more to go. Once I got out of the shower, I went and laid down.

I woke up extra excited this morning. Tiff said that we were going snorkeling today. The thought that I would be swimming with sharks and other fishes excited me. Well, the more I thought about it, the more I became nervous. It was something different, and I could take it off my bucket list. It was only 7 a.m., but I had a lot on my mind. I was an early bird anyway, and the heavy thoughts just didn't help. I got up, took a shower, walked out, and relaxed on the patio. I took some pictures of the view. Mike called. Mike is one of my best friends. There's nothing that we didn't know about each other. I love him like my brother.

"Yoooo! What's up?" I said excitingly. "How is it? I was waiting for you to call me to let me know you made it." He said sounding concerned.

"Sorry, bro. But Mike, we have to take a trip here together, either a guy's trip or with our other halves or whatever. It's absolutely amazing here." I expressed.

"That's what's up." He replied, "You know you and Chris are the only ones that have someone."

I answered, "Well, it's about to just be Chris in a minute."

"Yeah, yeah, yeah," Mike said.

I know Mike knows that I'm serious and he knows I'm all for love, but he knows me, and he knows that I'm done with Tiffany and her manipulative ways.

"You guys will love it. I exclaimed. We went ATV riding yesterday and we're going snorkeling later on today."

He asked, "Where is Tiff now?"

I replied, "Sleeping, you know she doesn't get up early. She'll probably be up at ten and start to rush. I'm already ready."

I continued, "So let me tell you, Mike. Yesterday, I took a stroll on the beach while Tiff was still sleeping. I saw this woman. My god, she was beautiful. The crazy part was I remember hearing her voice at the airport but never saw who it was. So, on the beach, she spoke while walking by. I said hi, but your boy froze up. You know I'm not the freezing-up type! But I was lost for words."

He asked, "You didn't even get her name?"

I replied, "Not even her name. But trust me, because of her

voice, I was able to put a face to her, and I'm not going to forget any of it, so I'll find her, and I will get her name."

"You're making me wonder how things are going with you and Tiffany." He inquired.

"It's going. I mean, I'm not going to lie; it started awkwardly; as you know, I didn't want to come. But I did. Everything was going fine until she decided to put the moves on me. I tried to resist, but I'm a man, and she was my girl. Yo, we're thousands of miles from home. So, I did what I had to do. I fucked the breaks off of her. I know it's over. I felt nothing. Then, when I went to take a shower, she came for more. I gave it to her, and she will never forget me. Mike, she had a whole fucking relationship, whatever you want to call it, with someone I knew very well, and she expects it to work. This is the second time she's been caught, but who knows within the almost four years how many other times she cheated. Maybe this is why she didn't want a family."

He replied, "I know this shit is hard, Jason. It was messed up on both their parts. You're a good man. That's why we told you to take your ass on that plane and enjoy it. For once, you didn't have to front the trip. Enjoy it. Plus, you met, well, let me rephrase. You saw a young lady. Who knows what can come out of it? She can be the future Mrs. McKnight and appreciate you for the man you are, or maybe you will find someone else. Just enjoy the moment. You know in your heart that it's over. Tiff has the right to know that, but not right now. Y'all are how many thousand miles away from home. That's not the place you want to tell her. Even though, in her heart, she may already know. Just let go for the moment and enjoy. Maybe lay low on the sex. We know that it carries a lot of emotions. Even though you may think you're detached. She isn't."

I replied, "You're right, Mike. I appreciate you for that."

"That's what I'm here for. He reminded me. I know you're going snorkeling. Have fun.

Yeah, and did I tell you it's with sharks? "Nah, you didn't, he laughed. Well, bro, have fun. I was just checking on you. Remember to not over think anything, and again, have fun, and most of all, be careful. Hit me up if you can. I'm hoping that I really won't hear from you, but if I do, I will be here. Be safe. Love you, bro."

"Love you too, man."

Mike is a therapist, a damn good one too. He has his own practice. I trust his words, not just as a therapist but as my brother and friend.

It was 9:30, and Tiff was still sleeping. I just didn't get it. I laid down and watched TV for a while and checked on a few things while I waited. Tiff finally woke up at 10:05. Thank God the meet-up spot was within walking distance. "Why didn't you wake me up?" She grumbled. I told her we had time, just to avoid it turning into an argument. She knew we had plans. I have told her on different occasions that she can't always rely on people, or else she will run into problems.

We made it there exactly at eleven. We got geared up, took some before pictures, and we were ready to go. What an experience this was. A few black-tip sharks swam by me; they were calm like I wasn't even there, but man in my mind, I shit myself like four times. If it were to really happen, it would be worth the embarrassment. I was so happy I knew how to swim. The water was beautiful, clean, and clear. The excursion took about two and a half to four hours. We were under the water for thirty minutes. They provided us with food and beverages. We were able to take pictures in the water. We took group pictures, selfies, you name it. I have always loved to take pictures since I was a kid. I believe in having memories, plus there was nothing like having pictures to go with your story. We got back to land at 3:30. I was tired. The water sure would do it to you. Walking back to the bungalow, we stopped to get a drink. Tiff got a margarita, and I tried a drink called Bora Bora. It was early. I didn't see the rush to get back to the room.

"Are you having a good time?" Tiffany asked me.

I replied, "Yes, I am, thank you. I appreciate it."

"You're welcome. Jason, look, I just want to let you know that I am really sor…"

I interrupted, "Stop, I don't want to talk about that now. We're here, let's just enjoy our time, and we will discuss it at another time and place."

In a low tone, she said, "Okay, I respect that."

We sat there, enjoying the music and the waves. We ordered two more drinks and then headed back to the room. I was tired.

I asked, "What's the plans for tomorrow?"

"I didn't really have much more planned. I thought maybe we would play it by ear. I was thinking about the beach, but we were in the water today, so if you want, we can just relax tomorrow, stay in, and then go to dinner tomorrow night. We can go to the beach on Friday or Saturday, and we can find some other stuff to do. It's up to you."

I replied, "Okay, that sounds good." I got in the shower, had a little bit of flashbacks of the trip so far, and before I could count to ten, I was out.

I woke up to the sound of rain. It was 3 a.m. I was thirsty, so I got some water and I lay down until I went back to sleep. I must say, yesterday was a refreshing day. Thank God we had no plans. I finally fell asleep after getting up at 3 a.m. and listening to the rain. I'm not one to stay still and sleep late, but I took advantage of it. I stayed in bed all day. I slept, woke up, and went back to sleep. At one time, I noticed Tiffany was gone.

When I woke back up again, she had brought lunch and dinner. I got up, ate, laid back down, and was out again. I got more than enough rest, so I was ready for the beach today. I just want to relax some more. I've been up for a few hours. We weren't going to head to the beach until 1 p.m. since we didn't have a special schedule to be on. I put the stuff down by the cabana and then went to order our drinks. When I got back, Tiff was already in the water. The beach wasn't crowded today. I looked out and saw a boat heading out with the snorkeling crew. I know they are going to have so much fun.

"The water feels great, Jason. Are you going to go in?" She asked.

I replied, "Yeah. But I'm just enjoying the scenery right now."

I was halfway done with my drink. She sat down and enjoyed the scenery as well.

I asked, "Are you enjoying yourself, Tiff?"

She replied, "I am. This place was a great choice."

"Yeah, it was." I agreed.

The tone of her voice was a little sad.

She asked, "Do you want another drink?"

"Yeah, but I'm going to go in the water first." Replying to her question.

She said, "Okay, go ahead. I'm going to go get it."

I went into the water. Tiff was right, it was warm and clean. I felt free in the water. When I got out, Tiff had already finished her drink and went for another. I didn't realize I was in the water that long. From her demeanor, I knew she wasn't all too happy. Maybe reality was finally kicking in for her. "Was I in the water that long?"

She laughed. "Not really."

"You drank that drink really fast and on to another," I said.

She replied, "Not that fast. I started at the bar, and Jason, I'm a big girl; I can handle it."

I laughed. "Okay, big girl."

We stayed out there until it got close to sunset before going back to the room. Tiff went straight to bed; it was still early. She was tired from our outing earlier, plus she drank a lot. I tried to sleep, but I couldn't. I felt restless, so I went for a walk. The night was still young, so why not? A lot was going on. I saw couples hugging and kissing. That could have been Tiff and I,

I guess this was the downside of the trip. Getting to one of the bars, I decided to get a drink. That was how I saw her, she was sitting there having a drink, alone, is what it looked like from here. I stood and watched before I approached her. I wasn't going to freeze up this time. Her hair was down. It was long. She had on a nice long orange dress with white sandals. I wondered why she was out here by herself. Where was her man? I laughed; one would wonder the same about me. Maybe she was waiting for someone. There's only one way to find out. I could hear her voice replaying in my head from earlier.

"Hi," I said. She looked at me; her eyes were sensual and welcoming. She looked shocked as if she wasn't expecting anyone. She had on some gold bracelets, and her nails were done. She stared for a few seconds before finally responding. "Hi," she smiled. She has a sexy smile, just gorgeous, and those dimples; you could see them from a mile away. I've always had a thing for dimples but, surprisingly, never dated anyone with them. I sat down. Maybe a little closer than I planned. She smelled sweet; I could eat her right now.

"I'm Jason."

She replied, "HI, I'm Nadia."

I loved it, and it was all coming together. I finally got a face to the voice and the name to the face. "Nadia is a beautiful name. I had never met anyone with your name before." I know it may have been a little cheesy, but it was too late to take it back. I ordered a drink, hoping it would help me relax. I had never been this nervous to talk to a woman before. I had always been confident in myself, but she did something and didn't even know it.

I said, "I hope it's not a problem if I'm sitting here with you. I don't want to cause any problems between you and your man."

She replied, "My man is the least of your worries."

I asked, "Why is that?"

She answered, "Because I don't have one."

Yes! That was the best news I had heard all day. I brought her a drink, and we talked and laughed; it felt unreal. I began to loosen up a bit. Nadia was great company. Not often do you run into someone and click right away. We were into a lot of the same things. While talking, we even found out that we lived in the same city. This has to be a dream. Someone pinch me.

How come we never ran into each other before, I thought.

"I see you're always smiling and blushing."

"I know. It's just who I am" she replied.

I said, "I'm going to start calling you Smiley, if that's okay with you."

"Smiley is cute, I like it."

This was one time I wished time could stay still. I ordered another round of drinks. There wasn't any silence between us, so I didn't realize how much time had passed.

"Would you like to take a walk?" I asked.

"Let's go."

We grabbed our drinks and proceeded to walk. We stopped at this spot, away from the crowd, and stared into the ocean.

"This island is so beautiful, relaxing, and stress-free." She said.

"It really is Smiley, and I'm so happy I made it here."

While she spoke to me, I just wanted to kiss her. I prayed she didn't ask me if I came here with someone. I wouldn't know what to say because I wouldn't want to ruin the moment, but I knew I had to be truthful. The only thing I was sure of was that I wanted to see her again; I wanted to know her better. She became quiet. "Are you okay, Nadia?"

She replied, "Yes, I'm good. Are you okay?"

I smiled, "Yeah, I am."

We were just about done with our drinks, and I felt great.

Looking at my watch, it's getting late, Nadia agreed. "If you are not in a rush, I'm not," I wasn't expecting that response. I felt something take over me, and before I could stop myself, I kissed her. I pulled her close to me; she was short compared to me. I gently placed my lips on hers; they were soft, she didn't resist, and she kissed back. Our lips parted; there was passion in this kiss. With my eyes closed, I imagined making love to her on the sand while saying her name with each stroke. I pulled her closer, not wanting to let her go. I put my tongue in her mouth, and she accepted it.

I had to stop; my dick wanted her too. I began to rub her back with slow strokes. *Stop Jay,* I said to myself. *As much as you may want her, you're still here with Tiff.* I argued with myself for a few minutes. This felt right; she felt right. I didn't want to stop kissing her. I gently pulled away. There was a shy but sexy look in her eyes. She smiled. Then I said to her, "You're going to be my wife. I promise you that." She laughed, but it was different.

She said, "You don't know me well enough to know if you

will even like me as your girlfriend, and that's if I even want to be that girl."

I replied, "Well, there's only one way to find out, right?" She chuckled. "Can I please get your number Smiley, and can we see each other again later on today if possible?" We exchanged numbers. She kissed me on the cheek, "Good night, Jason," and she walked into the night. I stood and watched her until I couldn't see her anymore. Smiling, I started walking back to my bungalow. I smelled her all over me. I was licking my lips, replaying that passionate kiss. It was 1 a.m. when I made it back.

I tried to hide my excitement. Tiff was up watching TV.

I said, "Hey, good night. I'm surprised you're awake as tired as you were when we got back in earlier."

Tiff replied, "I'm still tired. I got up to use the bathroom and noticed you weren't here."

"I couldn't sleep, so I went to explore a little. I heard music playing and wanted to see what was going on and see a little of the culture in the nighttime. We're only here for two more days. Well, one now, I'm trying to take it all in." I told her.

She said, "Oh, I only have something planned for our very last day, and that's dinner. So, if you want to relax or just hang out, just let me know."

I had plans to see Nadia again later today. Tiff obviously wasn't on my mind while I was making these plans. I'll figure it out. Once I woke up, I got us breakfast: pancakes, eggs, bacon, fruits, and freshly squeezed orange juice. I had to order more. I drank mine before I left the restaurant. We sat on the patio and ate breakfast. I was feeling a little tired and didn't sleep much once I got in. I guess from the excitement with Smiley. "There's an all-day spa I want to try out if you don't mind," Tiff said.

She continued, "I'm going to get a facial, body massage,

feet, mud bath, the whole works." "Sounds fun. Go ahead, I'll find something to get into."

Look at that; I didn't have to try. Within the hour, Tiff had showered and gotten ready to go. Once she left, I laid down on the bed and flipped over on my stomach. The bungalow had the floor set up where you could see the ocean, not the whole thing, but in certain spots. The view was mesmerizing. I looked at the fish as they played together. Before I knew it, Nadia and I were swimming together in the water. Her skin glowed as if she belonged there. We swam in unison with the fish. I got a hold of her, and we kissed; I ran my hands across her breast, and she whispered in my ear to love her right. She started to rub my dick, pulling me closer, "Be gentle with me and promise me that you won't hurt me." She started taking off her bathing suit and I jumped up looking around for her. Then I noticed the fish. Fuck! It was a dream. I looked down, and my dick was hard. I had to go take a shower. That dream felt so real. We were meeting at 2 p.m. I didn't make any plans. I was going to take her to lunch. They had a boat that sailed out on the water, and you could have lunch or dinner, depending on the time. It was 12:45. I finally went in the shower and stood under the hot water while the steam filled the room. Afterward, I put on a pair of shorts and a polo-style shirt from Armani; it looked like it came right out of the cleaners. I sprayed some of my Dior by Christian Dior. It was 1:30, and I was ready to go. I left early because I didn't want to rush. I took my time. The weather was just right. Oh, shit, I had to call Mike. I called, but he didn't answer. I waited a few minutes, and I called again, "Mike."

He replied, "Hey, everything okay?"

I answered, "Yeah, I just need a huge favor. Someone is supposed to drop something off for me tomorrow. Will you be able to grab it for me? You can go to my house if you want.

They will be there at about 3 p.m., but I'll let you know if anything changes."

He replied, "Yeah, I can do that for you."

I said, "Thanks. Do you know where the spare key is?"

He answered, "Yeah, I got you. You sound really excited, a lot different from when I last spoke to you."

I said, "Since I have you on the phone, I might as well tell you."

"Oh, you have something to tell me? He asked. I thought it was because you had one more day left.""No, not really, but that's a good thought." I laughed.

"Are things better with you and Tiff?"

"It's pretty much the same since we last spoke. We're okay, though."

He asked, "So, what is with all the excitement?

Okay, I can't stay long.

Is Tiff there?" He asked anxiously.

"No, she went to an all-day spa," I answered,

"So, you're hanging by yourself?"

"That's the thing, no. I found Nadia!"

He asked, "Nadia, who? The mystery lady?"

"Yes!" I chuckled. "I hung out with her last night, and I'm on my way to meet her now. We're going to have lunch."

"Jay, how did you pull that off? He asked.

"Tiff decided to go to the spa, so it gave me some time. I'll give you the full details when I get back in town."

He replied, "Okay, I'm happy that you were able to find her. Have fun, but please be careful."

I replied, "Thanks, I have to go. I'm almost there."

I got off the phone with Mike and couldn't believe it; Nadia was already there. That was a plus for me. She saw me coming and smiled. It was so contagious you couldn't help but smile when she smiled at you. She greeted me with a hug and a kiss on the cheeks.

"Good afternoon, Jason,"

"Good afternoon, Smiley. I said joyfully.

I ordered you a drink. I wasn't sure what the plans were. So, I'm starting us off with a drink. I hope a Long Island iced tea is okay."

I replied, "It's perfect."

She was glowing. Her dress was hunter green, mid-length, and it hugged every curve God had blessed her with, and her hair was in a bun. Let's not forget the brown sandals that slightly wrapped up her legs. She smelled amazing. I never smelled it before.

"You smell good. What are you wearing?" I had to ask.

She replied, "It's called Good Girl by Carolina Herrera."

I asked, "Are you a good girl?" "Wouldn't you like to know?" She said with a smile.

The boat was going to start boarding at 3 o'clock. It was to sail for two and a half hours. We started walking closer to the dock. They had tables and benches over there where we could sit and wait. I really wanted a picture with her, so I asked a man walking by if he could take a picture of us.

"Beautiful couple," he said.

"See, Nadia, we look good together. Even the man couldn't help but to give us a compliment" I said.

Ignoring what I just mentioned, she said, "Dinner on a boat, that's nice, Jay."

"Thank you." She called me Jay. I loved it.

Chapter 7

TIFFANY

"This mother fucker," I said to myself. Was I really seeing this shit? I moved closer to get a better view but far enough to where he wouldn't see me if he turned around. A large palm tree stood a few feet from where they were sitting, and it provided me with the perfect hiding spot. They sat staring into each other's eyes like they were madly in love. *Who is this bitch? Did he plan this? Did he meet her here? Did he bring her here?* A million thoughts raced through my head all at once. *No, he couldn't have brought her here.* I was boiling mad and couldn't think clearly. I knew I deserved it, though. I loved him but hadn't been fair to him in our years together. Jay is a good man and completely undeserving of everything I have put him through. He stayed with me because that was my Jay, loyal to a fault. As I stood behind that palm tree, watching him with another woman, I felt tears rolling down my cheeks. I loved him. I wiped my face. *Go get your man, Tiffany!* Before I realized what I was doing, I marched over to where they were seated. He was slowly caressing her arm with one hand while he took the other hand and kissed it softly. My lips, those were my lips. As I got closer, I could see how pretty she was. She smiled at him, and I could see the dimples protruding from her flawless, brown-skinned face. Jay was a sucker for some damn dimples. I didn't know exactly how I would play this out just yet: jealous, ghetto girlfriend, or calm and unassuming as though I hadn't been watching them flirt with one another for the past few minutes.

"Hey, baby, what are you doing here? I thought you were back at the bungalow," I said with as much enthusiasm as I could muster. Calm and unassuming it was. He snatched his hand away. His eyes widened. I stood there for a second, taking him in. He was sexy as hell! I love the roundness of his light brown eyes and bushy eyebrows that I insisted on shaping for him. "Men don't arch their eyebrows, Tiffany," he'd protest.

"We're not arching them, babe; we're shaping them. There's a difference." He obliged, but not without putting up a fight.

"Who is this, Jason?" the woman asked, bringing me back to reality. Before he could get a chance to respond, I quickly answered. "Oh, I'm sorry, I'm so rude. I'm Tiffany, his Fiancé."

"Fiancé?" she repeated. She sounded genuinely hurt. I could have said girlfriend, but fiancé had more of the dramatic effect I was aiming for. If she had any decency about her, she would stay away from a man whose about to get married. From what I saw between them from behind that palm tree, I needed to get rid of her quickly. "I'm sorry, Tiffany, I was under the wrong impression. Congratulations, and good luck with everything." She grabbed her purse and walked away. "Nadia, Nadia, please don't leave, please let me explain," Jason chased after her. I turned around to watch him, half in shock. Did he just leave me standing here? He grabbed her arm, but she yanked it away. They were too far away for me to hear what was being said. She walked faster. He could have easily caught up to her, but he gave up. Whatever she said to him must have really hurt. He stood there with his hands on his head.

Chapter 8

JASON

can't believe she did that! What the fuck was she thinking? I saw hurt, embarrassment, and slight anger in Nadia's eyes and facial expression. I ran after her, trying to explain; she told me she knew I was a mistake, that she didn't know why she thought I would be any different, and that I seemed too good to be true. It took me a few minutes to gather my thoughts, and I tried to keep them together! Tiffany was approaching me; of all our years together, I had never been out of character with Tiffany.

"Look, what was I sup…" Before she could get the words out, I snapped!

"What the fuck was that? My fiancé, really?"

"How could you be enjoying another woman while we're here together?" She asked.

"God damn it! Is that a trick question? I guess the same way you were fucking other men while we were in a whole relationship! Should I add, also living together"?

She seemed stunned by my response. Her expression

changed. "I thought we were here to put things aside and make things work."

"That's what you were here for! I was having a good time and didn't want to ruin the moment but thank you for fucking it up."

"Do you mean to ruin the moment with her or me?" she asked.

I started to respond, but my answer would have crushed her.

She continued, "So, you're just going to ignore me? What else was I supposed to do, Jason? I saw you sitting here smiling and enjoying the company of a beautiful woman, looking at her in ways you never looked at me!"

I said, "Tiffany, don't try to sell me that bullshit. I loved you, did everything for you, and looked at you like you were my everything, but you never appreciated it because you were too wrapped up in you! Thank you for making this so much easier for me. Don't wait up for me either."

She begged, "Jason, please."

"Tiffany, stop; we don't need to cause any more attention to ourselves."

I had to get away from her. I couldn't believe I still had another full day left here. I left her standing there calling for me. I started to feel a little embarrassed while walking past a few people. When I looked to my right, I saw two ladies standing there. They looked like the friends Nadia came with; one smiled. Oh shit, I wonder if she told them about me. Did she tell them what happened on the beach last night? Oh no, did they just see me with Tiffany and heard everything? I started to feel a rush of panic coming on. I really wanted to ask them for Nadia but couldn't. I felt so bad. It was still early. I didn't know what to do or where to go. I was no longer hungry, just angry now. I walked to the bar and drank more than usual. I just kept replaying it in my head. I was hoping I would see Nadia out here. I didn't know where she stayed. I felt like going and knocking on every door until I found her. She had tears in her eyes. I made her cry before I had the chance to show her how much I could love her. How was I supposed to come back from that? I should have told her. That night at the bar, I should have told her everything. Tiffany kept calling my phone, and I kept sending her to voicemail. She definitely outdid herself; someone had to give her an award for this. I felt like a fool for the first time; I was even ashamed to share this with Mike, Chris, and Eric. I couldn't drink anymore. It was now 2 a.m. The temperature had dropped, and I was drunk and ready to lie down. Fuck, I didn't want to go back to my bungalow; I should have gone over to one of the hotels and got a room earlier. I stumbled my way back to the room. I don't ever want to be this drunk again. I opened the door, and Tiffany jumped up. "Jason, thank God you're okay. I was worried." I walked past her and went to take a shower. I got out, grabbed a pillow and blanket, and laid on the floor. I couldn't wait for Monday afternoon to get out of here.

The sight of Tiffany made me sick to my stomach.

When I got up at 7:30, I had a hangover, it wasn't too bad, so I got myself together and I left the bungalow. I didn't want to be in this area; I was hoping to run into Nadia. I needed her to give me the chance to explain and take away the hurt, but I didn't. I scanned the crowd, but she was nowhere in sight. I went hiking; I might as well do something daring; everything else seemed to be going downhill. Hiking helped me; it took my mind off everything temporarily. Once I returned to my area, I stopped at a restaurant for dinner. I wanted a table outside. While sitting and eating my food, I finally saw the sunset. It was beautiful—still no luck with finding Nadia. Once I get back home, I'll try calling her.

On our flight back home, there were different people from the original flight when we came, which was expected. Some people stayed longer or shorter times, took a different flight in the morning or evening, or even missed their flight. This flight wasn't full, so I moved my seat and got comfortable for this long flight home.

Chapter 9

NADIA

Once we got back from Bora Bora, I started working out. With me being so busy, I kind of neglected it. I woke up today wanting to run longer; I needed to push myself harder. Plus, I had some anger to burn. I'm starting to believe that I'm meant to be by myself. That incident with Jason keeps playing in my mind. And to think I was going to give him some that night. The ladies always say, "Be a little more spontaneous." I'm wondering if I should have given it to him at the beach and just left it there. There's something about him; he's different, I know he is. Why didn't he just tell me he was engaged and wanted to have a little fun before he made it official? I just kept hearing. "I'm Tiffany, his fiancée." I began to pick up speed as I ran. The corner of my eyes was getting wet. He seemed just as shocked and startled when she walked up.

She's about 5 feet 8 inches, has a nice chocolate complexion, and is thick. Her hair was short, like a bob, but long on one side, short on the other, and the back shaved low. She was cute. From the bag she had in her hand, it looked like she had just come from the spa. The ladies went there today. I wonder if they saw her. I was going to go but canceled to be with Jason. I was amazed that he ran after me. Why would he leave his fiancée there and try to explain anything to me? Shouldn't he be explaining things to her? I was too embarrassed to stop. He grabbed my arm to get me to stop, and I snapped at him, possibly hurting his feelings. My words were harsh. He let go of my arms and stood there. Nothing made sense. I returned to my bungalow and didn't leave until it was time to get our flight. I refused to step foot out there unless I had to. When the ladies returned from the spa and saw me there, they were shocked. I didn't feel like saying anything at the moment; I just told them I didn't feel good. Eb and Terri kept looking at me like they knew something. Later that night, I couldn't hold it in anymore and told them what had happened. For the first time, they were speechless. They just gathered around me in a big group hug.

I had plans on starting back my open mic nights. I love poetry. I used to do it at least once a week, sometimes three times a week, depending on what I had going on. I finally made the time to continue working on my book. I'm supposed to be meeting with an editor next week.

This new area that I'm working out is great. It has a grass area. It's a very big park. I might bring my yoga mat one day and do a few things.

We've been back a month now. The second week, Jason started calling me. I wanted to answer, but I couldn't. Why is he calling me? Was my initial thought. I answered by accident one day, but I couldn't speak. The words just wouldn't come out. I heard him keep saying "hello." His voice was so soothing. He eventually hung up.

After my run, I saw a smoothie king and decided to go in. I got a Gladiator, which is a fitness blend. I tried the strawberry flavor with bananas and pineapples. I must say it was good. This might be my new favorite drink. Walking back to my car, I realized that today was a free day for me, but I had to find something to do.

While driving, I took another sip from my smoothie. I was still shocked at how good it tasted. I stopped at the supermarket on my way home. I stocked up with a week worth of food. When I finally got home, I peeled off my clothes quickly as I needed to take a bath; my body was aching. I ran the water, put Dr. Teals Epsom salt in the water, and got in. I lost track of time while I was there. That hot water was soothing to the spots that were hurting, and I didn't want to get out. Soon, I will be doing my first open Mic. I didn't know what I wanted to recite. Maybe I might use something I have already. Who knows?

Tonight was the night. I was nervous; I hadn't been in front of a crowd for a long time.

I made it there at about 7:50. The ladies were already there.

"Hey, Nadia," Terri said. "Are you excited?"

"A little," I replied. "For some reason, I am more nervous than anything."

Terri replied, "Sis, you got this."

Terri seemed a little more excited than usual, but then again, she gets like that occasionally, especially when she's extra happy. I thought maybe it was because the fashion show was around the corner. We were supposed to be going this week, but they had to change the date due to a minor problem with the location. I sat with them while a few poets did their thing. I love this. I love the different levels poetry can take you and the beauty of it; there's no right or wrong way to do it. I was next;

after the intermission, the DJ switched up the music a little and started playing 'OMG' by Usher. I ordered a shot of Patron.

"Okay, guys, I'm next. I'll see y'all in a few."

"Kick ass sis!"

"Thanks, Eboni." I shook my head and laughed. Did I mention how much I love these ladies? Sitting backstage, I went over a few lines in my head. I was using one of my poems I wrote after Andre and I broke up. The music was lowered. Then the DJ started talking.

"Right now, I'm about to introduce y'all to this phenomenal sister. She has blessed our stage many times before, and I'm honored to be able to say she's back. Please snap your fingers and welcome Nadia to the stage." I closed my eyes, and I let the words flow.

* * *

"The hurt I'm feeling I can no longer hide.

The pain I cannot deny.

Look in my eyes; tell me, what do you see?

Can you really see what you did to me?

Feel my pain, feel my sorrow; the way it hurts is like there's no tomorrow.

Take it away; it's what I need you to do, but

of course, you can't, and you know that it's true.

I loved you with all I had, and you betrayed me.

Got me walking around here looking crazy.

I wish you could feel how I feel for just a moment.

You wouldn't know what to do with yourself if you had to feel how I'm feeling right now at this moment.

This is something that just won't go away.

So, I won't even lie and deny and say

 that I'm okay.
Maybe we will make it, maybe we won't.
I tried so hard to push this aside.
But I can't
My brain goes a million miles a second.
And it's driving me crazy.
My heart is broken, shattered into pieces.
I'm so angry and full of rage.
I want to say I hate you, but in my heart, I really don't.
Just hurt and disappointed.
Another lesson learned.

 I heard the snaps.

"Thank you, thank you" and I walked backstage, wiping the edge of my eyes as I walked back to the table, that felt great. I'm so glad that I decided to come back. I didn't realize how much I missed it or how much it missed me. Walking through the crowd, I joined the ladies and had a seat. Mel had my Amaretto Sour waiting for me. I thought I saw Jason here; maybe my eyes were playing tricks on me. Or maybe it was wishful thinking. I'll blame it on my Patron shot and the fact that the lights are dimmed. I turned around to join the conversation, and this guy approached me.

"Nadia, I wanted to tell you that you did great tonight. You also look amazing."

I replied, "Thank you."

He asked, "Will you be performing again soon?"

"I plan on it."

"Great, I look forward to seeing you again." I smiled.

"What was that?" Mel said.

"Girl, I guess he was trying to get my number but probably chickened out, which worked out well for me, no complaints."

We hung out for about two more hours and then went home. I have a job to do on Monday.

A company wants me to redesign their office space. I'll show them three ideas I think will work well with the type of space they have, and once they give me the okay. I can get started.

Chapter 10

TERRI

I was low on gas, so I stopped at a gas station before heading to Tyler's house. Looking at the clock, it was 2 p.m. That's it. It felt later. I sat in my car for ten minutes. I didn't want it to seem like I was overly excited about today. I was, though, but I didn't need it to show. He lived on the 15th floor, the Last floor before the penthouse. Once I got out of the elevator, he was two doors down. I rang the bell. He opened the door with no shirt on with some sweatpants. It looked like he just got out of the shower.

"Nice to see you slim."

"Hey, Ty, I know I'm a little early."

"Nah, you're good. Come in." His home is very light. It's a two-bedroom condo. It didn't have much in here. It was just right. It was clean and smelled great. There were a lot of windows, so the natural light came in, making it bright. There was a big TV on the wall. He had music playing. There weren't any curtains so you could enjoy the view from any part of the house, and no one could see inside. It was really a lovely place.

"Nice place Ty."

"Thanks, slim; you know I'm not the fussy type. Less is more; plus, the only thing missing to complete it is you."

"You have a lot of game, Ty."

He responded, "No game, baby, just facts."

"Why are you single again?" I asked.

He laughed, "Terri, always remember I'm single by choice. Do you want something to drink?"

"I'll take some water if you have any," I replied.

He came out of the kitchen with a bottle of Fiji water and said, "I'll be ready in a few minutes. I want us to be out of here by three at the latest. In the meantime, please get comfortable, watch TV, listen to music, and change the station to whatever you want to hear." He disappeared into his room. He was playing Tyrese's 'Sweet Lady' when I got here. I left it just like that. It's really big here. I walked over to the window and admired the view. I imagined making love to Ty by this big window, him holding me in his arms and kissing me slowly. Me rubbing his chest and kissing him on his neck as he makes his way down to my nipples, caressing them slowly with his tongue. "Slim, I'm ready." He brought me back to reality sooner than I wanted. If he waited a little longer, I may have had a mini orgasm right there. He had a big duffle bag in his hand, then he went into the kitchen and came out with a smaller one. *What is he up to?* We took the elevator to the parking garage where he was parked. He has a Porsche SUV, black matte paint with some simple chrome rims. It sounds like he was jamming to some Tupac the last time he was here. "Play that song again," I told him. Once he played it back, I turned it up and we were rapping our asses off to 'California Love.'

* * *

Pulling up to the park, he backed in, pulled out a big umbrella, and grabbed the duffle bag, "I'll be right back, he said."

"Do you want me to help you?"

He replied, "No, stay right there."

After a few minutes, he came back again, grabbed a few other things, and went back. Finally, he made it back to me and opened my door, "Let's go." Holding my hand, he led the way. I was shocked. Ty had set up a little picnic area for us. The umbrella covered everything from the sun. There was an oversized blanket, cake, juice, water, and champagne sitting on ice, salad, chicken wings, and pasta, but I couldn't tell what kind from where I was standing. There were also some biscuits, and lastly, two candles and a vase with a dozen red roses. I was speechless.

It seemed like a lot of food, but the portion was enough for two, maybe three people.

"Surprised?" he asked.

I exclaimed, "Yes!"

"I just thought I would do something different yet simple for you. We sometimes forget the value in the little things."

I said, "This is different from all the dates I've been on. No one has ever done it like this. I love it, Ty. This is beautiful."

Once we sat down, he pulled out his wireless JBL speaker and let the music play. We caught up and laughed. The vibes were really nice. I enjoyed him. At this point, I saw Tyler differently. He could've easily taken me anywhere and spent whatever amount of money, or spend no money at all, but this took thought and was priceless. We packed everything up and walked back to the car. He had something else up his sleeves. He gave me a Macy's bag.

"I knew you were going to dress cute, which is okay with me, so I came prepared."

I looked in the bag. It had a pair of sweatpants, a tank top, socks, and a pair of sneakers.

"Thank you, Ty. You didn't have to! Why didn't you just tell me what I needed to wear?"

"And ruin the moment? Nah, I just wanted you to be you. As you can see, I got this."

"How did you know my size?"

"Terri, we've been friends for years. I know we've had some in-between times where we haven't seen each other, but I know. I pay attention."

We pulled up to an indoor hiking spot called Project Rock. I had heard about this place before. I was excited, and you could see it all over my face. I hugged him, He grabbed the bag from the backseat, and we walked in. Taking the bag, I went to the restroom and got changed. Once I walked out, he was standing there waiting for me.

He asked, "Are you ready?"

"Yesss."

He took my bag along with my purse and ran back to put it in the car.

When he got back, he said, "Let's go climbing."

"Let's go!" I said cheerfully. Oh my god, who would have thought this would have been so much fun? Thank God this was indoors, and we were strapped; I fell a few times. The cool thing was that live pictures were being taken. Talk about awesome. We were there for about an hour and a half. It went by so quickly. That saying is true. "Time flies when your having fun." Oh, that was a workout. Once we were done, he was cracking on me for falling and all the crazy facial expressions I had in the pictures that were taken. We brought all of them.

"Ty, thank you so much for this. It was different. I love it."

He replied, "Anything for you, slim." Without thinking, I

reached over and kissed him. It felt right. We returned to his place around 8:45. "Slim, are you in a rush?"

"No, what's up?"

"I have one more part of our date if you have the time."

"Of course I do. What do you have in mind?" I asked.

"A movie; I wanted to finish such a great night with a movie," he said.

Ty has a big 75-inch TV in the living room. His sound system made you feel like you were in the movies theater. He had a sectional with deep cushions, soft enough to make you fall asleep.

I answered, "Yeah, we can do that, a movie sounds good".

"What do you want to watch?"

I replied, "Something funny and romantic, or just funny, it doesn't matter. Surprise me."

"Are you hungry?"

I replied, "A little."

"I'll order some pizza and make some popcorn. And, we still have some cake left from earlier if you're in the mood for that type of dessert, and I have ice cream in the freezer."

"Sounds good,"

We decided to watch 'The Hangover.'

I asked, "Can you show me where the bathroom is?" He guided me to the guest bathroom, and he went into his room. He has great taste for a man. I wonder if his mom helped him out. Walking past, I got a glimpse of his room. He had a big king-sized bed, and it was high with a white comforter set and fluffy pillows. Mirrors were on one side of the wall. I didn't get to see everything. I didn't want to make it obvious that I was trying to be noisy. I washed my face in the bathroom. *Why did I let Tyler slip through my fingers like this?* I was just amazed that he still liked me the way he did. I was torn because I liked him, but I was also into girls, that is what I kept telling myself. I felt like I was trying to make excuses, not to anyone, but to myself. I don't think Tyler would be okay with that. To be honest, I wouldn't want to share him with anyone, either. I got back into the living room. I smelled popcorn. It was kettle corn, the sweet one. He had the blankets and pillows on the couch and the popcorn, chips, dip, the cake, water, and juice on the table.

"Impressive Tyler, you move quickly. I know I wasn't in the bathroom that long."

Laughing, "You might as well go back to the bathroom," and handed me a bag.

"Pajamas? Ty, you're killing me."

He replied, "Sorry, I just want you to be comfortable; we've been out most of the day and have been active. You can take a shower if you want to. I'll just make more popcorn for you; and the pizza isn't here yet. So, you have time. I'll get you a towel and a rag. Take your time."

The pajamas were cute: long, plush, pink and black pants and the pink and black tee shirt to go with it; let's not forget the fluffy black socks. I swear he was treating me like his girlfriend already. The pizza guy was just leaving when I walked out.

"Right on time, slim, let's get started."

Ty had taken a shower to; he had his pajamas on and smelled like Lever soap. He looked as refreshed as I felt.

He turned off the lights, grabbed a slice of pizza, put the bowl of popcorn and chips close to us, and played the movie.

* * *

"When did we fall asleep?" I woke up wrapped up in his arms. It was still dark outside; I didn't even know where my phone was. It had to be about 3 a.m. I curled up under him and went back to sleep. When I woke up again, it was about 8 a.m.

"Hey, sleepy head."

"Morning, Ty. Why did you let me fall asleep?"

"Why wouldn't I? Don't feel bad; I fell asleep right with you. That was the end of a beautiful night."

He must be playing mind games with me. He's such a gentleman. I was blown away because he did not attempt to make a move or sleep with me not once, as close as our bodies were, and he had ample opportunities. This felt so unreal. As the natural light came through the window, I was still lying on the couch. I loved and hated the fact that he gave me butterflies. *I need to stay in control.* Tyler, I think I imposed enough. I should get ready to leave.

"Can I have you for a little longer? You can't leave without eating something; what kind of man would I be? "

I exclaimed, "Tyler!"

"Yes, Terri."

Damn, he sounded sexy, answering me, in such a gentle tone.

I asked, "What are your intentions? I need to know! Are you putting this much effort in because you know I'm a virgin? I just don't want to be tricked or fall for you under false pretenses."

"Terri, how long have we known each other?"

"Since elementary school."

"Okay, how long have I liked you and made it known?"

"Well, you made it known since our sophomore year of high school."

"Okay. Here's my confession." He sat down next to me and continued, "I've liked you since 5th grade. I didn't want to say anything at that time. We've always been close, but I stepped back once I expressed how I felt for you, and you didn't react, not even leaving me with a hint of if you liked me or if you didn't. I know you always wondered why I pulled away from you, but the more I was around you; the more I fell in love with you. Then, when you told me you liked girls, I was crushed. I felt like there wasn't any chance for me, but my heart wouldn't let me stop. So, I gave you your space. I always said if you give me the chance to show you who I am in this way, I will. I was going to take every opportunity I had to show you how much you mean to me. All those relationships and sexual encounters can't compare to this one day I've spent with you. I don't have to run any game on you, Terri. I respect you. I respect you as a friend and most importantly I respect you as a woman! Even if you weren't a virgin, I'd want you the same way. The great thing about it is that I fell in love with you long ago. I'm not in a rush, Terri. I would rather have you when you're ready and the time is right than rushing into something because you feel like it's the right thing to do or that you're being pressured."

Fuck, fuck, fuck, he was making me cry. I wanted to grab him and make love to him now!

I asked, "Why are you single again?"

He laughed, "Slim, stop it."

"Tyler, that's the sweetest and most thoughtful thing anyone has ever told me,"

"Terri, what are you scared of?"

Now he was putting me on the spot; how could I not share with him when he had been so open with me?

He said, "If you are not ready to talk now, I understand. My number isn't changing, you know where I live, so I'll be right here whenever you're ready to talk. I'm going to get in the shower; you go take one too; we will go get some breakfast and get our day started."

We went to IHOP. I was in the mood for waffles. I ordered a Belgian waffle combo, Ty got a

T-bone steak with eggs, and we ordered a side of hash browns to share with some orange juice.

"Breakfast was great. Did you have a good time?"

"I had an amazing time, Ty. You gave me more than I expected."

We went back to his place so I could get my car.

"Can I see you again, slim?"

I was trying to control the excitement. I replied, "Well, you know we both have crazy schedules."

He replied, "That's not what I asked."

Smiling, I replied, "Yes, you can." I leaned in to hug him and to give him a kiss on the cheek; he held me in his arms and kissed me. It was short but sweet and then he helped me in the car.

Driving away, I saw him standing there, just watching me go. I had to blast the AC. I thought I was going to melt. I kept replaying everything in my head.

Once I got home, my mom was there.

I greeted her, "Hey, Mommie good afternoon."

"Hey, Terri."

"Where's daddy?"

"He went to the supermarket."

"And you didn't go?"

She replied, "He just went to get a few things; there is no need for me to go.

Quickly she changed the subject.

"I see you slept out."

"Mom! Don't do that!"

She replied, "It's true baby."

I knew that was her way of trying to find out where I've been.

We kept no secrets.

"Well, if you must know, I was with Tyler."

Laughing, she said, "Tyler! Little Tyler?"

"Yes, little Tyler". I told her everything.

"I always told you there was something special about him."

"I know, Mom. I don't know what to do. He's the type of guy that you just want to settle down and live happily ever after with, but I don't know if I'm ready."

"Try talking to him, Terri. Tell him what's on your heart, but don't sell yourself short worrying about things you can't control."

"I'm scared Mom."

"I know, Terri, but that's part of life."

"Thanks, Mom, you're the best." I have a great relationship with my mom, so sharing personal things with her, that may be uncomfortable for other young ladies to do with their mom didn't bother me, and I truly valued her opinion. I took another shower and relaxed for the rest of the day.

Tyler and I spoke every day. We became closer as time went by. We even hung out more. Nothing ever went past a kiss. I wanted him more. Vanessa was calling me, too, yearning for my time. "I need to see you, Terri. When can we hang out?" I didn't want to come across as a bitch, so I agreed to meet with her next week.

Tyler and I were hanging out more as friends, we really didn't want to put a title on each other, it was still to soon. we were just trying to enjoy the moment. But its funny because it seems like since Tyler and I were getting closer, now everyone wants to show interest in me.

I told Ty that I would go hang out with Vanessa; there was

nothing to hide. We had been as honest as possible, so why stop now?

"Are you sure you want to hang out with her?"

"Aww. Are you jealous?"

"Nah, I'm just saying, you know she wants you in all ways possible."

"So do you. And I'm still hanging out with you almost every day.

I couldn't hold back the laughter. I continued, "And we are doing great, aren't we?"

"Ughh Slim, what if she put the moves on you again?" He was right; what if she did? What if I couldn't resist and give in? Where would that leave us? I knew he was worried because Vanessa was a threat to him; at least, that's what he thought.

"I'm going to stay in my lane. Just be careful. Please. Terri."

I agreed to meet Vanessa on Wednesday. We went out for lunch. We hadn't seen each other in months. She looked nice. We caught up, and she's doing good for herself.

"I told you, Nessa, hard work pays off."

"I know you always said that, and I appreciate your push even when I didn't see it in myself." She reached over the table and kissed me—the first warning sign. "Terri, I have great news. With all this hard work, I can finally get my own place. I wanted to know if you could check out this condo with me."

"Of course. Congratulations."

"Thank you."

"When do you want to go?" I asked.

"Today, if you are free."

"Yeah. Checking the time on my phone. We can do that."

"I just have to call the realtor. She's a friend of mine. She told me she would give me the info, and I could do a self-walk-through, and if I liked it, I could get it ASAP. She said that the owner will be selling it next year, so if I wanted to, I would be first in line to buy it."

I replied, "This is great news."

"If you want, I can follow you back home, and you can ride with me. I wouldn't want you to leave your car here."

I wasn't going to leave my car here, even if she wanted me to.

I made it back to my house before she did. I ran inside to use the bathroom and spoke to my mom for a few minutes. She and Daddy were getting ready to go on their weekly date night. I loved that about them. They did whatever they had to do to keep their love alive. There was never a boring moment with them. They even switched up the days they went out. Nothing stayed the same. Daddy always said, "Whatever you did to get them, make sure you keep it up and add on as you go to keep them. Don't ever stop once you get the person." He was right. Mommie wasn't a fussy woman. She's laid back with a relaxed personality. So, he had it great. He would be the first to tell anyone that she is his best friend. They had their own friends but most importantly, they had each other. I love my parents and consider myself fortunate to still have both of them in the same household.

"You guys have fun, not too much fun. I winked at them. I love you."

They replied, "We love you too; don't wait up for us." I laughed. I wouldn't be surprised if they didn't come home for two days. Who could blame them? They didn't have any babies. They would call to say that they were okay, and when they made it home, they made it home. Surprisingly, Vanessa had just pulled up as I was getting ready to walk out the door. Here I was, thinking I had her waiting; she probably stopped to get something or pulled over to get information about the place.

I couldn't believe where the condo was, four blocks from Tyler's home. Awkward. We walked into the building. The condo was on the 10th floor. It was beautiful, a very spacious one-bedroom.

"This is a great starter, Vanessa. I said excitingly. This huge bedroom has an amazing walk-in closet that suits your profession."

"Yes." She agreed as she continued to explore the condo.

I continued, "The bathroom has a lining closet, and the lighting in here is what every woman would die for. I think you should get it."

She was all smiles. "Me too, Terri. I think I am really going to get it," she replied.

"Do you see this balcony? It's big enough to place a few chairs and a little table out there." I'm laughing at the fact that I sound like a salesperson.

She called her friend and told her she wanted it. They went over rental info and agreed to meet in two days to finalize everything. While she was talking, Tyler texted me.

"Hey, Slim, how's it going?"

I replied, "Hey, Ty. Everything is good." I told him where I was. He was shocked that Vanessa would be so close to him. I let him know that I would hit him up once I leave from hanging out with Vanessa. We locked up and went back to her car.

She said, "Now that I will finally have my own place, I hope to see you more." I didn't know what to say. I felt stuck. I kept thinking about Tyler.

"We will see what happens."

"That's fair enough. She said.

I know you mentioned you've been hanging out with Tyler. How is he?"

"He's great."

She gave me a look.

"Do you want a drink? I have a bottle in the trunk."

"Sure." I'm starting to feel like that wasn't the best answer and why does she have a bottle in the trunk?

"Okay. I'll stop at the store to get some ice. Where do you want to hang out?"

"Well, my parents will be gone for a few hours. We can do my house, your house. It doesn't matter."

"Well, we can swing by my house if it's not packed. If it is, we can just go to your house." She stopped, got a bag of ice, and we headed to her house. Her home was nice, but she had a lot of siblings and a few other relatives who lived there, so her house always seemed busy. Luckily, she had her own room, but that didn't mean much. We hung out in her backyard for a while; the traffic was coming and going. Then it started to rain. We finished up our drink, grabbed everything, and ran to her car. I didn't drive, so she still had to take me home. We should have just gone there, to begin with.

Once we got to my house, I told her that I have a sheltered patio in the back. So, we went back there and drank some more. We started looking at furniture for her condo online. She had some beautiful ideas.

I said, "Nessa, Nadia is also specializing in becoming an interior designer. You should let her help you. She can put her skills to the test."

She replied, "Okay. That's great. Can you let her know I would like her assistance, and we can go over what she will charge?

I said, "Now, you know you will be her first real client, so her price won't be too high, I'm sure."

"That's fine. I'm willing to pay whatever it is. Just have her call me as soon as she can.

Can I use the bathroom?"

"Sure. I was about to suggest that we go inside, anyway." The rain started coming down heavy.

We grabbed our things. Once in the house I put the ice in the deep freezer. We refilled our glasses and went to my room so she could use the bathroom. I knew I had too much to drink. I started feeling hot and bloated. Nessa came out of the bathroom; she stood there for a few minutes. I think she was drunk, too. My phone started ringing, it was Tyler. Vanessa saw that it was him, walked over before I could answer, took the phone out of my hand, and threw it on the bed; before I could ask her why she did that, she started kissing me, a kiss that said I missed you and no one was going to interrupt her time!

I didn't want to sleep with her again because I wasn't sure if she was what I wanted. I liked Tyler and wanted to see if we could have something together. She moved as if she had to fight for me. I didn't have the strength to fight her off. I kissed her back but, at the same time, tried to tell her to stop. It was like she couldn't hear me or wouldn't hear me. She stuck her hands in my underwear while still kissing me. Ahhhhhh, it felt good. I had to get her to stop. Pushing me back on the bed, she lifted my shirt with her free hand and began sucking my nipples while still having her way in my underwear. Moving her hand, she licked her fingers and went back in. "Tell me, Terri, how does it feel? Tell me I make you feel good; tell me, Terri." I tried not to think about Tyler, but I did. Why do I feel like I'm cheating on him? Vanessa got up and began to kiss me again.

"Vanessa, I don't think we should do this."

She replied, "How long are you going to keep fighting me off, Terri? Are you scared to fall in love with me? I know you want me! I need you, Terri, in all ways. Please."

I said, "Maybe we should take it slow, Nessa."

"How much slower does it have to be, Terri? It's been months since I had the pleasure to taste you. I need more. This is the first time I've seen and been with you since then. I know we're a little limited due to certain things, but I'm okay with just pleasing you if that's what you want."

"That wouldn't be fair to you." I said

"I don't care, Terri, I don't care."

I felt like I needed to let Tyler know. After being with him and him treating me like he did, I felt I owed it to him. *Should I just let tonight happen and worry about it later? This could very well be an option; Vanessa wouldn't go without a fight.* The only great thing was I was not with either one of them. I know Tyler knew something may happen; that's why he called. Vanessa felt like Tyler and I do have something going on; that's why she took the phone before I could answer it and is pushing to sleep with me tonight.

"Tell me what's on your mind, Terri," while kissing me on my neck. "Let me make love to you!" She moved down and pulled off my underwear. She was obsessed. She was having her way, and as much as I didn't want to, it was happening. I placed my hands on her head; she was going slow. I felt like my head was spinning.

"Damn, Terri, I miss this. She whispered. You taste so good." She got up, began to kiss me, and took one of my hands so I could caress her nipples, and she placed my other hand on her pussy. She was wet! I began rubbing and caressing it while she continued to kiss me. She bit my bottom lip softly. She placed her nipples in my mouth. I began to suck on it gently. She moaned, "Oh yes, Terri." I sucked more; this time, I got into it a little more; I nibbled on them, and she loved it. I pulled away, and she started kissing me more. She got up, opened my legs, and drove back in. She was enjoying it.

"Ohhh Nessa, ohhh Nessa." Me saying her name turned her on. She reached up while still enjoying her meal and rubbed my nipples. I couldn't hold it back; nor did I try. I let it out, and she licked it all up. "That's all I want to do, Terri, satisfy you. Please don't rob me of this." She climbed back on the bed to kiss me; I began to caress her breast and laid her on her back. She looked excited and confused. I drank some more of my drink and started kissing her again. I made my way to her neck, sucked her breasts, and she rubbed my back. I was a little nervous; this was my first time. *What if I didn't do it right? Screw it, I'm border line drunk, I don't think I can fuck this up. I started feeling courageous.* I kissed her stomach and made my way to her girl box. Slowly, I took my tongue and ran it across her clit; she moaned. I opened her legs, and I decided to have my way; I went slowly with my tongue up and down on her clit; I took two fingers and started stroking it in her. I picked up the pace, and her legs began to shake. I knew this was a possible mistake, but there was no turning back at that point we're already here.

"Terri, oh Terri, yes, oh my god, if I didn't know better, I would have thought you did this before. Oh yes, right there. I'm going to cum, oh, I love you, Terri." What did she just say? There was a moment of awkward silence. She wanted to spend the night. I told her it wasn't a good idea. She got herself together and left not to long after. About forty minutes later she texted me to let me know that she made it home. Right after another message came through and it said, "Terri, I really do love you, I'm in love with you, I hope that doesn't scare you off".

After she left, I took a shower and called Tyler.

Chapter 11

TERRI

He answered on the first ring. Was he waiting for me to call?

"Hey, Ty."

"Hey, Slim. What are you doing? I was hoping to see you tonight, but I understand."

"Don't do that, Tyler."

He asked, "So, is she still with you?"

"No."

"I'm not going to even ask. We're just going to let that one slide." He said.

I started to feel bad.

"Slim."

I replied, "Yes, Ty."

"You know I'm fucked up about you, right?"

"I know."

"Okay, I just want to make sure you know."

"Ty, you sound like you've been drinking."

"I have. When I called you earlier, and you didn't answer, it kinda did something to me."

"I've been drinking, too. Maybe too much.

Ty, how long have we been hanging out?"

"About two months, close to three months."

"Okay, two things. Can I see you tomorrow?"

"Slim, you know I'll always make time for you."

I continued, "Two, do you want to be my man?" There was a long silence.

"Hello? Are you there?"

"Slim. You know I want to; you know I want you. I've been trying to be your man for years. This is the best thing I've heard all night, but are you sure this is what you want to do? And it's not the alcohol?"

I knew it was a weird time to ask him, but if he was going to be the man to take my virginity and bring me into womanhood, he needed to be with me. Be my man!

"Yes, I'm sure, very sure."

"What time do you want me to come over tomorrow?"

"It doesn't matter. Just come over. I wish you could come now, but you've been drinking, I've been drinking so I'll wait."

"Okay. I'll call you when I wake up."

"Sweet dreams Ty. Sweet dreams Terri.

When I woke up in the morning, I replayed everything that happened last night down to the conversation with Tyler. *Was I moving too fast? Maybe I shouldn't have rushed and asked him to be my man. Was I really ready?* I never really had a boyfriend before. I had friends that were guys, yes, but boyfriend? No. Plus, I was bisexual. *What if I got the urge to want to be with a girl or even Vanessa? Oh god, what did I do? I know I can't have the best of both worlds.* I really liked Tyler, though; maybe this was my way of holding onto him. I was going to talk with him because I did not want to lose him either.

I didn't want to call Ty too early. After taking a shower and getting something to eat, I let some time go by and I gave him a call.

"Morning, Ty."

"Morning slim."

"I hope I didn't wake you."

"No. I'm cleaning up."

"Did you eat breakfast already?" I asked.

"Yeah, I had an early workout, so I just stopped and picked up something while I was out."

"Okay. That's good."

It's funny that I didn't want to call him too early and here it is he worked out, ate breakfast, cleaned up, probably took a nap, and ran a marathon in that little space of time. The marathon part tickled me because even though he didn't really do it, I felt like he could've, but for real, who does all of this after drinking the night before.

So, what time are you going to come over?"

"I was thinking maybe about another hour or two."

"Cool. See you soon."

I wanted to surprise him with lunch. I knew he loved Hooters. I ordered bacon-wrapped wings, naked wings, Baja shrimp tacos, onion rings, curly fries, and, for dessert, caramel fudge cheesecake. I know it seems like a lot of food, but it was not. We both liked to eat. I packed an overnight bag as well. I got dressed, grabbed my things, and left. Ty wanted me to start parking in the parking garage. He didn't like the idea of me parking outside in the guest parking, which worked out for me today. I pulled into his extra owner's parking spot and walked to the elevator. He opened the door. "Baby, why didn't you tell me you had all this stuff? I would have met you downstairs."

Laughing, I replied, "Ty, it's only three bags."

"I know, but still." I kissed him while walking in the door. He seemed shocked, but I wanted him to know I was serious. "I do hope you have something to drink. I forgot to order it with the food. I didn't remember until I was here."

He replied, "Yeah, I have juice and lots of water."

"Okay, good." He grabbed the food out of my hand and placed it on the table.

"I wanted to surprise you with lunch."

"You're all I needed for lunch," he said in a low tone but loud enough for me to hear.

"I hope I didn't disappoint you."

Blushing, he said, "No, no, you didn't."

We sat and we ate.

"Those bacon-wrapped wings were on point. I need to tell the ladies that we have to try them." I decided to tell Ty about last night with Vanessa. He didn't seem shocked but looked a little disappointed.

"Ty, I really like you. I want to give us a chance, so I'm being as transparent and honest with you as possible. You're a threat to Vanessa for her own reasons, so I don't want to leave you out of the loop with anything. Talking about transparency, I must let you know I'm also a little scared."

He asked, "Why?"

"Because Ty, I have never really been in a 'real' relationship. You're going to be my first, and I don't want to ruin it. You mean so much to me."

"Slim, you're thinking too much. We're not perfect, and all we can do is take it day by day. You mean a lot to me, too. We will figure it out together."

I loved his way of thinking. He is so optimistic and open-minded; he has been this way for as long as I have known him.

"Tyler, what if I feel like I'm missing out on something?

Here it is you have had a few relationships and experiences, and you will be my first. First, for everything."

"Terri, if it ever gets to the point that you feel that I'm not enough for you or you're missing out on something, talk to me. The difference between me and many other people, guys, ladies, or whoever is that I know you." I couldn't hold back. I kissed him.

I was officially dating. In my Chante Moore voice, I sang, Terri's got a man. We hung out all day. I went with him to get some groceries and other things he needed for his home. I went from spending one night to still being there till Saturday night.

I said, "Bae, I need to go home and get some more clothes. I'm down to my last outfit." Licking his lips, "You can walk around with nothing on. That's fine with me."

"Hey, that doesn't sound like a bad idea." I added.

"Hmmm," he was smiling like he had the image of me walking around naked.

"Okay, let's go." He said, and we rode in his truck to my house. My parents were home. "I'll just stay in the car."

"No, you won't! Get out of this car Tyler. Stop acting like you don't know my family. You're my man, so you will be here often." He looked nervous.

"Don't worry, I already told my mom about us. Not that we made it official, but she knows." He agreed to accompany me into the house. When we walked in, Mommie and Daddy were in the kitchen. I don't know what they were discussing, but they were laughing away. I loved their energy; hope to be like that one day.

"Good night," I gave my mom and dad a kiss. "You guys remember Tyler?" They were smiling from ear to ear.

"Yes. Hi Tyler, how are you?"

"I'm great, thank you, and how are you guys doing?"

My mom replied, "The same. It's really great to see you again. You look great. Terri told me that you do modeling as well."

"Yes, Ma'am."

"Great. I'm happy for you."

"I just came to grab a few things and will be on my way." They talked a little, while I got my things. When we were leaving, my dad shook Ty's hand, thanked him, and told him to take care of his baby girl.

Ty responded, "As long as she allows me to, I'll make sure she will always be happy." I kissed my parents and told them I'll see them soon. This time, I grabbed a few extra things to leave at his house just in case I was there on a random night. On our way back to his house, someone on the roadside was selling roses; he pulled over and bought five dozen. "What do you want to eat, slim?"

"Are we going to grab it to go?"

"Yeah, if you want."

"Okay, well, let's get Tijuana flats." We stopped by placing our order and had a drink while we waited. Once we got back, we placed the roses in a vase, put the TV on, and ate.

"I'm full."

"Me too" He said.

"I'm going to go take a shower because if I sit here any longer, I'm going to fall asleep." I went into Ty's room and took a shower. I had brought some 'Caress' body wash when we went shopping a few days ago. There was nothing like feeling fresh and smelling good. I heard when Ty turned on the music. I couldn't help but sing along; I love me some Sade. Her smooth velvet tone voice will do it to you, "You give me the sweetest taboo; that's why I'm in love with you." Did I mention that Ty could sing; I remember we had music class together in high school, and those girls would go crazy over his tenor voice. He could work the crowd as well. He always took part in school concerts or plays that allowed him to sing. I was surprised he didn't pursue being in the music industry. He was just multitalented. I got out of the shower; I didn't realize how long I had been there until I looked at my fingers. 'Love' by Musiq Soul Child was playing. Ty knew his stuff. "LOOOOOOOOVVEEEEE, so many things I got to tell you." I dried off, put some lotion on, and got ready to walk out, still singing. "Love so many people use your name in," I was stopped dead in my tracks; the room was dark, and there were scented candles lit around the room. There were rose petals making a trail on the ground to the bed. He put two of the roses on each pillow. This was a good way to utilize those roses. I slowly walked out of the room, where a trail of rose petals still flowed through the house. I walked into the living room, and there was no sight of Tyler. I peeped in the kitchen, and he wasn't there. "Tyler." No response. *Maybe he's in the other bathroom.* I checked. Not in there. *Okay, well, maybe he went to the car. I'm just going to go put my pajamas on and wait.* I walked back into the bedroom; Ty was standing there with two roses and a glass of wine. I said, "Babe, you scared me." Smiling, he walked over, kissed me, and gave me a glass of wine.

I said, "This is good! It was sweet. What kind of wine is this?"

He replied, "Manischewitz cream red concord."

"Everything is beautiful, Ty; I don't want to believe I was in the shower that long for you to have the time to do all of this."

"Believe it, slim, and it worked out for me."

I laughed. "You shouldn't have been playing all this good music. You know the outcome once I start singing and vibing. I was having a concert in the shower." I put on my PJs and refilled my glass while Ty took a shower. I so happened to walk into the room while he was getting dressed and just stood there watching; damn, he was fine; I wanted to move, but I couldn't. My eyes were stuck on him. He turned around like he knew I was there checking him out; I put my glass down and walked over to him. I couldn't fight it anymore. The romance was in the air, and the mood was set. I wanted him. I didn't want to wait any more. Kissing him gently, I rubbed his back. All he was wearing were his boxers. His dreads were hanging. He pulled me in closer; his body was damp. His kisses flowed down to my neck. I shivered. I had never been this far with him; I was nervous. I felt his manhood rising. Oh, he was ready for me like I was for him. My eyes were closed; I was enjoying the moment, taking it all in. He took my shirt off, and our eyes connected; he reached in and kissed me, and that alone made me moan. He picked me up and placed me on the bed; gentle kisses were placed on my stomach. He slowly pulled my shorts off, and I closed my eyes and let it flow. He kissed my girl box softly and wasted no time getting to work. I was moaning and holding onto the sheets. I came faster than I wanted to. His tongue game was on point. I laid quietly on the bed, as I felt my heart racing, and I continued to go back and fort with the thought that it's finally about to happen.

"Slim," he softly said while looking me in the eyes. "Are you sure you want to do this?"

I replied, "Yes, Ty, I'm sure." He got up and grabbed a condom. I didn't know what to expect; my emotions were running wild. I guess Ty picked up on my tenseness.

"It's going to be okay, babe. He said trying to reassure me. If at any time you want me to stop, please let me know, and I will. I promise I will be gentle and take it slow." He put the condom on and got some 'Ky jelly.' "Tonight is your night," he started to kiss me.

At that moment, Boys II Men's, 'I'll make love to you,' started playing. What perfect timing. While lying on top of me, he slowly penetrated my girl box. He took his time to make it in. It hurt but felt so good. "Oh my God, Ty," I felt every inch of him. My eyes watered as I held onto him tightly. I was trying to keep up; every stroke with him was sensual. He moved slowly and patiently. This was the best feeling ever! He stopped while still inside me. Sweat glistening on his face, he smiled. "Are you okay?"

"Um, hmm," was the only thing I could come up with. Looking into his eyes, I felt different. I saw his love for me, and at that moment, I realized I was falling in love with him, too. I will never forget that moment. I fell in love with my friend. We took a shower together once we were done. So, that was what it felt like to make love. I was so happy; I waited and didn't rush to experience a moment like this any other way. It was perfect. He was the perfect person to experience this with. Once out, we lay down, cuddled, and watched TV until we fell asleep. It was the wee hours of the morning when I woke Ty up wanting more of him. We made love again, this time even better than the first.

Chapter 12

TERRI

It felt good to be home. I had to get prepared for my big trip to Italy that was coming up. I had so much catching up and running around to do. I am headed to the supermarket right now because there is nothing to eat at home. I didn't shop much because I knew Ty and I wouldn't be there long. I didn't want anything wasted; I was not going to buy many things because before you knew it, I'd be gone again.

"Hey Travis, what's up?"

"You want to go with me tomorrow to meet a sports agent?" Travis had dropped his current sports agent and was on the hunt for a new one.

Travis continued, "I heard great things about Mr. McKnight. They said he has a different mindset and brings a different feel to the table. He was once in the game, so he knows what to look for and what the people want."

"You think I'm your security?"

"Nah, sis. I'm just trying to take advantage of some time with you. I know we don't have that much free time; one of us is always busy, plus I haven't seen you since you left for Bora Bora. I have to get you when I can. Can a brother get some love?!"

"Okay, you got me.

What time?"

"10 a.m."

"Alright, I'll be ready."

"Thanks, sis. I'll see you tomorrow."

"Good morning, big bro."

"What's crackalackin, sis?" I swear I love my brothers. When we're together, it's always a good time; even as we get older and have our own lives, nothing changes. Being the only girl didn't matter; we just connected.

"So, are you excited about this big move?"

He replied, "Yeah, I am. I need this for me and my career."

We got to the office. This was such a beautiful building, clean and classy. The office was on the 7th floor. Even the inside of the office setup was nice. The air wick they had plugged in here smelled like Gain fresh. The receptionist, Abigail, greeted us with a smile, "Hi, Mr. McKnight will be with you shortly."

Not too long after, he came out and greeted us both, "Good morning." He had pearly white teeth and was tall, that nice, sexy kinda tall. He was taller than me, so you know he's tall. You could tell he played sports. He's Handsome and carried his confidence well.

"Thank you for your patience. You can follow me," he led us back to his office. It was neat. He had a futon-style couch with three big pillows, and his desk was glass, with turquoise accent chairs. His chair was gray. He had some pictures on the walls as well. I had to give it to him; he did his thing. I could see Nadia coming in and killing this office with her sense of style and touch, but he did well. Travis introduced me as his sister. We engaged in small talk. The more I looked at Mr. McKnight, the more he looked familiar. I didn't think anything of it. I see many people all the time, so it would be hard to pinpoint him. Travis seemed excited to be working with him. I was excited, too. One thing about our family is that we push each other; we all have to win. It's never I'm on top, and I'm going to forget about you or not support you. He excused himself and stepped out to take a phone call. "Jason speaking, how may I help you?" His voice trailed off in the distance. While waiting I stretched my legs, walked around his office and looked at some of his pictures and accolades hanging from the wall. 'Jason McKnight, award for excellence in community outreach and so much more.' Mr. McKnight was quite successful and well-accomplished. I turned back to look at Travis, who was busy looking through something on his phone. Something caught my eye as I turned my attention back to the pictures on the wall. It was a picture of a small bamboo hut on a beach with the sun setting in the background. "Why does this look so familiar?" I whispered to myself. Just then, Mr. McKnight returned and found me staring. "I apologize. He said. I had to take that call."

Mr. McKnight then notice me standing looking at the pictures., "Oh, I see you've made your way to Bora Bora. Beautiful, isn't it?"

Bora Bora? Bora Bora! That was it! Jason! Nadia's Jason! That's where I know him from! "Nadia," I said. I must have said it very loudly.

"Excuse me?" He asked.

"Nadia," I repeated. "I think you know my best friend, Nadia." I had to snap back a little, remembering why I was here in the first place; I didn't want to ruin anything for Travis. His expression changed. He hesitated a little; he was being careful before he answered. *Remain professional, Terri, no matter what he says, don't allow it to make you come out of character.* I looked over at Travis; he looked confused; it felt like forever before Jason responded.

Chapter 13

JASON

Tiffany and I are officially over. That shit she did in Bora Bora just did it for me. We've been back for three weeks. I had her take all the things she had at my house and give me back my keys. I must say, I allowed her to let me get out of character a bit, and I didn't like that. I've been keeping busy. I have a meeting coming up with a football player named Travis Price, who wants me to be his agent. It's in a week and a half. I had to get my mind right. On my way to meet Mike one morning, I stopped to get some coffee at a small mom-and-pop shop. I came out of the store and thought my eyes were playing tricks on me. I stopped dead in my tracks. It was Nadia. She was working out at the park across the street. She was dressed in all black from head to toe. She started running fast. I thought for a second that someone or something was chasing her. Nadia looked just as beautiful as the last time I saw her. I replayed that moment at the beach in my head every day. I wanted to say something but decided watching her from a distance instead was best. I wonder if she runs here all the time. I never saw her here before, and I'm always in this area. She ran around the park a few more times. I wonder if she thinks about me. I can't stop thinking about her. She finally stopped and grabbed her things to leave. It looked like someone was calling her, she looked at it, hit a button and put the phone in her pocket. I was in my car, out of her view, but she was still in mine. She walked into Smoothie King; I wondered what kind of smoothie she was getting. Coming out this time, she was on the phone; I assumed that person finally got her to answer. I hoped she didn't notice me; I saw her smiling, those dimples. I wondered who it was that had her smiling, and I suddenly started feeling a little jealous. Did she look at my phone calls and ignore me the same way? Why wouldn't see just speak to me? Does she live in this area? Part of me wanted to follow her. Jason! Snap out of it. What's wrong with you? Just like that, she was gone. I was happy I got to see her; Confirmation that she made it back safely. I just wish that she was safely in my arms. My phone ringing brought me back.

I answered, "What's up, Mike?"

"Bro, where are you? I've been waiting for forty minutes already."

"I'll be there in ten minutes. I just had a little distraction."

"Everything okay?"

I replied, "Yeah. I'm on my way."

It was unusual for me to be late, so I understood him being concerned. I had promised to help him move some things out of his mom's house. She was getting ready to give his childhood home a face lift. Once we were done, we grabbed something to eat at Crafty Crabs. Mike said a client recommended it, and he wanted to check it out. Mike got a beer, and I had lemonade. I told myself I wasn't drinking for a while after I drank too much the last time in Bora Bora.

He asked, "How are you, Jay?"

"I'm good, hanging in there, just taking it day by day."

"I know we haven't had time to really talk since you returned. Have you tried reaching out to Nadia?"

"Yeah, she doesn't answer. One time, I called; I swear she picked up. Maybe it was wishful thinking, I don't know."

"Give her some time. If it's meant to be, it will be."

"You're a great man Jason." Thanks, Mike. "Did I show you the pictures of her?"

"No, Chris and Eric told me they saw the picture." I grabbed my phone eagerly to show him the one picture we had together, the one picture I had of her.

"She's beautiful, Jason! She also looks like I saw her somewhere before."

"I wouldn't be surprised if you have. I uttered. Crazy enough Mike, I saw her this morning."

"You saw her?"

"Yeah! That's why I was running late. She was at the park working out."

"Please tell me you spoke to her."

"I couldn't, Mike. I tried, but I just couldn't."

"She really does have some type of hold on you, are you sure haven't slept with her? I've never seen you like this."

"Mike, my intentions weren't bad. I was wrapped up in the moment; her vibes had me feeling like nothing mattered but me and her. I didn't want to tell her about Tiffany there because it would have ended just like this. All I needed was to make it back home. I would have told her everything in my comfort zone, where I had full control. Yes, I should have kept it real. I could have handled it better, but everything happened quickly; that's why I'm in this situation now, feeling the way I am feeling."

"Well, I don't think she hates you, maybe disappointed and, of course, embarrassed as you would be."

"Ha! I was," we laughed.

"If you really want something with her, get to where you can talk to her. You better talk and spill it; find a way to make her listen. Do not let her get away without a fight.

Talking about fighting, when was the last time you spoke to Tiffany?"

"Man, I don't even want to talk about her let alone speak to her. The last time I spoke to her was the week we came back, and she came by to get her stuff. She keeps calling me, and my mailbox is full because of her. I'm ready to block her and change my number. She even tried calling me from other numbers. It worked out where I missed the call, and when I returned it, they said she was the one who called."

"Yo! She called me a few times looking for you too. That's why I asked you when was the last time you spoke to her. I cut her short; she was trying to explain. I told her I didn't have time for it, that she didn't need to try and explain anything to me, and I asked her not to call me again."

"Thanks, Mike. I'm sorry that you had to be caught up in this. Enough about me. How are things going with you?"

"Well, I met someone."

"About time!" I exclaimed.

Mike have been single for a few years! He continued, "We've been dating for almost a month. She's really nice and we're taking it slow."

"I'm so happy for you, I said, taking it slow is a good idea and hopefully, we can meet her soon."

"You guys will. It feels right with her. Maybe we should have a BBQ, pool party or something, and I will bring her over."

"Noted."

I went back to the park every day to watch Nadia. I had to make sure no one messed with her. I was her secret security. She had the same routine; she switched it up from time to time, but nothing major: exercise, run some laps, get a smoothie, and then she will leave. Today was the day I was going to make my move. She exercised, ran, and walked into Smoothie King. I took a deep breath; *I'm going to walk in there, act surprised to see her here, and pray it all goes well.* I imagined walking in there; she sees me, and bam! Just like that, I have a smoothie thrown in my face. I couldn't do it. I chickened out. I almost got caught; she walked out before I could get back in the car. She stopped to sip her smoothie, making the cutest ugly face possible. My guess is she tried something new, and she didn't like it. She threw it away while mumbling something to herself.

I was waiting to meet with a new client named Travis Price at my office. He had reached out to me and said he was interested in me becoming his agent. I grabbed a cup of coffee and relaxed in my office until he came. I had just redone it a few months ago. I changed the carpet and got new furniture. It was lighter and more spacey; I loved it. The view from up here was nice. I could see everything going on outside. On my late nights, I could see the sunset.

Travis was accompanied by a woman when he arrived. He introduced her as his sister, Terri. She was tall and looked like she played Basketball.

I welcomed them, "Nice to meet you guys." I shook their hands. "Please have a seat." We sat down and went over some important details, and what he expected from me as his agent.

"I heard a lot of great things about you, Mr. McKnight, and I need you on my team." We went over numbers, but the whole time, I couldn't get Terri's face out of my head; she looked familiar. I had to have seen her somewhere.

I asked her, "Do you play sports too?"

She laughed. "No, I used to play Basketball in high school. I focused my career in a different direction. We have enough sports players in the family for now, so I went full force into modeling, but I still got game." We laughed.

I said, "You do look familiar."

"Maybe you saw me on a billboard or in a commercial."

"Yeah, maybe that's what it is."

We were getting ready to wrap things up, and I got a phone call, "Jason speaking." Once I was done with the call, I walked back to the office. I saw Terri checking out my wall decor.

I said, "So, Travis, it's going to be a pleasure working with you." From my peripheral vision, I noticed Terri had a strange look, more like a shocked look. I hoped Travis didn't have a change of heart. Terri was still viewing the pictures. She smiled at me, but it wasn't a happy smile. I was shocked by what she said next. I wasn't expecting it. All I heard was "Nadia," and then it hit me: Terri was one of the friends I saw when I was walking away from Tiffany at the beach. I started to feel embarrassed but excited. I swear my heart was racing, Nadia's best friend. How did this happen? The world is really small. I started to feel hot; it felt like I was sweating out of control. She was just starting. I couldn't even look at her. She seemed like a totally different person, no longer happy. I was in the hot seat and had to be careful with my response.

"Yes. I know Nadia."

"Oh, I know you do! Terri, can we exchange numbers? Can I explain in detail what really happened?"

"Why do you feel the need to explain this to me? I'm not the one you made look like a fool."

I felt that comment in my bones. I kept hearing "look like a fool," playing repeatedly. I must really look like less than a man to her friends. *She wouldn't talk to me! At least if I can get someone to hear me out, whatever happens from there, I'll respect that. I don't think this is the time at the moment.* Travis had a 'what the fuck' look on his face. Everything seemed like a blur.

"Okay, I'll exchange numbers with you, just know I'm not with the bull shit, so come correct." I was so happy that she agreed to talk to me. I had never been happier for a meeting to be over in my life. It started off about one thing and ended about something else. I walked them to the door, "Thank you guys for coming. I look forward to seeing you soon. Have a blessed day."

I walked back to my office. I took a deep breath. I had two more clients coming in and then I would be free for the rest of the day.

Chapter 14

EBONI

Since I got back home, I have been busy. We still have to plan to go again to support Terri in a few weeks. I had a lot of running around to do. I went to Macy's to get a few things. It felt amazing seeing my brand and my product there. Hard work does pay off, but I won't stop there. I wanted more I want to create more. I have a few other plans and ideas in the making. I strolled around the mall for a little; I was enjoying my personal time. We were supposed to see Nadia perform in a few days. I was so excited. I wonder how she comes up with those words, the way she puts them together. Her mind is amazing.

I finally made it home; I ate the salad I bought from Sweet Tomatoes and checked my phone. I had missed calls from Dante and Carlos. I noticed Carlos was trying hard to get and keep my attention, but Dante wasn't playing about my time with him either. He's been trying to come around more, and I've been trying to avoid it, but it's getting harder and harder to resist him.

Tonight, at the lounge, was nice. We hadn't hung out much

since we got back from Bora Bora, not because we didn't want to, more so because we had some catching up to do work wise, business wise, and the few of us that had men, needed to catch up, especially in the bedroom, if you know what I mean. We will be getting ready for our trip to Italy soon; I know it will be fun. Nadia owned that stage. As vocal as I am, I don't think I could do it. All the performances were great tonight. The vibes are always nice here. After we left, I met up with Dante at his house. He had been trying to see me for some weeks now. He wanted to meet me at the lounge but then he would want to be clingy like we were together. I had experienced this many times before with him. I understand why he may be that way sometimes; after all, we were fucking, and he wouldn't want to see anyone try to hit on me while he was right there, and I wouldn't want to see anyone hitting on him; I don't want to have to check anyone. I didn't care that we were just fucking, but we understood where we stood and what we had. If I tell him right now that I'm ready for a relationship, he will drop every girl he has. I think, though, at this point in my life it's time. I can't say that I haven't had fun. I've lived, so I know when I do settle down, I won't feel like I missed out on anything, and that's exactly what I wanted: no regrets. I don't have to answer to anyone. I've never been the type to allow anyone to change me, nor do I want to change anyone unless we are bettering each other. So, if we don't match, that's cool. I have that free spirit; let's live and have fun. I guess that's why Dante has been the only person to be around because he's free like me and the only person who can handle and is not intimidated by me, my mouth, and my independence.

Nadia once told me, "You keep pushing everyone away; there won't be anyone there when you're ready." I felt her on that, but then I used to think, maybe I'll never be ready, which

I knew deep down in my heart wasn't true. Maybe I was just scared, and when Dre broke Nadia's heart the way he did, I was like fuck that, I'm good by myself. I know I won't hurt myself. I don't want to be the one who gets hurt and can't find my way out of it. We're all strong until we are put in a situation where we feel defeated. I guess you can say I'm still scared and don't want to waste my time. I'm woman enough to admit that. I do have a lot of thinking to do. I'm getting older, and everything else is falling into place, so maybe trying to be in a relationship won't be so bad. Plus, I may want a baby or two somewhere down the line. I was shocking myself with these truths that were surfacing.

I made it to Dante's house. I sat in the car for a few minutes to get my mind right. I had all these different emotions going on. *Is it the alcohol or maybe it's the fact that Nadia has a man who barely knows her, trying to find her so he can explain himself?* Terri told me everything about running into Jason. It takes a real man to want to clear his name even if, in the end, it may not work in his favor. She absolutely deserves a man, a real man. We forgive people for the worst things, so I hope she doesn't show off on him when he shows up. We agreed not to tell her anything because he deserves a real reaction, and she needs to give him exactly that. So now it's just me who needs to get it right.

I could see Dante moving around the house. I finally got out of the car and rang the bell. He opened the door, he had on a wife beater, and some blue sweatpants; I could see the print of his dick just waiting for me to touch it. I was already imagining what we could be doing around the house. *Stay focused, Eb. Take your eyes off the prize and focus on his handsome face.*

I greeted him, "Good night, Dante." He kissed me.

"I was just about to call you. I figured you weren't going to come again."

"No, I've been outside for about twenty minutes."

"Are you okay?"

"Yeah, I was just thinking about some stuff."

He hugged me while placing his hands on my ass and said, "I'm glad you came. I missed you. I don't understand why you give me such a hard time."

"None of your floozies are going to stop by randomly, right? I hope they know tonight is my night, okay" He gave me that look like 'Don't fuck with me.'

One time, I was here, probably about a year and a half ago, we were just chilling, and some girl, I guess he was fucking with, fucked, or was going to fuck popped up. I remember hearing him say, "How the fuck do you know where I live?" That's one thing he doesn't play with. He has to be fucking you on a different level for you to possibly know where he lives. He doesn't bring anyone to his home. He will hotel the shit out of you or go to your house, car, whatever, but his home was off limits. He went off on her and told her she better not show up again. So, from time to time, I mess with him about her. He told me he saw her after that, and she tried to talk to him like everything was cool. I told him he couldn't be fucking them like he was trying to make a baby and expect them not to come looking for him. You know women can be the best detectives ever when need be.

"Well, if you let me give you that baby, we won't have these problems, right?" and I ignored him as usual.

"Do you want something to drink?"

"I'll take a bottle of water, please. I don't need any more liquor."

"I'm going to get you a towel so you can get comfortable.

He said." Once I got out of the shower, he gave me one of his T-shirts and some socks. I love socks, especially when going to bed; they make me feel complete. I couldn't wait to fuck him tonight! I haven't had any dick since Carlos in Bora Bora. He had been calling me a lot; when I called him back earlier, he told me he would be here in about a month and a half and wanted to see me.

Dante and I started watching a movie in the living room; I dozed off. I had been going all day and then drinking, so that shower was the final touch. I felt Dante pick me up off the couch to carry me into the bedroom, and I woke up laughing.

"Look at you, sleeping beauty; you can't even hang." He laid me on the bed. I asked, "How long was I sleeping?"

"About forty-five minutes."

"Really, why didn't you wake me up?"

"Why should I? You were doing exactly what I wanted you to do: relaxing. You were so relaxed I almost left you there on the couch."

"So, you didn't want me to come over so I can ride that dick while you moan for more begging me not to stop as you cum?"

His expression was so cute.

"Damn Eb, he smirked, then he leaned over and kissed me. I almost asked you to repeat that again, but seriously, your presence is good enough for me. I love being sexual with you, but it's not every time you're here that it has to be for that reason. Everything about you turns me on, not just your pussy. So, get your butt under that blanket and take your tired ass to sleep."

He turned me on in so many different ways.

"Dante."

"Yes?"

"Thanks."

He smiled. *God, is this a sign?* I was thinking about all these different things earlier in the car, then I'm here now, and he just wanted me to come over to be here with him. Ugh, this is so hard. I thought it would be much easier than this. His phone rang. He didn't bother to answer it. The person called again; this time, he sent them to voicemail. Whenever he was with me, I got all of him, his time, and his attention. No other woman could get his attention or mattered when he was with me, and they have tried. We never questioned each other, but he knew, and I knew what it was. The crazy thing was if he was with someone, and I called, he answered. If I wanted to see him and he was with someone else, he found his way to me. Why was I playing around? All along, the answers had been right in my face. I was starting to feel bad and a little foolish thinking about everything. I knew I needed to figure it out quickly because I wouldn't know how much more of this I could take if it were the other way around.

I heard Nad in my head again, "You keep pushing everyone away; there won't be anyone there when you're ready."

I slept great that night, and I woke up to the same thoughts from the night before. Dante was still sleeping. I went to the bathroom and decided to take a quick shower. Once out, I put on my dress from last night.

"Are you leaving so soon?"

"You scared me."

He asked again, "So, are you?"

"Well, yeah, and no. I couldn't go back to sleep, so I just took a shower. You looked like you were still sleeping, so I was going to leave you a note to call me when you got up."

Getting off the bed, he walked over to me, "What's wrong, Eb? Are you upset that I didn't sleep with you last night?"

I replied, "Honestly, no. This was different, and I liked that."

"So, what's wrong? You seem unlike yourself."

"It's nothing."

"Okay, I'll take your word on that." He kissed me. "Well, if you want to leave, you can, but I'll be at your house around 2 p.m. to take you to lunch, so be ready! Let me know if you have somewhere you would like to go."

"So, how do you know I don't have plans already?"

"I just know, and if you did, he would have to wait. I take my time with you very seriously."

I thought, *Damn, Dante, I don't know what has gotten over you, but I love it.* He stopped asking and started demanding my time. Something else to think about. I laughed.

"What's funny, Eb?"

"Nothing. I'll be ready."

"Don't have me waiting."

"Have I ever had you wait before?"

He answered, "No" alright then.

We made it to the door, and he kissed me the way he would when he was about to give it to me, making my knees shake and my eyes roll to the back of my head.

"You're trying to make me stay?"

"I never said you had to leave," he placed my hands on his dick. "You see what you do to me? So, if you're worried, don't be."

I got into my car, and he was still standing there. *What am I going to do with him?*

Once I made it home, I ate some frosted flakes. It had been a while since I had some cereal. I wanted something quick and light since we would be going out to lunch. I found this denim dress in the back of my closet that I had been waiting to wear. It was a little above my knees and had thin straps. Any reason not to wear a bra always made me happy.

I was ready for later; all I had to do was take another shower. It was still early, so I laid down and watched TV. I jumped up to my phone ringing; apparently, I fell asleep at some point. I looked at my phone, it was Carlos. It was 10:25 a.m., so it was 7:25 in Cali.

Hello.

"*Buenos dias te desperte?*"

He likes to speak to me in Spanish.

"No, I've been awake."

"Why are you awake so early?"

"I had to take my sister to the airport. I'm on my way home now, and I thought about you. How is it going?"

"I'm doing pretty good, I can't complain. How are you?" I asked.

"Great, I can't wait to come see you; as a matter of fact, I might be coming sooner, but I'll keep you posted."

"How long are you coming for?"

"Four days. It's me and a few of my boys."

"What do you guys have planned?"

"Nothing yet. We will take it day by day." We spoke for a little longer. I started to wonder if he was coming here for me or if he was coming here and just adding me into the mix. I needed to find that out because four days was a long time for me to keep him company.

I put my music on. Once I got out of the shower, I did my makeup. *Girl, you look hot!* I always hyped myself up, not waiting on anyone else to do it. I rubbed the lotion on my legs. *It's almost time to go get another wax.* I checked to see how I was doing with time, and I had another twenty minutes before Dante would be here. I put my dress on and found some accessories. I was having a hard time choosing between my gold wedges and pink heels. Time wasn't on my side, so I went with the wedges. I looked out the window, and I saw Dante pulling up. I grabbed my purse, put some perfume on, and made my way to the front door. I opened it, and he was standing right there. Dante was wearing some white jeans and a blue jeans shirt. If I didn't know any better, I would have thought we planned our outfit.

"You didn't have to come out; I was going to come to the car."

"I wanted to come out and greet you like a man should. You look beautiful by the way."

"Thank you. You look handsome as well."

I locked the door, and we walked to the car together.

"Did you decide on where you want to eat?" He asked.

"No, I didn't."

"Cool. I have somewhere in mind." We pulled up to Coconuts restaurant and got a table outside to enjoy the beach view and take in the beautiful weather. We engaged in a great conversation; our phones rang a few times. None of mine was important enough for me to answer; he didn't answer as well. I looked at him, and he seemed to have a little concern in his eyes.

I asked, "Are you okay?"

"Yeah, just thinking."

"What's up? You know you can talk to me."

"I know I can, Eb. I know I can do a lot of things with you, but you won't let me. It's like you keep shutting me out." Why did I feel like this would come up? It was just sooner than I expected, wanted, and planned. I walked right into it. I think my phone ringing was the final straw. Yes, a few guys called me, but I was with him. His phone rang more than mine. Not that I was counting, but I didn't make him feel any kind of way. I let him vent, and I listened.

He continued, "I would drop everything for you, Eboni. I know you know that I love being around you. I know that you have had some fucked up experiences in life which has caused you to shut people out or just push them away. The amazing part is you've let me in more than you know, and I take it when I can. I'm not putting any pressure on you because the last thing I want you to say is you were forced, rushed, or pressured, but I'm falling in love with you more and more every day and trying to fight how I feel is getting harder as the days go by. I have felt this way for a long time but just pushed it aside. I want to be your man and only your man and make love to you and only you. I don't want to be playing these games any longer. This is just something to think about; like I said, I'm not pressuring you, I'm not expecting you to make a decision overnight. If you feel settling down is something you may not want to do, and it's not for you, I could respect that. I will know where I stand or what to do, but at least you know how I feel."

My heart was racing as Dante was expressing his feelings. *What is going on? What's in the air?* We both felt the same way. No wonder he had been so 'take-chargeish.' I respected his honesty; at least I was not just a piece of ass to him. I heard Nad's voice echoing in my head again.

He continued, "Eboni, as we both know, me getting pussy isn't a problem, the same way I know you getting dick isn't a problem, but the thing is, I would rather give it all to you."

I had to take a drink on that one because that dick was everything. Sometimes, I wonder if he gives it to them the way he gives it to me, the way they are calling and stalking. He probably would have had me going crazy if I didn't know how to control myself.

"None of those women got me like you do."

I wanted to tell him how I felt. He did say no pressure. The waiter came with our food. "Thank you, Carlos," Dante said. *Oh, shit, Carlos.* He slipped my mind immediately. I ordered another drink.

"This is the last thing I'm going to say, Eb. Last night was just my confirmation; if I had to change my number to show you how serious I am, I would."

I replied, "Dante, you have left me speechless. I really like you, too, and I have been feeling the same way. I just have some thinking to do."

Smiling, "As I said, there's no pressure, but it's nice to know that we're on the same page," he stood up and kissed me. "Just say the word and know I will be your man, all of me."

"I'm scared, Dante." There I said it.

"I understand, let's just take it one day at a time. Like I said before, no pressure. You know how I feel, and that's important. Now, let's eat before our food gets cold."

We took a walk on the beach after eating. For the first time, Dante being clingy didn't bother me.

Chapter 15

JASON

It's been two days, and I haven't heard from Terri. I was hoping that she would reach out first, but then again, why would she? After all, I needed her help, and I was the one who "made her best friend look like a fool." Those words still make me feel ashamed. She was right, though. There isn't any excuse or anything I can say to justify it. I was pacing back and forth. *Should I call her now, or should I wait? Screw it; I'm going to call her now. I don't need to let any more time pass by.* I checked the time—4:30 p.m. I took a deep breath; it was now or never. The phone rang, "Hello."

"Hi, Terri, this is Jason." There was a silence that felt like an eternity.

"Hi, Jason. How may I help you?"

"I was wondering if we could meet up, where I can talk with you face to face. Are you free tonight?"

She replied, "No, not tonight, but tomorrow evening around six-ish, I will be."

"Great, is there a special place you would like to meet?"

"No, just let me know where you choose, and I will meet

you there." She was not making this easy for me at all. That's okay. I was willing to fight for what I wanted.

"There's this restaurant. I heard they're really good. I could meet you there at 6:30 p.m."

She replied, "That's fine."

"I'll keep in touch. Thanks, Terri." I felt a little at ease because the first step was over. I was already home, so I stayed in for the rest of the night. I cleaned up a little and then worked out for an hour to ease my mind. I began to wonder if Terri told Nadia that she saw me. All these different thoughts were running wild. Getting out of the shower, I heard my phone ringing. I hoped that Terri was calling me back, willing to meet me tonight. I was quickly disappointed. It was Tiffany. Why wouldn't she leave me alone? This is ridiculous. I didn't get this many phone calls when she was my girl. I threw my phone on the bed, got dressed, and heard my text notification go off. I was going to delete the message, but I read it just for the hell of it. "Jason, why are you ignoring me? Please talk to me; I miss you and that BIG DICK! I need to taste it in my mouth, cum all over my face, baby! I know you miss this pussy too. Come over to my house and give it to me. Please, Jason, please. I'll do whatever it is you want. I'm horny and craving you, Jason, PLEASE!" I sat there, not sure if I wanted to laugh or cry. This woman was crazy! How did I not notice before? She did an amazing job of hiding that shit. I can't believe this is the woman I wanted to be my wife. Oh my god. I walked into the kitchen to grab a shake I made earlier. My phone rang again; I hoped that it was not Tiffany again. I've been trying to be an adult about this, but she will make me answer this phone and read her all of her rights. I grabbed the phone, "Hello."

"Hey, Jason."

"Who's this?"

"It's Michelle."

"Michelle?

Michelle Johnson, oh yes, sorry, I just have a lot going on. I didn't look at the number. I thought you were someone else. So, how are you?"

"I'm good, Jason, and you?"

"I'm good as well; I can't complain. So, what did I do to deserve this call tonight?"

"I was just checking on you. I haven't heard from you in a while."

"Oh, okay. Yeah, just been busy, but that's nothing new."

"So, I heard you're single now."

I laughed, "Wow. Word do spread quickly, don't it?" I could tell she was smiling.

"Yeah, it does, so I'm taking from that comment that it's true."

"Yes, it actually is."

"So, why don't you let me take you out and occupy your time for a little?" I had to look at my phone for a second. I couldn't believe she was hitting on me like this.

"Michelle, I'm flattered but I don't want to lead you on. Besides, I have my eyes on someone else."

"Okay, is she your girl yet?"

"No."

"Are you guys dating?"

"No."

"So, what's the problem?

"There's no problem."

Does she even know you like her?"

"Yes, she does."

"So, until she shows you, she's interested, why not hang out with me?"

"Well, Michelle, you are a nice person, but the reason why I wouldn't bother to do that to you is that I don't want to waste your time getting you hooked on me, and when she decides that she wants me to be her man, I have to drop you like a hot tamale."

"Hmmm, you're that confident that she will want you."

"Yes, the same way you want me."

"So, how do you know I can't get you hooked on me?

"I'm not saying that you can't; what I'm saying is that I won't give you a chance to, but let's just say I did; all she has to do is say, "I'm ready," and I'm out of there."

Michelle laughed, "Jason, if anyone else told me this, I'll feel offended, or should I say pissed, but one thing I always admired about you was your honesty. Whoever she is, she's one lucky lady whether she knows it or not. I couldn't let a possible opportunity pass by and not give it a try."

"I understand; you're a good woman, Michelle; that lucky guy will come around soon."

It was 6:10 p.m. I changed the original location. I pulled up to Brewfish Bar and Grill and went inside. I told the host I was expecting some one and I just sat at the bar to wait. The basketball game was on; the Heats were playing the Brooklyn Nets. I wanted to order a drink just to kind of ease my anxiety. I know I said I wasn't going to drink for a while, but tonight, I deserve a pass. I ordered a Rusty nail. I was on a one-drink maximum. As I focused more on the game, I heard someone say my name. I turned around, it was Terri. I smiled. She showed up. I honestly thought she would have left me hanging, but she didn't.

"Hey, Terri, how are you?"

"I'm good."

"Thank you for coming." I let the host know that we were ready to be seated.

"Would you like something to drink?"

She replied, "Sure, why not?" Terri ordered a blue martini, and I ordered some appetizers. I took a sip of my drink. "Thanks again, Terri, for coming." She sat there silent. Were they all this way? This is tough. Then she smiled.

"Jason, it looks like you're having a little trouble, so I'll be the icebreaker. If you are having a hard time talking to me, I don't know what you would do if it were one of my other sisters."

Was it that obvious that I was nervous? Did she basically say the others were tougher than her? Wow!

She continued, "Obviously, you like Nadia, or else we wouldn't be sitting here. No one goes out of their way for no reason. I'm here, and this is your opportunity to plead your case." I took a deep breath.

"The lady I was with in Bora Bora is my ex. I caught her cheating again, so her way of trying to beg for forgiveness was to take me there. I wasn't going to go, but I did. I'm so happy I did. I knew it was over, but I didn't feel like that was the place to address it. One night, I was stressed about everything. I couldn't sleep, so I decided to stretch my legs. The crazy thing is you guys were on my flight, and I remember hearing Nadia's voice. So, when I saw her on the beach for the second time, I had to talk to her. The opportunity was there. Everything about Nadia was welcoming. I felt myself falling for her quickly. We had such an amazing time in those few hours we spent together than I had in months with my ex; honestly, my ex wasn't even on my mind, just Nadia. I had to see her again. Being with Nadia allowed me to sleep peacefully that night compared to the whole time I was there. I couldn't wait to see her again, hear her voice, talk to her, touch her, be in her presence. When Tiffany came up to us, I was shocked, but what pissed me off was the fact that she lied, said she was my fiancée, and made it seem like we were so happy. She was barely my girl. She was hanging by a thread. If the way Tiffany felt mattered to me, I would have never run after Nadia. I know I'm wrong for not letting her know up front, but everything was going so fast, and I didn't want to ruin the moment. I never planned for her to get hurt. If I could go back, even if it meant removing myself from the picture and never speaking to her, I would so she wouldn't feel the hurt and embarrassment she felt. I apologize to all of you because you are the ones who had to go through it with her. I tried calling her to explain, but as you already know, she wouldn't talk to me. Honestly, I want the chance to apologize. I don't want her to feel like I was out to use or hurt her. If she still doesn't want to talk to me again after, as much as it hurts to say, I'm okay with it."

"Jason, you're a good guy; I heard a lot about you. Even after meeting with you, I did my research, and a lot of great things were said about you. The way Nadia glowed in the little time she spent with you is beyond explainable. Believe it or not, you are the closest anyone has gotten to her in years; that means something. You did something to her in a good way, so when that incident happened, she went right back into her shell. I know I may be sharing a little too much, but we need her to be happy. I can't make any promises on how the outcome may be, but I'll help you. Only Eboni knows I'm here and as long as you mean right by Nadia, you have my support.

"Listen, Nadia is a writer and a poet. She will be performing next weekend. I think you should stop by."

"I will. I'm familiar with that place but haven't been there in a long time." We had a little small talk. Terri shared that they will be going to Italy soon for a few days for her fashion show.

"If Nadia is who you really want, Jason, don't give up! If you're doing this to save your face, I advise you to stop right now."

"I want her, Terri; no, I'm sorry; I need her, and I'm not going to stop until she's mine."

I felt like a load was off my shoulders getting my truth out to someone other than my boys. Now, I had to get my mind right to make things happen. I called Eric and Chris to find out if they wanted to roll with me tonight. I should be going by myself just in case I get shut down, but I'll take my chances. Mike went away for the weekend with his new girlfriend. I'm happy for him; it was long overdue. We got to the lounge around 8:30. The atmosphere was so poetic if that makes sense. There was jazz music playing. We sat at a table in the back where we weren't in sight. It was perfect; it had a great view of the stage. The waitress walked over, and we ordered a drink. I saw Terri with two other women, but Nadia wasn't in sight.

"Jason, relax! You look nervous," Eric said.

"I'm good."

"You sure?"

"Yeah, yeah, I'm sure." A few poets performed. They were great, so into it. Then there was an intermission. I got eye contact with Terri. She smiled and nodded my way.

When I heard the DJ say her name, my full attention went to the stage. She looked beautiful, and my heart was pounding. She wore a knee-length black dress, her hair was in a bun, and she wore these fuchsia pink heels with matching lipstick. She looked like she belonged up there. I heard Chris and Eric in the background say, "You never told us she looked this damn good. We see why you are hooked." I didn't even bother entertaining them; Nadia had all my attention. She grabbed the mic and smiled, "Goodnight, everyone. It's been a while since I touched the mic, but here we go." Her voice was smooth, and you could feel the emotion in her voice. Did I come on the wrong night? I felt her pain, and I felt worse than before. Did I contribute to this hurt, or was this something she randomly wrote? Once she was done, I saw her come back out and walk over to Terri. Not too long afterward, a guy walked over to her, they hugged, and spoke for a while. I couldn't take it. Chris and Eric were enjoying themselves. "You guys don't have to leave, but I have to go.""What's going on, Jay?" They asked.

"What happened to the plan?" Eric asked.

"I just can't do it. I'll talk to y'all later. Thanks again for coming." I got back to my car. I can't believe I did it again. This was my chance, and I possibly blew it. I sat in the car for thirty-five minutes, debating whether I should go back in or not.

Monday morning, bright and early, I was parked waiting to watch Nadia do her normal routine, and like clockwork, she was there; then Thursday rolled around, and she never showed up. I began to worry. Maybe she's tired. I know sometimes your body can do it to you. I know firsthand because I love to work out. The next day, the same thing happened; no Nadia. Worried, I picked up the phone to call Terri. *What are you doing?* I hurriedly hung the phone up. I can't call Terri; I never told her this part. I didn't want her to think I was weird. I'm worried now. I hope she's okay.

Chapter 16

Once I met Jason and he explained what happened; it made sense with what I heard and saw from inside the spa, leading to the episode on the beach. Sadly, I'm not the one he needs to get to believe him, though. I am willing to help because no one will go through this length of trouble to prove themselves if he didn't really like Nadia, and the best part is, you can't say it's because of the sex because there wasn't any.

When I saw him show up, I was excited; whew, finally, we can get to the bottom of this. It looked like he came with some friends, maybe a support system. Hey, whatever it takes to make it happen. Once Nadia finished and returned to the table, I was sure Jason would be walking over. I turned around, and some random guy was in her face. Fuck! I noticed Jason leaving. His friends were still here, so I thought he went to get some fresh air: ten minutes, twenty minutes, no Jason. I kept looking at the door, but he never came back.

"Terri, are you okay?"

"Yeah, Nadia. I was expecting someone; I was just keeping an eye out."

"Oh, okay."

I wanted to walk away and call him, but I'll wait until we leave. Some more poets performed. We talked for a while and then we left. I couldn't wait to get in my car. I didn't care what time it was; I'm calling Jason and he better answer.

"Hey Terri."

"What was that, Jason?"

"What was what?"

"That's my point exactly. Where did you go? Your leaving wasn't part of the plan!"

"I know. I'm sorry. I got scared and a little annoyed when I saw that guy walk up to Nadia, and I wasn't sure who he was, so I felt like the best thing to do was leave."

"First off Jason, what are you scared about? Obviously, you like each other; keep being scared, and see what that would do for you! You think you're worried now, keep that scared shit up. That guy was a nobody. Yes, he was trying to hit on her, and he couldn't even do that right, which worked out for you because if he did have a good pickup line, you may have lost your spot! I'm telling you, the longer you wait, the more space you are making for someone to come in. I know you don't want that, right?"

"You're right, Terri. I don't. I'm going to get it together."

"You better! Had me looking crazy looking for you. I still can't believe you left! You asked for my help and I'm trying."

"I appreciate it, Terri, I really do."

"Look, Nadia will be performing again next weekend. Hopefully, you can make it."

"I plan to unless something comes up."

She said, "Please pull yourself together, Jason. No more being scared or annoyed. Nadia doesn't bite."

"Terri, Thank you."

"No need to keep thanking me. Save it for that speech on your wedding day." He laughed. "I needed that, Terri. It's a deal," Once I was done talking with him, I hit the shower. Jason does come across as a nice guy. Genuine but he better get it together, quickly.

"Hey baby, you answered the phone like you miss me."

"You know I miss you, Slim."

"I miss you too. I was hoping you would be home tonight."

"We don't get back for another four days."

"It seems so far away Ty."

"I know baby.

Then I will be leaving for a few days."

"Ty, I don't know how much of not seeing you I can take."

"I've been feeling the same way, baby."

"I've been thinking about doing some local work for a while."

"No, that's not fair Tyler."

"It's not fair not being able to wake up next to you for weeks at a time."

"I know Ty. Let's talk about it when you get home before you make any decisions.

"I love you."

"Love you too Ty."

Tyler and I have been going strong for six years. It was rough at first, more so on my end. I was confused and wasn't sure what I wanted, and he really hung in there. Stuck with me. I love him so much. Best decision I ever made in my life.

Chapter 17

JASON

I woke up extra early today. It's Saturday. I'm telling you, today couldn't come quick enough. It felt like forever for it to get here. I couldn't wait to see Nadia tonight. Especially since I couldn't see her for those two days that she didn't go to the park. I hope she's okay. I had a few things planned for tonight. I'm excited! Tonight, I'm going solo; I didn't invite the guys. I didn't want to bother them, and they had their own thing going on. I walked into the lounge the confident man I knew I was. I almost thought I was losing my touch for a second. I'm glad I snapped back to reality with Terri's help. I couldn't believe how packed it was; it wasn't even 9 o'clock yet. I'm wearing the same cologne I had on the first time we met. On my way home last night, I went to the barber to get my tape and my beard freshened up. I found a seat in the back where I sat last week. It's the same table if you want to get technical. When the waitress came over, I ordered a rusty nail. I didn't see Terri, Nadia, or the other ladies that was with them the last time I was here. The crowd is thick, so maybe I missed them. I know Terri wouldn't have speeched me off the way she did for them not to be here tonight. What if something really did happen to Nadia and that's why they aren't here tonight? I kept calm, and I enjoyed the sounds and rhythm of the people blessing the microphone. There wasn't any discrimination on age. You had young and older people sitting here; I understood more why this place was so packed. It was vibrant; smiles and laughter were in the air. I checked my phone to see if I missed a call from Terri, but she didn't call. I went to the restroom, came out, and ordered another drink. I looked up and saw Nadia walking in with Terri. I watched her every move. To me, at this point, it was like the room was empty. I kept her in sight. They went over to a table where a group of people was already waiting. She had a funky, cute look going on tonight. Her hair was braided like a mohawk where all the braids met in the middle. Instead of the braids being braided down, it stopped halfway, and the rest of her hair that was left out was curly. She wore all white; her jeans were rolled at the bottom where they stopped at her calves, with her white fitted t-shirt that said, 'Melanin Poppin' in green, red, and black. She wore green shoes with the toes out and that popping red lipstick to compliment it; talk about a traffic stopper. I wonder what she's going to perform tonight. Nadia is really a social butterfly. She knows how to work the crowd. More people made their way in. I finished up my drink and made my way through the crowd. The closer I got to her, the more confident I felt. Her back was to me. Terri saw me coming and her facial expressions told me she was glad I made it.

"Smiley."

She stood there for a few seconds, which felt like minutes. Slowly turning around, she looked very surprised to see me. "Jason?"

I smiled, "Nadia, I'm so happy to see you."

"I'm not sure I could say the same."

"Ouch. I can't say that didn't hurt."

She had a confused look on her face. I knew exactly what she was thinking.

"Why are you here, Jason?"

"I had to see you. I've been searching for you and that was like running into a brick wall. I have to talk to you. I need to talk to you! You won't answer my calls and I didn't know what else to do."

"So, how did you know I'll be here?" I stood silent. I was trying to figure out what to say next, not wanting to blow Terri's cover.

"All I want is a few minutes of your time, Nadia. Please."

"Fine," she said. Looking at her watch, "You have five minutes starting now."

Shit! She wasn't playing.

The lights were dimmed. That was my cue. The spotlight was on her. Shocked, her eyes were on me, and my eyes were stuck on her. I pulled the mic out of my pocket. I stopped by yesterday and coordinated everything. The manager agreed to help me. So, I knew the timing and when to do everything.

"From the day I laid eyes on you

I knew you had to be mine

With that twinkle in your eyes

To the smile on your face

I knew you were the one for me.

I want to love you forever and a day.

Give me the chance to show you.

Show you how it's really supposed to be

To be loved, to feel love

To never have to shed a tear again.

I want to hold you close and never let you go.

I want our minds and bodies to become one.
I want to protect you from the world.
Let me make love to your soul.
While exploring your universe
I fell in love with your voice before
I had the chance to meet you.
I need to wake up next to you
Indulging in your scents
I want to see you at your worst
Not just at your best
We have a lifetime of memories to make
There's no need to rush
The way you made me feel inside
Makes me want you more
I could never get enough of you
That I won't deny
Tell me that you will be
My lover, my friend
One day, my bride

"Nadia, I know my writing isn't anywhere close to yours or anyone in here for that matter, but I just need you to know that this is from the heart. It may sound crazy, but you already have my heart, and I promise to make you happy and keep you happy. I know things went sideways, but I promise it will never happen again. I'm begging for your forgiveness in front of everyone here tonight. You don't have to take my word for it. I will prove to you every day that God blesses me with life; I will show you."

She didn't react when I touched her. She just kept looking at me. I hope I didn't embarrass her; maybe this was too much. This idea seemed great when I replayed it in my head a thousand times. I hope I didn't make a fool of myself. The last thing I need or want is to be rejected in front of all these people. I noticed a few people were recording. It's so quiet in here; you can hear a pin drop. Everyone is staring at us. Most likely wondering the same thing as me. Nadia is exceptionally great at hiding her expressions. I thought I had a breakthrough earlier. I wonder if they sit and practice with each other how not to show expressions. Terri showed me her preview and said she wasn't the worst of the bunch. At this point, I won't be surprised if Nadia is an undercover lawyer. I laughed to myself with that one. I saw a worried look on Terri's face; another one of her friends had her hand on her mouth. My heart picked up its pace; it was pounding. *Can anyone else hear it? Jason, just breathe;* I repeated it a few times. Her eyes are still on me. *What is she thinking?* I feel like I've been standing here for hours. *Should I just back away now and save the little bit of dignity I have left?* A lady in the crowd screamed out,

"I don't know what he did, but please forgive him." That broke the silence. She smiled. I smiled. Nadia was getting up out of her seat. *Is she going to walk away?* I was hesitant, but it's now or never. I stretched my hands out to hold hers; here goes another moment that seemed like an eternity. I'm starting to wonder if I like the thought of being or getting embarrassed. She smiled at me after hesitating and took my hand. I thought my spirit left my body. Her touch was so delicate. This is what I had been waiting for. I kept screaming yes, yes, yes in my head. Finally! Finally! I didn't want to let any more time pass. I wasn't giving her the chance to change her mind. I exhaled while pulling her close to me and staring into her eyes. I saw it. All the emotion she had been hiding. I was still not sure, but there was no turning back. I kissed her, and she leaned in and kissed me back. Everyone started clapping and was just as excited as I was. I stepped back and looked at her, still smiling. I hugged her and picked her up.

I whispered in her ear, "Let me make love to your mind while exploring your universe because I'm never letting you go. I know I have a lot of explaining to do but I'll worry about that when it comes."

Chapter 18

NADIA

It felt so good to be back. Getting on that stage did something to me. Why did I deprive myself of this for so long? I was ready to start this back full-time. I kept up my routine of working out, but I just couldn't do it when I got up this morning. My body told me, not today, and I had to listen; the last thing I needed was to be running and pass out, and no one knew. I'll just start fresh on Monday. I laid in bed all day. I took a sick day from the world. It was needed, and I took advantage of it.

Terri and I rode to the lounge together tonight. We hung out all day today. Mel and Jeff had plans, and Eboni had a few things to do, so we would meet them and a few other friends later. Jeff had a friend that he kept insisting that I meet. I told him to bring him tonight. At this point, why not? What do I have to lose? We were running a little late, so when we got there, it was packed. Thank God we already had a table there. I felt great tonight. We made our way through the crowd. I spoke to some people along the way. Once there, I remembered Jeff and his friend. "Nadia, I want you to meet Rick."

"Hi, Rick. How are you?"

"Great. I've heard a lot about you."

"Really? I hope it was all great things."

He smiled. "Are you performing tonight?"

"No, not tonight. I'm just going to enjoy the atmosphere tonight."

Rick and I spoke for a few minutes. He's cute but not really my type. Hell, maybe that's what I need. Someone that's not my type because baby, my type doesn't seem to appreciate me.

I was standing there talking to Eb when I heard someone say, "Smiley." It sounded like Jason; nah, it's not him; maybe someone else in here has the same nickname. That's not impossible. I turned around, and it was Jason. I couldn't believe it. What is he doing here? He looked so damn good. And that cologne, I know he did that on purpose. I tried to stay focused. I zoned out. I couldn't hear anything for a few seconds. Then I heard Terri say, "Hear him out, Nad. He's already here." Then other people started chiming in, "Hear him out, hear him out." So, I did. I sat down so I could "hear him out." Before I could blink twice, the spotlight came on me. I know they said the last performer was about to get on stage, so maybe they were having difficulty adjusting the spotlight because the performer wasn't me. I originally was going to perform but changed my mind. I couldn't believe it. My heart began to race, looking at everyone looking at me. I couldn't believe he was doing this. My heart was pounding. He looked nervous. You could tell. Hearing him speak did something to me. It's amazing when someone steps out of their comfort zone. I almost forgot that I was upset with him or even why. I did say "almost," laughing to myself. It got to me, though; he used something I loved and was passionate about to get to me. I loved it. I may have to show him a thing or two. I was enjoying this moment. Jason took the time to address me through me. '*Stay strong*' is what I had to keep telling myself. I felt my eyes getting watery. I never had anyone go to this measure to get my attention.

We definitely had a lot of talking to do. He placed his hands on mine while expressing his thoughts. Am I wrong to say that turned me on? I'm still trying to be tough. I can't let him know my heart is melting for him. His lips, the way it moved, I wanted to kiss it. Why are these thoughts running through my head? I'm supposed to be mad! He came in closer. I got another whiff of his cologne. It made me want to rip his shirt off. *What's wrong with you, girl? Control yourself.* My eyes never came off of him. He was doing an amazing job. I was impressed. There was passion with every word. I swear it won't be hard to fall in love with this man, but I had to make him sweat a little.

I know I was making him more nervous. I started to feel bad, but I had to test him. I'm not going to lie; I was a little hesitant. I was going to let him finish and silently reject him, but why? I had to remind myself that no one is perfect and not many people go through this length of trouble just to get your attention. I deserve to be happy, and that's what he was trying to do. What do I have to lose? For a long time, I've been walking around here, manless, lonely, making love to Tristan the dildo because I was scared. I allowed it to have to much control. Life is about taking chances, and Jason made me realize this tonight. He took that chance. I am good enough. I am worth it. If, after a month, I was still on this man's mind, he at least deserved me to hear his side of the story or just hear whatever it is he needs to say. I really wanted to jump in his arms. Then, when that lady blurted out her comment, I thought it was cute and right on time. When he kissed me, Lord, I had to remember where we were. I think if we were alone, he would have gotten all of me tonight. I'm glad it turned out the way it did; absolutely perfect. At this point, I am choosing me.

We hung out here at the lounge afterward, and I introduced Jason to everyone. They happily welcomed him and told him what a good job he did. Poor Rick didn't look too happy but respected what it was. My girls looked at me and there was joy in their eyes. Jay didn't let me out of his sight. He had a glow of happiness all over him.

"Nadia."

"Yes, Jason."

Pulling me close, he asked, "Will you come home with me tonight? Please. But first off, before you answer let me say this. I want you to be comfortable so, if you're not comfortable coming right now I understand; I just want to, you know, talk. Make sure everything is clear."

"I would love to talk with you and make sure things are clear as well, so, yes, I'll spend the night with you." We hung out for another ten, fifteen minutes, and we left.

Making our way to his car, he opened the door for me. He is such a gentleman. He has a nice SUV, clean and it smelled like he got it washed today.

"Are you okay?" he asked.

"Yes, I answered. Are you?" "I'm great. Is there anything special you would like to listen to?"

"No, I'm in your space; allow me to see what you like."

He smiled, "Okay." He turned on his Spotify and started playing 'Love Riddim' by Rotimi.

"I love that song, Jay." I sat back and enjoyed the ride.

We pulled up to his house. Beautiful, beautiful, beautiful. He pushed the button to open one of the doors to the garage. I see why we probably never ran into each other before. We lived on two different sides of town. I live in a nice area, but Jay lives in a nicer one. He pulled in and closed the garage once we were safely in. He got out, walked around, and opened my door.

"Watch your step."

"Thank you." Holding my hand, he led the way. From the garage, we walked into the kitchen. He had an island in the middle with a stove in it. On the wall were a double oven and a deep double sink. The cupboards were glass. A separate door led to the pantry, which was like another room with a walk-in fridge. The kitchen table is off to the side. Mel would love this kitchen.

"I will give you a better tour of the house tomorrow if that's okay."

"That's fine." It was really late anyway.

"Are you hungry or thirsty? Or maybe both?

Do you want anything before we go upstairs?" He asked.

"Do you have water?"

"Yes, baby. Let me go grab a few bottles; wait right here."

Hmm, did he just call me baby? I'm not gonna lie; it felt right.

"Okay, let's go. I usually have some in the fridge in the room, but just in case I grabbed a few." Damn, he has a fridge in the room. The stairway was beautiful. You could access the stairs from either side of the house. These are those type of stairs you can take beautiful pictures.

We walked into the bedroom.

I took a look at the room. First off it was big. He had a King-size bed with a blue bed set on it. There was a door that led to the balcony, A balcony where you could sit and look out into the huge backyard. I saw the little fridge in the corner.

"Would you like to take a shower?"

"Yes, thank you." That would be great. He gave me an oversized towel and led me to the bathroom. There was a "his and her" sink. The tub is separate from the shower. He had a toilet and a bidet. The decor was simple. It said a man lives here. I turned on the shower and got in; there were two thermostatic shower systems with a dual-function showerhead and six body jets. This shower felt amazing. I couldn't believe I was here. This man could have any woman he wanted, yet he was on a mission to find me. I could cry, I did cry. It felt like a fairytale. I couldn't wait until the morning when we could talk, and I could know everything and what was really going on. I hope he doesn't have any children. Sorry, not sorry, it's for my sake. Sadly, people make you feel this way. I got out of the shower and dried off.

"Damn, I don't have any clothes." I said to myself while I slowly opened the bathroom door.

Jason was standing there.

"I know you don't have any clothes, so I have one of my T-shirts for you to sleep in tonight. Tomorrow, I'll get you something to wear."

"You know I could just go home and get something."

"I know, but I didn't ask you to go home. I'm going to go take a shower; please make yourself at home."

Once he went into the bathroom, I put the shirt on, placed my towel on the basket he had by the closet, temporarily until he came out of the shower, and I climbed into the bed. It was soft. The mattress molded to my body, and I felt like I sunk right into it, hugging my body like it was telling me, "Welcome home." The blanket was soft and fluffy, everything was just right. I was trying to stay awake until he got out. I dozed off but heard when he opened the door. I had to stay alert; this was our first time being together completely alone.

Jason brought the bottle of water and placed it on the nightstand. He had on some basketball shorts and no shirt.

Licking my lips, I said, "Damn, Jason, you don't want to put a shirt on?"

He laughed. "You took my last one." I giggled.

"Thank you for coming, Smiley," he kissed me. "I'll be back. I'm going to make sure the alarms are set."

Once he got back, he got in the bed and pulled me close to him.

I woke up the next morning to the sun shining through the window. Jason had me tight in his arms. This was different and new to me. It had been a long time since I woke up in a man's arms. I didn't realize how much I missed that feeling. It was nice.

"Good morning, Smiley."

Wow, he's awake already? "Good morning, Jason" I turned around to face him. He looked like he'd been up for a while.

I hope I don't have bad morning breath. I thought to myself.

"You're up early."

"Yeah, that's every day. He replied but I didn't want to wake you."

"What time is it?"

Looking at the clock, He replied, "A few minutes to eight."

"Yeah, this is late for me." I said

"Are you hungry? Because I'm starving." He asked.

I laughed. "Yeah, I'm a little hungry but not starving, yet."

"I wanted to actually take you out, but I know we have a clothes issue right now, which I will take care of later. I have a few things planned for today if that's okay with you."

I replied, "Sure, whatever you like to do. I'm down." I could have made up all the excuses of why I would have to leave but I decided to stop fighting and resisting so much. I will miss out on life if I don't loosen up. I'm not saying my guard is down, but I'm going to enjoy it a little more and take more chances regarding relationships.

"So, what do you want to eat?"

"What do you have?"

He laughed. "What's so funny, Jay?"

"Nothing. I'm going to order us some breakfast."

"Oh, I thought we were going to go into that beautiful kitchen and make things happen."

"Not today, but I do look forward to many days of being in the kitchen and making things happen with you." He kissed me. "I'm going to go ahead and order breakfast. Is there anything special you want?"

"Ummm, waffles and definitely bacon. I love bacon," I laughed.

"Anything special to drink?"

"Tea, Mint tea preferably, but I'll take French vanilla cappuccino if they don't have any."

"Sounds good." He had stepped out of the room to place the order and I laid in bed analyzing everything. This room seemed bigger now than it did last night. He had two chairs in the corner, not side by side. There was an extremely big walk-in closet. The room wasn't cluttered, he was a clean man. Thank God. I felt at ease. I went to wash my face and take a shower. He had a toothbrush waiting there for me. This shower will make you want to stay in there all day. It's big. I imagined us making love in here, and then I began to wonder about last night. We both had to be tired because I was laying in the bed next to this fine man, who wore no shirt, and I had no undies on, yet nothing happened. I came out the bathroom with just my towel on. Jason was sitting on the bed.

"Breakfast is here," he said, licking his lips.

"Nadia, let me help you put this robe on." He stood up and

opened it, and I put my arms in; he turned me around, fixed my collar, and pulled me in for a kiss; I came in as close I could, rubbing his back; I felt his manhood rising, I couldn't get enough of him, he took his hands and grabbed my ass. I felt like I was about to have an orgasm. I need to stop. I slowly pulled away, "Let's go downstairs to eat before the food gets cold." He said.

We sat in the kitchen, and everything was laid out on the table. Jay told me everything that happened with him and Tiffany, why he was in Bora Bora, and the most recent incident. I understood his predicament at the time. He kept apologizing.

"Jay, there's no need to keep apologizing. Yes, the situation could have been handled differently, but it wasn't. The great thing is I'm here now, and I am happy that you were man enough to tell me the truth."

"So, Smiley, does this mean you're going to be my Queen?"

"Hmm, well, let me see. I don't know if we would truly be good for each other;" his mouth dropped, and his eyes were deadlocked on mine. I couldn't hold in my laughter any longer.

"Yes, I'll be honored." His eyes lit up. We sat and talked for hours, getting lost in time. While getting to know each other better.

We went shopping and then came back to his house.

"I would like to take you out to dinner tonight; what type of food are you feeling for?"

"I'm not a picky person. No matter where we go, I'll surely find something I like on the menu. We can even stay in. So, the choice is yours Jay."

Sadly, I haven't looked at my phone since I've been here. We were sitting in the backyard when I remembered, so I finally took the time and checked my phone and the group messages started flowing.

They said, *"Just checking on you; we haven't heard from you in almost twenty-four hours."*

"I hope he didn't blow your back out so bad that you're in the ER."

"Yes, let him blow it out."

I laughed and responded, "Ladies, I'm great. Thanks for asking, EB; no, he didn't blow my back out yet! He's respectable but I'm not going to lie, having a man in my presence as fine as he is, staying in control is hard. I'm looking forward to our trip on Thursday. Love you guys."

They replied, *"Love ya." "Love you too." "Love you."*

The weather was beautiful. It was not too hot.

"So, I should let you know that I'm going to Italy on Thursday."

"Really?"

"Yeah, Terri is going to be in a big fashion show on Saturday, and she wants us there."

"How long are you going to be there?"

"Oh, we should be coming back Sunday night."

"Thank you for telling me. If it's okay, I can make sure you get to and from the airport."

"I don't want to put you through all that trouble Jason."

"Who said anything about trouble? I will never offer, ask, or say anything I can't or don't want to do. You're my lady, so you're my number one priority. I have a driver on days I'm busy or don't feel like driving. So just let me know what time and we will be at your house on Thursday." The more he spoke, the more I was turned on and it wasn't so much on the sexual side. I loved his concern and his manly attitude.

"What can I really say to that, but okay." I understood more why Tiffany didn't want to lose him, but it was obvious she didn't appreciate or want to keep him either because she couldn't stop or, should I say, didn't want to stop the cheating. I may need to shake her hand one day.

We got up extra early today. Jay had a few appointments this morning. He told me I could stay at his house if I wanted, but I had things I needed to do. He got me home at about 9:30 a.m.

"Thank you for such a relaxing weekend." I said softly.

He came out and walked me to the door.

"I hope to see you before you leave on Thursday."

"You will. Have a great day at work." We kissed. I know I'm trying not to rush into having sex, but if I keep kissing him like this, it will happen sooner than planned. This weekend was everything.

Chapter 19

MEL

That trip to Bora Bora was everything. There weren't any disappointments at all. I missed Jeff, but I always enjoyed the time I spent with my girls. Once we got back home, we went back to Nadia's house. All our vehicles were there. We spoke for a while, put our things in the car, stayed outside talking, and went our separate ways. I was tired. That flight was long; it seemed like coming home was longer than going. I guess it was because all of the excitement wore out. I pulled up to my house, and I was hoping to see Jeff's car in the yard. It wasn't. I got all my things into the house. I just wanted to get in the shower and lie down. *I will call Jeff once I'm out and settled.* I took my clothes off and took a hot shower. I heard music playing. *I know I'm tired, but I know I didn't tell Alexa to play anything. Man, I knew I should have brought a gun like Jeff told me to months ago.* I walked out of the bathroom slowly. *Where did I put my phone? Lord, I'm going to have to fight because I'm not dying tonight. I hope my neighbors can hear me if I scream.* I turned the corner. I felt someone touch me; I screamed and swung the first blow. My towel fell, and I ran to my bedroom door. The shit was locked. While rushing to unlock it, I heard, "Alexa, turn off the music."

"Jeff? Alexa, turn the lights on.

Baby, what were you thinking?" I ran over to him naked.

"Sorry, babe. I guess I didn't think it through well enough."

"I could have killed you, Jeff!"

"Really, Mel."

He couldn't stop laughing. "I'm sorry, babe. I was trying to get here before you, but the traffic was crazy. I noticed you were here, and I still wanted to surprise you. I turned Alexa on by accident. You had already come out of the shower at that point, so I had to leave it on. I had the candles in my hand. I wanted to light them so you would see them when you came out, but you turned off the bathroom light. Smart move, by the way, but you walked past me while I was trying to move, and at that point, I guess you thought you were Jackie Chan."

"Very funny, Jeff." We laughed, him, a little harder than me.

"You could have surprised me with food or by lying naked in bed. You had me wishing I brought a gun like you told me to many times before."

"Well, I'm glad you didn't have it now, but that's another point I'm trying to prove. Anyway, come here with your naked, sexy self. I missed you so much."

"I missed you too, baby. I'm so happy to be home. I brought you back something, too."

"Thank you, but the only thing I wanted from that trip was you." We kissed, lay in bed, and talked until I fell asleep. I knew that would happen. Thank God I didn't have anything planned for a few days. I'm just going to stay home, relax, and enjoy my man.

The date for Terri's fashion show got pushed back, so we had to change our flights and hotel reservations. Thank God we had insurance, so it was free. I'm a little glad it got pushed back; I'm able to have more quality time with my Jeff. I was so happy. Everyone's life is falling into place more and more as the weeks go by. Terri has her man, I have my Jeff, Eb is still confused and not sure if she will ever settle down, and Nadia has a man. That night at the lounge left us all holding our hearts. We didn't know what she would do, but I'm telling you, if she didn't hear that man out, I was going to tell her about herself, and not in the nicest way. Everything was beautiful. She deserves happiness, and I believe it finally found her.

I didn't have plans today, and Jeff had a job to do.

Let me call my sister. "Hello."

"Hey, sissy."

"Nadia! You even sound different." I knew she was smiling on the other end of the phone.

"So, how was your weekend?"

"Honestly, Mel, it was amazing. He's perfect! I never thought anyone could get me this excited again in life."

"So, did you guys have sex?"

"No, he didn't even try."

She exclaimed, "What!"

"I know but listen his manhood was alive and well, but he controlled himself. He treated me like a queen. I didn't want for anything. He has a beautiful house. When I saw his kitchen, I thought about you."

"Yes! Nadia, this is long overdue. I'm so happy for you."

"Mel, I'm scared."

"Scared! Why?"

"What if I fall in love with him too soon? What if I sleep with him, then he doesn't want me anymore? I think that's another reason why I don't want to rush to cross those lines with him, yet. Mel, what if I mess up"?

"Nad, are you kidding me? She blurted out. This man is clearly fucked up about you and he doesn't even know what your insides feel like. You have been on Jason's mind for over a month and all you did was talk to him. So clearly, he sees way more than you can imagine. He is ready to show you that love still exists. Yeah, so what if you fall in love with him too soon? What is too soon exactly? I'm no psychic, but I don't see him not wanting you after you sleep with him, especially after all the trouble he went through to find you and to explain himself when we both know he didn't have to. I'm not saying you can't be scared; I get why, but don't sell yourself short worrying about the "what ifs" if it's too soon or if he wouldn't want you after sex. If sex is what he really wanted, he had all weekend to get it, and let you go but out of your own mouth, you said, "he didn't make a move but treated you like a queen." So, when the time comes and you feel like you are in love with him, accept it, embrace it, and let it be known. There's no specific time for love. We know that so many people are not fortunate enough to experience this. You are always worried and concerned about everyone else's life and happiness. Now it's time to accept yours. Choose you, don't rob yourself." And that part about you messing up, girl please. I'm not going to entertain that, but I will say this. No one is perfect but we can be perfect for each other. I know you're worried because you haven't been in the game for almost four years, but the problem was never you, you just allowed yourself to suffer like it was. Andre sadly wasn't your person, and honestly, we don't know if Jason is but there's only one way to find out and so far, sis, it's looking good. I don't know what your definition of messing up is, but I don't see it being a problem for you. Talk to Jason, keep it real and you will be just fine.

"Thank you so much sissy."

"That's what I'm here for and I'm serious, Nadia."

"I told Jay that we were leaving on Thursday. He didn't verbally express it, but I know he was a little sad. He said he would provide our transportation to and from the airport; there wasn't any debating."

"Nad, you got you a real man. Hold on to him."

"I know, I know."

"I am so happy for you sis."

"What are you doing today?" I asked.

"I need to clean up a bit. Then try to relax."

"Mel, soooo, are you cooking?"

"Yes, fatty. Good, I'm coming over for some food later. It's been a while since I had some of that good food. Let me know when you're done."

"Love you sissy."

"Love you too, Nadia.

I cooked fried chicken, mashed potatoes, green beans with bacon bits, seafood pasta salad, and yellow rice. I called everyone to come over. Eb was going to eat and run. She had a date with Dante tonight. Jeff was hanging with his boys but asked me to save him some food which he knew I would anyway. So, it would just be Terri, Nad, and myself.

"Terri, are you excited about this fashion show?" I asked.

"Yes. I can't wait. Three days of fun somewhere different. I'm hoping our next trip will be a couple's trip. Eb better stop playing with Dante."

"She needs to go ahead and make it exclusive with him." I agreed with Terri.

"They are actually perfect for each other. Dante can handle Eb."

"She told me once we come back from Italy, she will get it together."

"Okay, we will see. We all know how she can get."

"So, Jeff said he wants to start a family."

"Mel, that's great!"

"I know, Nad, but I don't know if I'm ready yet."

"What do you mean?"

"I don't want any restrictions right now."

"Well, it doesn't have to be now. Set a time, maybe the next two years or three years, etc. Starting a family is a big step. We're here for your support. We are still going to be able to live, but seriously, talk to him and tell him what your expectations are if a baby comes into the picture so there are no misunderstandings, and if he is the man you plan on spending the rest of your life with you better start talking and letting it all out now. And the fact that he brought it up might just be a good thing."

"You guys are right. I'll talk with him again, but I'm still on the fence."

Everything was packed and ready for Italy. We were all going to meet at Nad's house early in the morning since Jason would be sending the car there to take us to the airport. I only had one suitcase and a carry-on because it was only three days, and I knew we would also be shopping.

"Baby, you want to drop me off at Nad's in the morning?"

"Sure."

"Don't look so sad Jeff; it's only three days." I walked over to him and sat on his lap.

"We are going to be planning a couple's trip soon. Why don't you and your boys plan a guy's trip?"

"Really Mel?" I know he was being sarcastic.

"Yes, baby, stop acting like guys don't travel together even if it's local. Go have a good time. You work hard. You deserve it. Once we come back, I'll start looking into nice places for couples. If you have any ideas, let me know."

"Forget about that for right now. I have something better in mind," he said.

He picked me up and laid me on the couch. We made love. I was nervous because I didn't want to get pregnant. We stopped using condoms months ago and we have been very sexual these past couple of weeks, a little more than usual. Was he trying to give me a baby now or remind me of this good dick I have at home to hold me out until I got back? Either way, once we get back from Italy, I'm going to talk to him because I really don't want any surprises, none whatsoever.

I made it to Nad's house at about 7:15 a.m. She was up and ready, and coffee was being made.

"Good morning." Nad greeted me as I walked into the house.

"Morning." I placed my bags by the door and went to get my coffee and croissants. I would have made breakfast if we had time, but the croissants would do. Eb and Riri pulled up at the same time. They just left their bags in the cars instead of bringing them into the house. Nad was on the phone with Jason; he was on his way and wanted to know if we wanted anything to eat. Riri and Eb sat down while drinking their coffee.

"We're going to have so much fun, I can't wait," Eb said.

Fifteen minutes later, Jason showed up.

"Good morning, ladies."

"Good morning." He then walked over to Nad, hugged and kissed her. You could tell he was crazy about her, and she couldn't hide her feelings for him. It showed. They walked into the kitchen and stayed in there for a few minutes, coming back out he was drinking coffee, and she had her tea. They look good together. He introduced us to the driver; Alex and they began putting our bags into the SUV. The SUV was an eight-seater. Jason sat with Nad in the back row, and the three of us sat up front. Back there, he had his arms around her, and she looked comfortable like that was where she belonged. Joy can come from pain. Andre broke her to the point she thought she could never love again; while we thought he hurt her, all he did was make room and prepare her for a real man. We made it to the airport and found our Airline. We were traveling with American Airlines. We had two connecting flights before we could make it to the beautiful city of Milan. Jason helped us carry our luggage in. We had a few flights to catch, so Nad and I sat together on the first flight.

The flight had taken off. We were still awake for some reason. Nad looked at me, "Mel, I'm very proud of you." Even though I heard this from her many times, it was always like the first time. Nad has been my number-one supporter from day one. She always pushed me when I felt it was becoming too much; she didn't just agree and allow me to give up.

"Thank you, Sis. You know that means a lot to me."

She smiled and continued playing Candy Crush. We made it to the first stop, where we caught our connected flight. We were trying to save our sleep for the longest flight. Finally, hours later, we were on the flight to Italy. I was tired and ready to get there. I was never a fan of having to take connecting flights, but it's the least I could do if I want to see the world. On this flight, I sat with Eb.

"I'm so excited, Mel, we're going to Milan."

"Yes, girl, let's take one for the books." We took a few

selfies. I slipped my shoes off, pulled my blanket out, and got comfy. Eb did the same. Eb was doing something on her tablet. I stayed up as long as I could, and then I was out.

We landed at Milan Malpensa Airport; this place was beautiful. Milan, Milan, Milan. What a beautiful name. Maybe one day, if Jeff and I have a daughter, that may be her name. Milan or Milani. I laughed to myself. I can't believe I just had thoughts of a child. Ughh Jeff.

We caught an Uber from the airport to Mo.om Hotel. That's where we'll be for the next few days. It's not far from the Airport, thank God, the flight was long enough, who wants to deal with a long ride to a hotel after that. This hotel is amazing. It's… how can I describe it? Modern and futuristic. The design of the building is open, luxurious, yet still inviting. We are sharing a room, which we usually do anyway since it's just us. Why waste unnecessary money that we can use to shop and have a good time? It's morning here. We left in the morning, and we got here in the morning. Once we got to our room, we took turns taking a shower. I called Jeff to let him know we made it safely. Tomorrow is Riri's Big day. In a few hours, she has to meet up with the rest of her fashion crew to do a fitting and rehearsal. After that, we're going to find something to get into. We aren't going to be here long enough to explore and do much here in Milan how we would like, however if we can get to see something somewhere, it would be nice, whether it's going to see The Duomo, possibly getting to see the original last supper photo by Leonardo Da Vinci and of course finding a mall to shop.You know shopping is our middle name. I heard of the Brera district, Galleria Vittorio Emanuele ll, and a few others.

It was almost noon, and we were starving. We are going to get a head start and leave now.

"Let's get pizza," Eb suggested.

"Why not," Nad said. "We're in Italy."

Cool. We gathered ourselves and stepped out to enjoy Milan's beautiful weather and sites. There were a few pizza restaurants we could choose from, but a lot of them don't open until later in the evening, and that's not going to do anything for us. We found one that was open, called Strapizzami. We ordered two pizzas and a shrimp salad. Nad wanted the salad.

"Nad, can you tell me again why in the world we are in Italy, and you want a salad?"

Laughing, she replied, "I have to maintain this figure for that fine-ass man I have at home."

Terri said, "Oh please, Jason will love you no matter your size! You can go back home looking like the Pillsbury doughboy, and he would love you the same."

Terri took the words right out of my mouth. Jason is crazy about her. As long as she made it back home, that's the only thing he's worried about. She ate some of the pizza, not much, and we tasted the salad as well it was big. She wouldn't have been able to finish it by herself. From there, we checked out a few stores and then went straight to rehearsal with Riri. It ran a little longer than planned, but they were ready. The show was tomorrow night, so we have tonight and tomorrow morning; our flight is early Sunday morning, so we have to squeeze in the time to do and see everything and anything we can.

On our way back to our room, we stopped and got some food. We all got something different so we could eat it together. I got Risotto alla Milanese. It was so good. I took a shower after and went straight to bed. We woke up extra early today so we could go to the Duomo. It opens at nine. We were on a tight schedule. We would have gone last night, but they close at seven. We were dressed and ready to go by 7:30, thanks to our drill sergeant, Ms. Nadia. The Duomo is a sight to see, pleasing to the eyes. It took us almost three hours. The rooftop was a wonderful experience. We took so many pictures. This is the type of memories you should want to build.

Terri left before we did. Once we arrived, we found our seats. So many people were here. They all looked amazing. We saw some interesting pieces; I'm not sure where you would wear them, but hey.

"Ladies, do you see all these fine, handsome men in Italy?"

Nadia replied, "Eb, behave."

"What's wrong with looking and admiring Nad? Now, if one of them comes over here, thennnn…" We couldn't help but laugh; technically, she is single, but if she's serious about Dante, she will eventually have to fight the urge and get her mind right. It may not be easy, but it will be worth it. Once it was over and people started leaving, we returned to wait for Terri. We gave her a group hug.

"You ripped that runway, Riri."

"Thank you, Nad."

If nothing else, we are big supporters of each other and wouldn't hesitate to promote, praise, or do whatever it may takes to make sure we get the recognition that we deserve.

"Thank you, guys, so much for being here, especially since my parents couldn't make it."

Her parent was coming but when the dates were changed, it happened to be the same time they would be flying out for their yearly mini vacation. They were going to reschedule but Terri insisted that they stuck to their original plans. So, we made sure to take pictures and videos to send them. At one point Eboni called Terri's mom on video call so they could see her when she walked the runway.

"You know we wouldn't miss this for the world Terri."

It was pretty late once we left. We headed back to the room, got our things together, and slept for a few hours.

"We have to come back here again, ladies, for maybe two more additional days."

"Yes, Terri, we do. I agreed. The good thing is we really didn't come for fun but more for support, and we still had a great time."

Nad called Jason, letting him know we would land at about 11:14 p.m. Sunday. I fell asleep while they were talking.

At about 2:30 a.m., Nad was getting ready to take a shower, and she woke us up so we could follow suit. Our flight is for 7:30 am, so we have to be out of here by at least 4:45, another reason I'm happy we are close to the airport. I must say, I wish Nadia would sleep late for a change, but her early bird tenancies have saved us many times. The three of us are horrible; we would have missed many flights if she wasn't around. We're getting better, though, but not on Nad's level yet. We checked out and made it to the airport at 4:55. We were still on good timing. We checked in and waited to board.

Chapter 20

JASON

I was so excited when Nadia said she would come home with me. Shocked, that's the better word. The heart is a crazy thing. I barely know her, but I feel like I have known her all my life. I should have asked her if she wanted to stop home to get clothes, but we were both in the moment, and I didn't want her to have any reason to change her mind. When we got to my house, I wanted her to feel like she was home. Damn, she looked sexy in my T-shirt. That is something I could get used to seeing. Waking up next to Nadia felt different in a great way. I felt wanted, needed, appreciated, and she seemed to be comfortable, especially in my arms. She was sleeping peacefully, and I didn't want to move to wake her up. "Nadia," I whispered, but she didn't respond.

When I say a load was off my shoulder once I explained everything to her. I was expecting her to be, I don't know, upset still, but she calmly said she understood. Where has she been all my life? I know one thing she said that will stick with me, "If you ever feel the need to not want to be with me anymore, please let me know. If something is on your heart, please let me know. I want to be your best friend, no secrets." Nadia opened up to me about why she's been single for so long and why her guard is always up so very high. I understood now why she felt so hurt when Tiffany put on her show. Not saying that anyone else wouldn't be upset as well, because I know I would be, But I had a better understanding now. I started to feel angry with the dude Andre, but quickly reminded myself that he did me a favor. He did Nadia a favor, too.

"Well baby, I promise to never hurt you. I'm not saying we may not have rough times, but I promise you I will never hurt you."

"Jay."

"Yes, baby."

With innocence in her eyes, she asked, "Do you have any children?" I stood quiet for a few minutes. She looked antsy.

"Are you pregnant?"

"What?"

I repeated, "Are you pregnant?"

"Of course not, Jason."

"Well, there goes the answer to your question."

She playfully hit me on my arm, "Jason. You play too much". We laughed.

"Thank you, Nadia."

"For?"

"For giving me a chance. Now, let's go to the store and get you some clothes."

"Baby?"

Nadia calling me baby, it gave me chills. *Baby* sounds so succulent rolling off her tongue.

She continued, "I can't go into the store looking like this!"

"I know. I called one of the ladies who comes in and cleans for me to tell her she didn't have to work today. But I did ask her to grab me a pair of tights and a T-shirt from the store. She brought it for me while you were in the shower. Come put it on while I get ready."

She replied, "I don't want to sound crazy, but I don't have a problem keeping this on."

I smiled. "That's cool; you can keep it on, but we're still going."

She looked good in those tights; it grabbed her curves perfectly, and the t-shirt stopped slightly over her ass. I may have to agree with her, she might have to keep the clothes on a little longer. After I dressed, we left and went to the mall and a few boutiques. In the first store she was ready to pay for her things herself. She pulled out her wallet at the register and even tried buying me something. I had to find a way to say it nicely and not make her feel bad.

I said, "Baby, I appreciate your independence, but if I'm taking you shopping, please let me pay."

"I'm sorry. I'm just not used to this; I've been single for a long time, it's an automatic thing for me."

"I know, but I am your man; expect and accept that I will do for you."

After we left the mall, we were driving by an ice cream shop.

She asked, "Do you want some ice cream, Jay?"

"Sure, why not?"

"Great! I'm paying." She laughed.

I shook my head. "So, what kind of ice cream do you like?"

"Your ice cream," is what I wanted to tell her. Behave Jay; I told myself, you guys are going to take it slow.

I said instead, "I'll try what you're having." We had Pistachio ice cream. It was my first time, and it was really good. We made it home at about five. I had plans on taking her to dinner later. I gave her a full tour of the house when we got home. I wasn't sure what to do tonight. I wanted to go out to dinner and maybe a walk on the beach. She said she was okay staying at home, but I wanted to take her out of the house. I had to figure it out. We were so relaxed that I went ahead and ordered Chinese food. We're just going to stay in, watch a movie, and enjoy each other's company. I already knew she was going to go to Italy. Of course, I couldn't let her know that, but now that she was here with me, I really didn't want her to go. I know there would be some days that we won't be around each other, but her being in a whole different country without me was going to be hard, but I'm going to keep my cool. The bell rang. I went to get the food and tipped the delivery guy. Nadia was still in the backyard. I had two clients to meet the next day. I will take Nadia home and see if we can plan to hang out again before she leaves for her trip. I placed the plates on the table and walked out to the backyard to meet her. She looked peaceful while lying on the lounge chair. "Food is here."

She looked up and smiled, "I take it we're staying in?"

"Yeah, we have many nights to go out. So, we can eat in, relax, and watch a movie."

The food was great! I went upstairs to get a blanket and some pillows. We went into the movie room. I had it designed to have two two-seaters and the rest single seats that recline back. I have fallen asleep in there many times. I set everything up, and we began to watch the movie. At some point in time, the movie was watching us.

"I woke up and wanted us to go to bed. Smiley," I said softly; she opened her eyes. "How was the movie?"

She smiled; "It was great. What was your favorite part?" I told her my favorite part was right now.

Smiling with her, I said, "Let's go to bed."

I got to the office at about 10:30. Abigail, my secretary, was already there when I walked in.

I greeted her, "Good morning, Abby."

"Morning, Mr. McKnight, you seem to be really happy this morning."

I replied, "I am Abby. How was your weekend?"

"It was good," she said, "and yours?"

"Different and amazingly amazing."

"That's nice to know, Mr. McKnight. Haven't heard that type of excitement from you in some time. Oh yeah, just a reminder, you have 11:15 and 2:15 today."

"Okay. Thank you. If it's not a problem, can you hold my calls for about fifteen minutes? I just want to settle in and prepare for this meeting."

"No problem, sir."

"You're the best Abby."

I got my coffee and walked into my office feeling brand new. I couldn't wait for Nadia to come here and see this part of my life. It's amazing how someone can have such a positive effect on you. The meetings went well. I had a few brand-new contracts which were working well for me. The second meeting was just a follow-up to my first. We needed to sign some papers and finalize everything. So that wasn't too long. I decided to close the office a little early, and I met up with the guys for a drink.

On my way to Flanigan's, I called my baby, "Hey Smiley."

"Hey babe."

"How was your day?" I asked.

"It was good. I did some cleaning and just relaxed. I'm going to go to Mel's house later. She's cooking, and I love her cooking. I can't wait for you to try it. How was your day?"

"It was great. I decided to close the office early."

"I know your employees were happy."

"Yeah, I don't stress them about anything; their environment is way better than many. I need to make sure they are happy at all times."

"I love that." She said

"It's definitely the way to be."

"So, Jay, what are you about to get into?"

"I'm about to meet up with my friends to have a drink at Flanigan's; I may just grab something to eat there."

"If you want, I can make a plate for you, and you can stop by and get it."

"I would love that, but I'll just eat there because I'll be drinking and not sure how long we are going to be there."

"Well, if you change your mind, let me know."

God knows I wanted to take her up on that offer, especially if it meant I would be able to see her, but I didn't want to seem like I was invading her girl time. When I made it to the Flanigan's, Chris and Eric were already there. Mike was running a little late because he had a patient who ran a little later than planned.

"What's up, guys? Looks like y'all got the party started without Mike and me."

"You might as well get yours too. Mike would just have to play catch up."

I laughed. "You know he can,"

I ordered my drink and some wings. We talked about sports as usual. Mike came before we got too deep into it.

"Well, nice to see you, Mike," Chris said.

"Yes, nice of you to finally join us."

We called the waiter over so Mike could place his order and get his drink. He sat down; it was a long day, and this drink was more than needed.

He looked at me, "Jason, you look refreshed."

"Yeah, I had an amazing weekend. I finally mustered up the courage to approach Nadia, and we hung out all weekend."

"She didn't smack your ass in public when she saw you?" That was Eric's smart ass.

"Yo! I was ready for anything, but thankfully, it didn't turn out that way." I know they were waiting for me to say that we had sex. They kept looking at me like I was holding back.

"We didn't have sex."

"What!" They said at the same time. I laughed while calling the waiter over for another round.

"So, you're telling me you had this fine ass woman in your house with you alone all weekend, and you didn't hit it?"

"Chris, I know it's hard to believe, hell it was hard as fuck to resist her, there were a couple of times I had to walk away to keep it together, but she's different, and I don't want to rush and ruin anything. I want to take it slow. She has me captivated just by her presence, so I could just imagine when we do have sex what the fuck will happen to me."

They laughed and shook their heads. We all knew what would happen. You're going to be whipped! Eric exclaimed.

We had a few more drinks, and I wound up ordering a meal. I didn't need to have this liquor take over, especially since it's only Monday. Well, we definitely took advantage of happy hour and got our moneys worth. When I got home and walked into the house, it felt like something was missing. I went to my room and took a shower. Once I lay down, I smelled her; she was all over my bed. *Should I call her?* I don't want to seem like I'm obsessed. Fuck it. I grabbed my phone, called and she answered. I imagined her lying in my arms while we spoke. "I just wanted to let you know I made it home."

"Thank you for letting me know. I was going to give you another hour before calling you. Now I can go to sleep."

"Wait, so you were concerned about me?"

"Of course, I was. You told me you're going out to drink, and you are my man, so damn right I'm concerned."

"Can your man see you tomorrow?"

"Hmmm, can you?" I could see her smiling. "Sure, okay, I'll be free any time after 4 p.m."

I replied, "Okay. I'll call you to let you know what time."

"Sounds good. Sweet dreams, Jay."

I replied, "Sweet dreams, baby." I fell asleep with her voice replaying in my head and her scent on the pillow.

Chapter 21

NADIA

Italy was short but amazing. We were getting ready to land, and Jay said he would be at the airport by 11:30 p.m. The flight was on time, which is great. I wouldn't want him out there waiting for a long time. Oh, it felt great to stretch my legs. If I could stand up while going home, I would. These long flights will definitely do it to you. Before we went to get our luggage, I had to pee. I had been holding it for some time. Thank God the line for customs wasn't long because I couldn't hold it much longer.

"I can't wait to get home, take a bath, and lie down," Riri said.

A nice hot bath did sound good.

"Please, for the next trip we plan, let it be a little shorter in distance for now." We had to agree with Eb—Bora Bora, then Italy. Yeah, we really tried something. We made our way to baggage claim; I was getting my phone out of my purse to call Jay then I felt Riri touch me, then say, "Ohhh shit Nad, look!"

I was scared for a minute. Hoping I could see from my

peripheral view, so if I had to grab her and run, I would, but I couldn't.

I turned slowly. It was Jason. He was waiting by the baggage claim, holding a bouquet of roses and a few single roses with a sign that said in big bold red letters, **I'M WAITING FOR MY QUEEN, SHE'S ON THIS FLIGHT.** I was stuck in my tracks. Mel had to pull me to move. "Come on, Nad." He walked over, gave each of them a rose, and then gave me the bouquet. Smiling uncontrollably, I hugged and kissed him. Fuck! What is he trying to do to me?

"I missed you, Smiley."

"I missed you too." I don't know which one of them it was, but they were taking pictures of us. Jay placed all the suitcases on the cart and pushed them out to the car. "Sissy, he's just full of surprises."

"Yeah, I'm noticing that."

"Remember what I told you: if you feel like you're falling in love with him, accept and embrace it. Do not rob yourself, Nadia. I'm serious. Don't you start crying either. The last thing you want is for Jason to think something is wrong with you."

She stopped me while everyone continued to walk.

"Nad, you deserve happiness; he is here to show you what that is and doesn't care who knows it. That's a beautiful thing. Please don't rob yourself or him. It's okay to be scared; no one is perfect."

I hugged her.

"Thank you, Mel, for reminding me."

"I love you, sissy."

"I love you, too."

"Nadia, girl, he held up a sign that said he was waiting on his queen."

"Yes, Nadia, he values you! He only has eyes for you!"

We laughed and caught up to them. They had the bags in the car and were waiting for us. Jay helped us in the truck, and then he came and sat with me.

"Thank you for the roses. I love them."

"You are welcome, baby." I kissed him on the cheek.

"How was your day? You look tired."

"It was pretty productive. After we spoke, I slept for a few hours and was up and out by 8:30. I went to the office and did a few things. I was out by 1 p.m. My mom needed me to help her get some things done, so I spent the day with her. After that, I went home at about 9, took a shower, and now I'm here with you." He couldn't say that last part with a straight face. He continued, "Oh, I told my mom about you, and she said she can't wait to meet you."

"Really? You don't think it's too soon?"

"Not at all." He touched my face gently so we could have eye contact. "I need her to see the woman who makes my heart do flips. Remember I told you; you are going to be my wife."

Oh, he just gave me chills saying that.

He continued, "So, you might as well get to know your mother-in-law from now. Plus, she's nice, and I'm not saying that because she's my mom. She will be the first to let me know if I'm wrong about something, but you will see for yourself. We can plan a barbecue maybe in a few weeks."

"I'll give it some time. Let us enjoy each other first."

"You can invite the ladies and your family; I'll invite my people, and we all can get to know each other."

"That sounds fair," I said. "We can talk more about it at another time."

We made it to my house. Jason and Alex, the driver, placed the luggage in the rightful cars and then placed mine in the house. We hugged each other; they thanked Jay again for the ride and then went home. I know they were tired. It was after one in the morning. I want to take a bath and lie down.

Jay came out of the bathroom, "Babe, I know it's late, but do you mind coming home with me tonight? I will bring you back in the morning. I promise, but if you don't want to, it's okay, it's just…"

I walked up to him, placed my finger on his lips, and said, "Yes, I'll come." I packed a bag, grabbed my laptop, and we left.

As tired as I was, we talked almost the whole ride to his house. Alex dropped us off in front of the house and then parked the SUV; Jay paid and thanked him again. He then jumped in his car and left. "I could always count on him," he said.

Jay opened the door, and we walked in, "Babe, do you have any tea?"

"Yeah, I do."

"I bought some yesterday when I went shopping."

"Mint tea, right?"

Smiling, "Right."

"I see you remembered."

"I'll never forget," he said.

"Would you like some tea?"

"No, thank you. I'm okay. If you want to take a shower, I'll bring it up, so it won't be cold."

"Thank you, Jay," I replied. I took my things up to the room. On the bed were two Victoria's Secret bags and two gift bags. Across the bed were letters saying, "I missed you, my queen." Awww, I opened the Victoria's Secret bags. It had a robe, slippers, pajamas, and underwear. The gift bags had perfumes and a nice pastel peach cross-body purse. Finally walking into the bathroom, I took a shower, just what I needed.

I walked out of the bathroom with the robe and pajamas on. Jay walked into the room at the same time. He handed me the cup of tea, "I see you got your gifts."

Blushing, "Thank you so much, baby; you know you didn't have to do all of this."

"Oh, I know."

"So, you just knew I was going to come over, huh?"

"Well, I wasn't sure, but if you said no, I would have slept in another room until you came over."

"In that case, I'm glad I came. I wouldn't want you to be inconvenienced."

He laughed. I put the teacup down and I walked over to him, "I'm happy I can make you laugh."

He pulled me close to him and we kissed; I began to rub his back; neither of us wanted the kisses to stop. He removed my robe. Gently, he began kissing my ear and went down to my neck. Fuck! I was horny and turned on; he was kissing all the right spots that makes me weak. He then returned to my lips; we kissed a little deeper this time. His manhood was ready. He laid me on the bed while our lips stayed intact; I wanted him. It had been three-plus years since I had been with a man. And I'm not even talking about a kiss, but hell, I needed him. I needed him to make love to me while holding me in his arms. I needed him to make me drip while screaming his name. He rubbed his hand on my breast. I was lost in a trance. I was imagining what he could be doing to me, and I didn't realize I let out a little moan.

I pulled away.

"What's wrong, Nadia? Are you okay?"

"Yeah, I'm sorry; I just can't do this right now. It's not you at all." I picked up my robe and went into the bathroom. I washed my face. *What's wrong with you, woman? It's clear you want him, and he wants you. You can't keep running away. You have needs, too, and deserve to have a triple orgasm in the first round.* I started to feel embarrassed, like, really embarrassed. I couldn't believe I stopped him. I wish I could climb out the bathroom window and disappear.

Then there was a light knock on the door.

"Baby, are you okay? I'm sorry." *Oh god, now he thinks he did something wrong.* I felt like I ruined a good night.

"I'm okay Jay, and you don't have to be sorry. You didn't do anything wrong." Shit, if he only knew how right it was. I just want to scream!

"Please open the door. I warmed up your tea again."

I stood there for a few minutes; he warmed up my tea. Taking a deep breath, I opened the door. "I'm sorry, Jason." He smiled, "No need to be sorry. I understand. I know this is a new situation, and I am confident that touching, tasting, and feeling you will happen in time, but you can't blame me for trying." He kissed me, gave me my tea, and led me to the balcony. Jason is truly different, but I know I can't keep holding out for long. It's not fair to him.

The stars were beautiful while staring into the sky. I wanted to get up and sit closer to him, but I didn't want a possible replay of earlier.

I asked, "Are you okay, Jay?"

"Of course I am, baby."

"Are you working tomorrow, well, today?"

"Not really. I do have to run in for maybe an hour, but that's it. I did most of what I needed to do earlier today."

"Okay. I was wondering because you're still awake."

"Are you ready to go to bed? I know you may be tired from your long flight."

Smiling, *If he only knew how awake I was.* "Honestly Jay, I'm good. I just want to be with you."

"Come here, Smiley." My heart started racing. I'm trying to keep my distance from him, and now he wants me to come over to him. I kept my cool, took a deep breath, and walked over to where he was sitting.

"Sit with me."

I laughed, knowing I couldn't sit with him, but more like sit on him. My mind was thinking dirty already: *how many ways I can "ride" him while he's sitting on this chair.* As he held me in his arms, we talked more. I told him about our time in Italy. "I'll have to show you the pictures, later." When we went to bed, it was about 4 a.m.

The next morning, we made it back early to my house.

"I bought you something." I went to my suitcase and got the outfit I had bought when we shopped around and a souvenir that said 'Milan Italy.' He was so happy.

"Do you mind coming with me to the office?"

"I have a few things to do, but I could do it on my laptop. Let me change."

"We will only be there for maybe an hour or so, so you can set up in my office if you want or another office, conference room, or wherever you like."

"It isn't a big deal, Jason. I just don't want to be in your way."

His office was nice and well put together. His secretary is nice and very welcoming. She greeted him, "Good morning, Mr. McKnight; I wasn't expecting you today."

He replied, "I know, but I have a few things I need to take care of. I'm supposed to have someone meet me here in about twenty minutes. So, I'll probably be here for two hours max, so please hold all my calls. You can send them to my voicemail if necessary, and I'll check it and follow up tomorrow.

Abigail, I want you to meet my girlfriend, Nadia."

"Hi, it's a pleasure to meet you, Abigail."

"Likewise," she replied.

I followed him back to his office.

"The space is nice and comfy."

"Thanks, I did it myself."

I was impressed but not surprised; his house was beautiful.

"I may have to hire you to do some work for me."

"You know I will, and I'll do it for free, but it doesn't look like you need me."

Thanks baby. It looks good now, but I just know you'll have it looking like a page out of a magazine. He might have a valid point.

"I'm going to meet my appointment in the conference room, they will be here in ten minutes, and I'm also going to order Chipotle for lunch." We kissed and he left.

Checking out the view on this beautiful sunny day. Suddenly, I started to imagine making love to Jason in this office, lifting my dress, with no underwear on, he's on his knees tasting my womanhood, and then he slightly lays me on top of his glass desk as he gives it to me from the back. He switched positions, picking me up, and holding me against the big glass window with the possibility of someone seeing us. Seeing my ass on the window as I slide up and down on his dick. I realized I was still imagining this when Jay returned with the food. "If you need anything else, let me know. You can dial 718, and it will call the conference room." I think I'll have to make this imagination a reality one day.

"Thanks, babe, I'll be fine." While in his meeting, I was able to get a lot of things done. I utilized his office space to my full advantage. I have three clients I'm working on designs for, so I was able to send them some ideas, call for pricing, and order some things. An extra computer and phone did come in handy. I continued to admire the view from his seat and saw the world from his eyes. I looked at the pictures he had up around the office. I wasn't in a rush, so I started looking up more designs, print a few things and checked my email.

"You look good in that seat," looking up, Jay was standing by the door. "You compliment the room." What could a girl do but smile? "I just wanted to let you know that I'm all done, so we will be leaving soon." I gathered my things and waited.

Four and a half months have passed, and I could count on one hand how many days and nights we spent apart. Jay spent nights at my house; I went with him to the office a few times out of the week, and I would work from there and he came with me to the lounge to support my readings. The ladies and I would have our girls' nights, and he respected that. Last night, he invited his friends to come out to the lounge. They were nice and carried themselves well. We all mingled. The night was nice. These past months have been amazing. We had moments where resisting each other was hard, like trying to resist eating your favorite chocolate, but we overcame it. I'm ready to jump on top of him and ride him into the sunset, but I want this relationship to be different. I want to fall in love with him, and for him to fall in love with me, and then the sex seals the deal. I know I am falling for him big time already. He's everything and more. We are so wrapped up in each other that we still haven't planned the barbeque. After the lounge, we returned to my house; it was closer. I got up the next morning, made breakfast, and brought it to the room. He was still sleeping. He looked so peaceful lying there. I hate to wake him up. Especially since he doesn't sleep late. I leaned in and kissed him. Suddenly, he wrapped his arms around me playfully, pulled me on the bed, and kissed me.

"Morning, Smiley. You thought I was still sleeping, huh?"

I had to laugh, "Well yeah! I did."

"Nope, I felt when you got up; I figured you were up doing something." I jumped up, and we started playing around a little.

"Well, surprise anyway. Breakfast in bed!" He sat up while I brought the tray over to him. He didn't notice that part when he pretended to be sleeping, so my surprise worked. I swear I wish I could take a picture of his reaction.

"I never had anyone do this for me," he said.

"I'm happy to be your first, so get used to it because there will be many more days like this, my king."

Chapter 22

JASON

I was so happy when Nadia finally came back from Italy. I was like a little kid in a candy store. I made sure to keep myself busy. We talked almost every day she was gone; the calls were not long, but hearing her voice helped me. Seeing her in the airport made me feel at peace. I knew she was okay, and she made it back safely. We've been inseparable since she got back. It's getting harder and harder to fight the urge of being unable to make love to her, but I'm telling you, when that day comes, hmmm. I do like that we are waiting and not rushing into it. We're taking this time to get to know each other better, on a different level, but truthfully speaking, I'm in love with Nadia already. I'm not surprised. From the first time I saw her, I just knew she was different; she was special. I know she feels the same. I can see it in her eyes, how she looks at me, speaks, and touches me. There's no doubt. When the moment is right, it will reveal itself. We've been together for over four months, and it feels like four wonderful years.

Today is the BBQ Day. Finally, we were a little nervous. It's the reveal day. Everyone meets each other today. We already met each others' parents because that was important to us, and some friends then we agreed to wait before introducing each other to anyone else. We just wanted to get to know and enjoy each other first before allowing anyone else in. Hopefully, everything goes well, and everyone gets along. It won't ruin anything between us, I know that for sure, but it will make life easier. We have been up prepping the food since last night. Mel and Jeff are making a few dishes, so we brought what they needed and dropped it off to them about three days ago. Smiley made a few cakes last night and two cheesecakes. I helped as much as I could. We had so much fun. At one point, I thought we had more flour on us than in the cake. My mom makes really good potato salad, so she will be bringing that and something else. She said she would surprise us.

We were going off very little sleep.

"Hey baby, good morning. I have to go buy the ice. Is there anything else we may need?"

"Jay, don't you think it's too early for the ice? It's almost 9 a.m., and people won't be coming until about four. I just don't want it to melt."

"You're right, baby."

"Unless you want to buy it, put it in the deep freezer, not in the cooler, if there's enough space."

"No, I'll wait and go a little later. So, what else do you have to make?"

"Just the macaroni and the seafood rice. You already seasoned the salmon and chicken last night, and that's going on the grill. I forgot we were doing shish kabobs, so I have to season the shrimp and beef. We should have enough peppers and onions for that. The baked beans can be the last thing we make. When you get the ice, you can please get some Hawaiian rolls. Do you want me to make cornbread?"

"I really want you to get out of this kitchen, baby; take a break."

"I would love to, but I'd rather get everything out of the way and then relax."

"Okay, well, let me help."

I seasoned the fish, shrimp, and beef. I chopped up the onions and peppers. We worked well together. Smiley made a big pan of cornbread, and two pans of rice, and grated the cheese for the macaroni.

"Are you going to make the macaroni now?"

"No, about 2:30; I'll make it and the baked beans."

"So, are you done?"

"Yes!"

"Good, it's a little after 11." I made sure everything was turned off and grabbed her hand.

"Let's go take a nap." I set my alarm for 2:30, but she was already knocked out before I could tell her to get some rest.

My alarm went off, and I looked over; she was still sleeping. I had a few missed calls. I went to the kitchen and put the macaroni to boil and the baked beans on the stove. I put it on low. Then, I started to return some of the calls.

"What's up, Chris?"

"I'm going to be on my way soon. I'm going to bring two bottles, some chaser, orange juice and cranberry juice. I still have to go to the store, so is there anything else you may need?"

"You can grab some Hawaiian rolls. I have to go get ice in a little."

"I can grab the ice while I'm there; that's no problem."

"Thanks, bro, I appreciate it. See you soon."

Since Chris was bringing the ice, that saved me a trip to the store. I put everything in the deep freezer to get cold while waiting for the ice. I returned the other calls. While stirring the macaroni, I felt Nadia's arms wrapped around me as she laid her head on my back. It's 3:15 and I know she's still tired.

"You look sexy in the kitchen, but why didn't you wake me up?"

"Because you looked so sexy and peaceful while sleeping, plus you need your rest."

"We're having a party, baby; there's no such thing as rest." She finally let go of me. "Thanks, babe; now move over; let me finish this." She hooked up the Macaroni, and I let her know that Chris was bringing the ice and the rolls.

She said, "Jay, I need you to go take a shower and start getting ready. It's almost 4 p.m."

"We're getting ready together!" I said.

"Well, babe, I still have to finish cooking."

"Put the oven on low, and let's go. Chris may be here first. When I have parties, they usually go through the side gate. I will leave the back door open, and they'll know what to do. So, we're good." We already had our clothes laid out since yesterday. I jumped in the shower first since most of my guests may be coming first. I tried not to stay in long, but this water kept me longer than I planned.

The bathroom door wasn't closed all the way and I heard Nadia fumbling with something in the bedroom.

"Are you okay?"

"Yeah!" Her voice was traveling closer until she made her way into the bathroom. "I decided to come and join you since you were taking so long. I thought you might need some company."

I was stunned. We have seen each other partly naked but never full body. Nadia came in the shower, and I welcomed her. Her body was perfect to me. Her stomach was flat. She has a sexy birthmark on her thigh. You can see the tan marks from her bathing suit with a few stretch marks. I couldn't take my eyes off of her.

"Aaaahum," she noticed me staring. She was smiling when I finally brought my attention to her face.

"You see something you like?"

"You know I do." Her nipples were hard like it was ready for me to suck on it. *Why is she teasing me like this?* I don't know how much more fighting off I can do. How in the hell did she not have sex for so long? My dick was already hard. She grabbed my rag and began to scrub my back. I allowed her to take control. She turned me around to face her. She rubbed the rag across my chest and stared at every inch of my body. But she didn't stop there; she took her other hand and went up and down my abs. I feel like my dick is about to explode! She's killing me. She moved her attention from my chest and started to stroke my dick so goddamn gently. One more stroke and I feel like I'm going to cum in her hand. *Jason*! "Take control" is what I kept repeating in my head. I tried to think about something else, and finally, I grabbed her rag and started soaping her body. I needed the attention off of me. I rubbed her breast, watching her bite her bottom lip. I wanted to kiss her all over! Fuck it. I turned her around; her back was facing me. Since she's been here, we've worked out almost every day. I can see the pleasant results. I leaned her on the shower wall, hands upright, kissing her neck while her legs shivered; the water was dripping from our heads; she wasn't resisting. Is she ready? Am I really ready? It's now or never. My heart is pounding. I'm hearing my phone ringing one call after the other. I didn't care who it was. Then the doorbell rings. Fuck! We were lost in the moment and didn't realize the time. I heard the music playing. That's either Eric or my brother Jayden. I wanted to run out there and tell everyone the BBQ was canceled, but I couldn't. I'm excited for everyone to meet my queen.

We rushed out of the shower and didn't bother addressing what happened. We were color-coordinated. I had on some black shorts and a yellow T-shirt; she wore yellow shorts with a black T-shirt. The way those shorts hugged her curves made me want to take it right back off of her. While she finished getting dressed, I walked out on the balcony. There was a good amount of people here already. I can't express the last time I've been this happy or excited.

"Sexy Mama, are you ready?"

"Yes, sexy daddy, I am."

Chapter 23

EBONI

I can say Italy was nice. Besides the awkward moment when Terri went to rehearsal, and we noticed that Vanessa was also there. From the look on Terri's face, she was just as surprised. She remained professional, as she should. This is her job. Terri and Vanessa's friendship/ relationship, whatever it was, ended on not the best of terms. Vanessa was really upset when Terri didn't choose to be with her. Who can blame Riri? She got a feel of that good dick and couldn't let it go. We didn't bother to ask her about Vanessa being there. We knew she would talk about it when she was ready, but she let that go long ago. Tyler was the best thing that ever happened to her. Since we have been back, I've been thinking about Dante and what we discussed. Carlos called me yesterday to remind me that he will be here in four days, and he's looking forward to hanging out. I am not a hundred percent committed to Dante yet, but I think I'm going to give it a chance. We have a movie date tonight. We wanted to see John Wick 2, I'm excited. The movie was so good. Afterward, we went back to my house. We talked and got to know each other more on a different level. We have had many conversations before, but this time, it was different. We talked about everything. He really opened up. He's really smart.

"Dante, one of my friends will be coming to visit me in a few days. I'm going to show him and his friends around town."

"Him?" His mood quickly changed; I should have known better and kept it to myself. I really didn't have to say anything. I hurried and found a way to smooth it out. I continued,

"Yes, him. Listen, if you are going to be my man, I have to be able to share things with you. I'm very open and honest, which you already know. I have nothing to hide." This was planned before feelings were put on the table.

"So, am I going to be your man?" Just like that, the conversation got back on track but then led to another conversation I wasn't quite ready to start yet. He had a little twinkle in his eyes. I leaned over and kissed him.

"We can give it a try if you like. You should understand that this is, in a way, a big step to me."

"I know. We will get through this together Eboni."

I felt naughty tonight. "Let me show you how much I missed you!" I unzipped his pants and placed his dick in my mouth, sucking and licking like an ice cream on a cone on the verge of melting. "Stand up!" I began taking his pants and shirt off. I got on my knees and began to suck on it some more while playing with his balls.

"Yes baby, right there," he struggled to talk between moans.

"Baby lay down on the carpet." I'll put the condom on. Sitting slowly on his hard dick, he held me tight.

"Damn, Eb. I missed this pussy." Starting to pick up the pace, he moved, wanting to switch positions. "I want it from the back."

"Yes, Daddy, I don't have a problem getting on all fours for you." He got behind me and slid right in. "This is my pussy." He was right; my pussy has always been his, and so has my heart. I just knew how to control my emotions, and I stayed distracted. He knew how to work it. No one has hit spots or made me ever feel the way he does, sexually and emotionally. I started feeling like he was touching my throat while giving it to me from the back. There has never been a time where he didn't make me have at least two orgasms in the first round. I threw it back at him. I knew he was ready to cum.

I called the ladies on a group video chat. I needed to get my message out all at once without repeating myself four different times.

"Good morning, my sisters."

"Well, you look exceptionally happy this morning."

"Well, I am, Nadia. I have some news to share and wanted to let y'all know all at once." I decided to play around with them a little, dragging it out.

"Oh my god, Eb, what is it?"

"Okay, Mel, since you insist, I decided to make it official with Dante!"

They started screaming, laughing, and talking at the same time.

"We are so happy for you. On a serious note, Eb, you know we love you."

"I know, Terri."

"Do you think that you are ready?"

"I honestly don't know, but I have to give it a try. Guys, I'm getting older, and as scared as I may think I am, I want and deserve to be happy too."

"Yeah, you do."

"And, Dante and I have been fooling around for years just without a title, and no matter how we tried to pull away from each other, we can't. Then, when he expressed his true feelings to me the other day, I figured why not. I need to stop sharing my goods with these dudes who is really not about anything and can't stimulate my mind and body the way I need it to be."

"You're right; you deserve it, and I think both of you are a good match, so give it a try and enjoy each other."

"Thanks, Nad; I can always count on you guys regardless of what."

I'm home just relaxing, a little tired. Tonight is the first night that Dante and I weren't together in about four days.

"Hello, hey Eb."

"Hey, Carlos."

"I just wanted to let you know that we are here. We just made it to the hotel. We're staying at the Hilton hotel."

"Okay, great." It slipped my mind just that quickly that he was coming today.

"Do you think I could see you tonight?" He asked. For the first time, I didn't want to go. I could have, but I didn't.

"Oh, Carlos, I'm tied up tonight, but we can meet tomorrow if you like."

"Oh, okay. I really wanted to see you, but I'll wait. I'm going to settle in for the night, and I will call you mañana."

"Dulces sueños hermosa."

"Dulces sueños."

Carlos is a sweet guy; we have spoken often since our encounter in Bora Bora. I believe we could be best of friends, but that's where it would stop. The biggest problem is we live on two different sides of the world. Even if Dante and I didn't agree to give it a try, I would still feel the same way. I woke up to my phone ringing. What time is it? Looking at the clock, it was 3 a.m. I answered my phone.

"Hey, baby. Sorry to wake you."

"Dante, why are you still awake?"

"I came home from work, fell asleep, woke up to use the bathroom, and I just couldn't get you off my mind. I just wanted to hear your voice."

"Aww, you miss me? Or are you trying to make sure I was really home?"

He laughed. "I just knew you would say that! I know you all too well. So, let's clear it up. I miss you, and if I wanted to make sure you were home, I could have stopped by."

"Okay, if you say so. I miss you too." I swear, I love that manly 'let me check you in a sexy way vibe' about him. Like I said, not many men can deal with me, but he handles me all too well. We talked for a little while longer. Then we went back to bed.

I told Carlos that I would meet him at about six. He wanted to know if I had any girlfriends who could come along so his friends could have company. I had to let him know that my circle is extra small and the ladies that are in it are all accounted for. I felt weird having to meet up with him. Even though we were just friends, I didn't plan on sleeping with him, and most of all, I told Dante about the visit. I laughed to myself. Well, that's what made him become my man officially. It still felt like I was doing something wrong. I would have never thought it would bother me like this, but a promise is a promise, and one thing no one can say about me is that I said I would do something and didn't do it. So, I'm going to just put my big girl panties on and get this night over with. I met Carlos in his hotel room. They were in a suite. The hotel was really nice. I knocked on the door. While waiting, I still had that gut feeling that I should have kept my ass home. Carlos finally came to the door. He looked nice. He had a fresh haircut.

"Hey, Eboni," he greeted me with a hug. "Thank you for coming. Te ves Hermoso, just like the last time I saw you.

Gracious. I responded.

"Come in." He introduced me to his friends. "We're almost ready. Would you like a drink? We stopped at the liquor store last night when we grabbed something to eat."

"Sure, what do you have?"

"We have Patron, Cîroc and Henny."

"I'll take the Patron."

He smiled. "There was a nice restaurant within walking distance that I wanted to try. The guys said they would explore the area, and then we could meet back up and go to a club or bar. Is that okay with you?"

"Sounds good." As I finished up my drink, I didn't realize it was just going to be the both of us. But it made sense. Why would they want to sit around me having dinner at a restaurant?

Dinner was nice. He told me about his students and a few plans he has and that some of his Family are coming to visit. One thing we did great was talk. We had no choice due to distance. I wanted to let him know I was off the market, but I didn't know how. We walked back to the hotel. The weather was perfect for just that. We got back to the room, and the guys hadn't come back yet.

"I told them we would be back in two hours max. Now, no one's answering. Would you like another drink?"

"Sure."

"Patron again?" He asked.

"Yeah. I know I shouldn't drink so much because I do have to drive home."

"Sorry about the wait."

"It's okay. They were probably having fun and got sidetracked with the time. They did come to have a good time."

"You are right, Eboni. I'll give them about thirty minutes and try again."

"Where's the bathroom?"

"Two doors down."

"Okay. I'll be right back." I joined Carlos back in the living room and I finished up my drink.

I asked, "So, you haven't found that lucky lady yet?"

"Nah, not really in a rush." I got up to refill my glass, and I asked, "Do you want some more Henny?"

"Well since you're up, sure." I gave him his glass and sat back down.

"So, how about you? Have you found that lucky guy yet?" Well, his eyes were locked on me.

"Yes."

"Really? And he's okay with you being here with me?"

"Not really, but this trip was planned before, so he had to respect it," Carlos smirked. I touched his shoulder, "I'm so sorry."

"No need to be."

"Are we cool?"

"Of course we are. I really like you, Eboni, but another man beat me to the finish line." I felt bad. Ughh, I definitely didn't want the night to be like this. I had to use the bathroom again. This Patron is just running through me. Once I came out of the bathroom, I noticed my glass was refilled, and Carlos was by the window on the phone. He said, "I tried calling them again. I finally got an answer. It was not too much of a good reception, but they said they would be back in an hour and a half max. I wonder where they went."

I replied, "Me too." This is like my fifth glass of Patron, plus I had two drinks at the restaurant. I was starting to feel the effects of it. Carlos turned the radio on to lighten up the mood,

I guess. I can tell he was bothered even though he was trying his best to hide it. I tried to lighten up the mood too.

"If you want, we can go without them."

"We should leave their asses, but then I'll never hear the end of it."

Laughing, I said, "I know what you mean because I would be talking shit too!"

"You know, Eboni, if you still want to come out to Cali, you can."

Smiling, "I appreciate that."

He reached in and kissed me; I was caught off guard. Before I could move, his hands were in my panties, playing with my clit as his tongue played around with mine. I wanted to stop, but I couldn't, the alcohol had the best of me. I knew I should've stopped drinking after the third glass. He made his way down to my no-bra-wearing breast and sucked on it as we moaned together.

"Carlos, stop, this isn't right," he looked up and kissed me again.

He replied, "He doesn't have to know." He was right; I didn't have to tell Dante, but it still didn't feel right! He made his way down to my pussy and ate like he was trying to prove a point. I came twice, and he wanted to go back for the third. I was so mad at myself. How could I betray Dante like this? Carlos put a condom on and climbed on top of me. He worked it like he wanted me to feel that choosing Dante was a mistake. He turned me around to get in my favorite position to finish up. We fucked for about another ten minutes. His dick is really good, and his head game is spectacular too, but truth be told, he has nothing on my Dante. He did make me realize two things; I would be giving up the freedom to fuck how I please with no explanation, and then I also realized the person I was giving it all up for was more than worth it. For the first time, I felt disgusted, not with Carlos, he's a nice guy, but with me. I went and got in the shower. I felt sick. The guys still hadn't gotten back, and it was already after 12.

I asked, "Are you sure they are coming back?"

He had a concerned and confused look on his face, "I hope so."

"Well, it's already late, so I'm going to go."

"Do you have to?"

"You know I do."

"Eboni, Lo siento."

"*Es genial Carlos.*" I kissed him on his cheek and walked away.

"Let me walk you to your car."

"No. It's okay." I knew he was staring at me. I felt it. I looked back at him, and he smiled. I made it to my car. My mind was racing. *How am I supposed to tell Dante what happened?* I don't want to ruin our trust. I don't know what to do. I cried. I was scared of losing someone for the first time in a long time. I texted Carlos to let him know I made it home. He deserved that much, and I went straight to sleep. I'll figure it out in the morning.

I didn't sleep well last night. I woke up this morning with last night on my mind, along with a few text messages from Carlos. He let me know that he was leaving, that he hoped to hear from me again, and he had a really nice time. I thought he was here for one more day, but maybe he changed his flight. After all, he did come here to hang out with me and obviously that didn't go as planned. I need to talk to someone. I don't know which one of the three personalities I want to deal with right now. I know neither will judge me, but I'm going to play it safe.

"Morning, Eb. You're up early. What's wrong?"

"Why does something have to be wrong? Can't I just wake up early?"

"Because I know you, sis, and, out of us all, I'm the only one who wakes up early." We laughed.

"So, what's up?

Are you home?" I asked.

"Yeah, I'm here."

"What! Jay didn't kidnap you?"

"He spent the night here last night. He had an early meeting, so he left already."

"Oh, okay. I'm so happy for you, Nad. I really am."

"Thanks, Eb."

"I need to talk. Is it okay if I come over?"

"Of course, Eboni. I don't have any plans, so whenever you're ready, I'll be here."

"Okay. Thanks."

I made it to Nad's house around 12. I bought us lunch from Charley's. We love that place. Their three bacon Philly cheese steak and loaded fries are everything, and let's not forget about their strawberry lemonade. I had to get that in a large.

"Hey, Eb. You're looking good, love the hair."

I had got it done a few days ago. Nadia continued,

and I love that short set you have on. Let me help you."

Nad was outside checking the mail when I pulled up. "You came right on time. I was just thinking about ordering some food. I am hungry. I haven't eaten since last night, me to Nadia. Well, if you had ordered food that would have been okay too, I'm sure we would have found space to eat it later." We walked in and sat at the dining room table. We had small talk and then I decided to ease my way into what I wanted to talk about.

"Nad, I need your help." The tears began to roll. I couldn't stop it. Nadia jumped up.

"Eb, what's wrong?" She hugged me and just waited until I was ready to talk.

"Man, Nad, I fucked up." She sat down and pulled her chair close to me. We both took a sip of our juice.

"Talk to me, Eb. What happened?"

"I fucked up!"

"Yeah, I get that, but could you tell me how and why?" I took a deep breath, and I told her everything. She hugged me and looked at me for a few minutes; she had me wondering what in the world she was thinking, and then she smiled. The crazy thing with her is she smiles for everything, happy, mad, sad, angry, so you really don't know what to take from it.

I asked, "Umm, why are you smiling?" She stared at me for a few more long-drawn-out minutes that felt like forever. She hugged me again and took a deep breath.

"I'm proud of you!" I had to give her that 'Scooby doo what the fuck type of look.' I was confused. She laughed at me.

"Eb, I know it may sound weird, but when I say I'm proud of you, I mean, I'm proud of you for caring; I'm proud of you for not just putting yourself first. By your reaction to the whole situation, I know you love Dante, which is expected. You have been messing with him for a long time, and now that you guys have decided to make it official, this happens, but sometimes obstacles happen to test us, prove our strength, our love. Eb, tell me, when was the last time you cried for a guy for any reason?"

"Man, I can't even remember. Maybe high school."

"That's my point. That means something. You have always been that free-spirited woman. I'm going to live, and I don't care what anyone thinks of 'Me' type of woman. Trust me when I tell you, we all love that about you, but now look, you're crying because you don't want to lose Dante. You finally fell for someone, and you messed up. Now, messing up is okay. We are all human, but you have to ensure you don't do it again and be ready for the outcome and consequences."

"Nad, I don't know if I should tell him."

"I can't tell you what to do. You have to follow your heart. Question: does he know that you met Carlos and slept with him in Bora Bora?"

"No."

"Okay, well, I don't think you should tell him that part only because it was before his time; it will look like you had intentions of sleeping with Carlos because you were intimate with him already. You're a very honest person, so the only thing that will have me concerned is if you don't tell him now about what happened last night, and once you guys are together somewhere down the line, then he happens to find out."

"Nad, I'm not perfect, I was just trying to do the right thing, and I screwed it all up."

"Don't beat yourself up. This is new to you, and he could at least give you that. Eboni, we're in this together and you have our support all the way. So, are you going to tell him?"

"I really don't want to, but my heart is telling me it's the right thing to do, and Dante deserves the truth. I want a relationship built on trust."

"Well, if you feel it's the right thing to do, then do it. Have you spoken to him since the incident?"

"Yes, this morning. He gave me my morning call as usual."

"How did he sound?"

"He sounded the same. Happy to talk to me. Cheery."

"Okay, so he may not suspect anything. That's good."

"Nadia, I'm not ready to share this with the ladies yet. Can we keep it between us?"

"Of course, your secret is safe with me." She hugged me again. Tight. She knew I needed it. A few hours later, Mel came by. We hung out in the backyard, and they had a drink.

"Why are you not having a drink?" Before I could answer, Nad said, "She's not feeling good." She wasn't lying. I felt sick to my stomach. Not physically, but emotionally.

"Are you okay?"

"Yeah, Mel, I'm okay. It will pass." I left Mel and Nadia talking. "I'm going to go home and lie down."

"Call me," Nad said.

"I will."

At home, I took a cold shower. It was needed. I called Dante.

"Hey, I'm just calling to say good night. I'm not feeling too good, so I'm just going to lie down and watch TV until I fall asleep."

"Are you okay?"

"Yeah."

"Are you sure? Because you don't sound like it. Do you need me to come over?"

"No, babe, it's okay."

"Well, I will keep checking on you until I see you tomorrow."

"Okay, that's fine." I had so many missed calls and text messages from different people. I tuned everything out until I fell asleep.

Dante came over this afternoon. I was so happy to see him. It's been a few days. Once he came in the door, I just hugged him. We didn't have any special plans today.

"You don't look like yourself, baby. What's wrong?" I just brushed his question off. He went over to the bar and made a drink.

"Do you want me to make you one?"

"I'm good." He looked at me with slight concern. I went to the bathroom and washed my face. *Get it together, Eboni.* I walked back out and watched as Dante got comfortable.

"Come here, baby," he said. "I missed you. This is how you treat me when you don't see me in a few days?" I walked over to where he was sitting, and I kissed him. The way he kissed me back, I knew it would lead to more. We have that type of chemistry. Before it went any further, I stopped.

"Baby, we need to talk." My heart was pounding. He made another drink and sat next to me. All these thoughts were running through my head. *Are you sure you want to tell him?* I have to, for my peace of mind. Whatever the consequences are, I'll have to deal with it.

"Baby," I grab his hand. "I could sit here and make up all the excuses in the world, but I need to let you know that a couple of nights ago when I went out with my friend, we slept together." He instantly pulled his hand away and threw the glass. I was startled by the glass breaking on the wall. That was not like him.

I started to regret telling him. I saw the hurt and anger in his eyes.

"Eboni, what the fuck do you mean you slept with him? You mean to tell me you couldn't control yourself!"

"Dante, I'm sorry. I didn't go out with the intentions of sleeping with him. Maybe I had too much to drink."

"Fucking, really? That's the best you got. Too much to fucking drink? And to think I trusted you enough to let you go and not pressure you about it. I thought this shit was strange. I knew I should have kept my feelings for you to myself. We shouldn't have crossed the line and tried to become something more than what we were, FUCK BUDDIES!" Oh, those words hurt. I couldn't hold back the tears anymore. I can't believe he said that.

"Dante, I'm so sorry."

"Keep your sorry because I know you are not. I'm sorry for thinking we could work. I'm sorry for thinking my feelings meant something to you. Funny, since we're confessing, while I was sitting home missing you, and you were getting your brains fucked out, one of my old fuck buddies called and invited me for a drink, and I went." I interrupted, "Shut up, Dante!"

He continued, "Oh, I'm not done; after a few drinks, we went back to her house."

I exclaimed, "Shut the fuck up, Dante!" The tears rolled down even more, but this time I felt the anger coming on.

He continued, "And I fucked her; as a matter of fact, she fucked me better than you ever did, had me second guessing…," before he could finish, I slapped him. He was shocked. So was I. That was out of my character. I didn't mean to slap him.

"I can't fucking believe you!" I could barely talk from crying; his eyes were watery, too. He was trying to hold back his tears.

"You know what, you're right. We should have kept things how it was. Silly me for thinking we could be different. Here it is: I was beating myself up because I hurt you, not on purpose, but I'm not making any excuses for it, and I know I possibly ruined our trust. I could have kept it to myself, and you wouldn't have suspected shit; sorry for being honest." I stood up from the sofa and grabbed my purse. "Sorry for trying to do the right thing because I'm fucking in love with you!"

"Eb, you love me?" The tone in his voice was now gentle.

"Dante, don't talk to me."

"Wait, Eb! Where are you going? Eboni! Come back,

please." I had to leave. I was hurt, upset, angry. I had to get out before I said something I couldn't take back. I sped off. He kept calling me and I sent him to the voicemail. He texted, asking me to answer. I just turned my phone off. I couldn't take it. It was still early, about 7:30. I went to a bar at the beach and sat there for hours. I had about four drinks and I cried. This is why I don't open up to anyone, this is why I just do me! Like Nad said, you must be prepared for the outcome and consequences. She was right. I thought I could handle it, but I couldn't. I didn't want to go back home. What if he was still there? I tried to check on my camera, but it wouldn't connect for some reason. I never in all these years saw Dante like this. He has never spoken to me out of character before, let alone raised his voice. He was always gentle. I know I hurt him. I know I was wrong, but I wasn't prepared for those hurtful words. Every word felt like a stab in the middle of the heart. Maybe I was meant to be alone. I knew at this moment without a doubt that I loved Dante; I was in love with him. It made no sense trying to fight it anymore. If anyone else had told me about fucking someone, I would care less. I would probably laugh in their faces. I felt lost and confused.

It's midnight. I'm just sitting in my car still by the beach. I wanted to call Nad but didn't want to burden her, especially so late. Eventually I turned my phone back on. I had about fifteen voice messages from Dante. I know he called more but just didn't leave a message. Then he sent text messages. I didn't read it. I just wasn't in the mood to be bothered. I didn't want to read anything else that may hurt my heart. I was lost in time; before I knew it, it was 2 a.m. I started feeling sleepy, so I headed home. Halfway there, my phone rang, it was Carlos. I sent him to my voicemail, too. *Why is he calling me so late?* I don't want to answer and let my anger out on him. I'll give him the benefit of the doubt because of the time difference. Maybe he didn't realize he called me, or maybe he was calling the wrong person. I know he called me earlier as well and may have been following up on that call or butt-dialed me. Right after that, Dante started calling me again. I sent his ass to voicemail too. I just don't have the energy. I want to take a shower and go to bed.

I pulled up to my house, creeping. Like I was doing the stalking. I needed to make sure he wasn't there. Thank God he wasn't. If he was, I was going to go to a hotel for the night. Walking into the house, I felt a heavy feeling in my heart. I slowly walked around the entire house. He cleaned up the glass that was on the floor. I sat on the couch, trying to re-evaluate everything that happened. I didn't bother to put any clothes on when I came out of the shower. I just went straight to bed. I woke up feeling tired. I went to grab my phone, and it was dead. I put it on the charger and went back to sleep. Today, I'm going to shut the world out. I closed every blind in the house, made a cup of coffee, and curled back up in bed. I slept for the rest of the day and half of the next day. When I woke again, it was 3 p.m., and I was starving. I didn't want to go out into the world, so I ordered something to eat through the app, and had it delivered. While waiting for my food, I took a quick shower. I came out just as the doorbell rang. Putting my robe on I checked the camera since the blinds were still closed. Yes, it's my food. I said excitingly. I grabbed the cash on the table to pay for the tip, ran to the door, thanked the young lady, then returned to my room and stuffed my face. I knew I was hungry; I didn't leave any crumbs. In fact, I still felt hungry. I should have ordered something else for later. Finally, I picked up my phone: I had over a hundred and fifty missed calls. I didn't know that was possible. I'm not in the mood to talk right now to anyone, maybe later. I put a movie on and laid down. I started to feel restless. I had to get up. I turned the TV off and the music on. Music always does it for me. The first song that came on was 'Just Fine' by the one and only Mary J. Blige. That song got me going a little. I started cleaning. I didn't realize how low on food I was. I guess I have no choice but to leave the house tomorrow. A woman gotta eat and I love my stomach. Everything was going well until 'Someone Like You' by Adele came on. I was in my feelings, but I still sang along. Sang like it was my song. My stomach started to growl. Where can I order from at this time with delivery? I grabbed my laptop and went on a search. I settled for TGIF. I got tired of looking, plus I can really do with their loaded mashed potatoes and their Jack Daniels ribs. Their Jack Daniel sauce is really good. The music changed to reggae. Now, I'm in the mood to dance. I haven't been to a good Island party in a while. I'm starting to feel okay now. I wonder if it's the music or the thought of food. Hmm, maybe both. I finished up in the kitchen. The bell rang. My food is here finally. Just the thought of the food made my stomach growl. The bell rang again. This person is impatient. "I'm coming." I was trying to find my cash to tip them. I knew I had twenty dollars in cash but only found five. I emptied my purse on the table. I found another five. Okay. Ten dollars will work. I prefer to give cash tips than to tip in the app. I ran to the door and opened it. I was looking down, because I almost dropped the money rushing to the door.

"I'm so sorry; I was trying to get money too." When I looked up, Dante was standing there with my food. I stood there, stuck for a few seconds.

"What are you doing here, and why do you have my food?"

"I've been out here for a while, and when I saw the guy pull up with the food, I saw it as an opportunity. So, I took the food, tipped him, and here I am."

"How much did you tip him?"

"Why?"

"So I could give you back your money!"

"Really, Eb?" I just stared at him.

Did you really say that, Eboni? That was the first thing that came to mind. I could slap myself. He was still holding my food.

"Are you going to let me in?"

"I don't know if that's a good idea."

He asked again, "Eb, can you please let me in? We really need to talk." I gave in and let him in. He walked in, locked the door behind him, and then placed my food on the table in the dining room. As I went to turn down the music, you would think the next song was planned. The song that came on was 'Foreigner; "I want to know what love is."' It felt a little awkward. I turned it off.

"Eboni, I love you, I'm madly in love with you, and I'm sorry. I never meant to hurt you or make you cry. I was hurt and so angry with you for sleeping with someone else." The tears began to roll down my face and he wiped them away. It's not just about the sex to me Eboni.

"Dante, I'm the one that should be sorry. I violated your trust, but I swear to you it wasn't intentional, so I had to tell you. I needed to tell you. It bothered me."

"I believe you, Eboni. I went home, and I thought hard about it."

"I really wanted us to work, but now I'm not sure, Dante." Maybe I'm not cut out for this.

"Baby, stop crying. I don't like to see you like this. Everything will be fine. We will be fine. There's something else I need to tell you." I wonder what else he has to say, and I don't know if I can handle anything else. He took a deep breath and sat down. I started feeling like a crybaby. He wiped my face again.

"I never slept with anyone, Eb. I was so angry and wanted you to hurt like I was, possibly worse. I wasn't thinking in my right frame of mind; it was straight emotions, but when you reacted the way you did, I knew you loved me then you said it. You ran off so quickly before I could tell you it was a lie. Then you wouldn't answer the phone. I was worried. I knew I fucked up because I added fuel to the fire, and I prayed that I didn't lose you forever. I stayed here waiting for you until 1 a.m. When you didn't come, I figured you went to one of your sisters' houses." He never called the ladies my friends but my sisters. "Every time I called your phone, it went straight to voicemail. I couldn't sleep. I came here yesterday, and once I saw your car in the yard, I knew you were okay. I sat out there wanting to knock on the door, but at the same time, I wasn't sure if it was a good idea or the right time. Then I said I would wait to see if you would leave, but you never did. I tried calling you again and again and got no response. While I was sitting outside, I heard the music, and I saw the lights on. Then, when I saw the delivery guy, I knew I had to take my chances. I'm hurt but I couldn't and wouldn't let you go like that."

I couldn't hold back my smile. I'm so happy he really didn't sleep with anyone. I wish I could have said the same for myself. I truly felt his pain and I wish I could take it away.

"Eboni, do you forgive me?"

"Dante, I should be the one asking for forgiveness. My heart shattered with the thought of you sleeping with someone else. I felt your pain, the pain that I caused and sorry will never be enough, but I want to start here, by saying that I'm sorry and I promise you it won't happen again."

"Baby, I know because you opened your heart for the first time and welcomed love in." I hugged him so tight. I didn't want to let him go.

"I love you, Dante."

"I love you too, Eboni. On another note, you have a mean right hook. Now you know that I love you, Eb, but we're done if you ever do that again. I want this to work, and I know you were hurt, but know that I will never put my hands on you, and I expect the same amount of respect in return."

I apologized, "I'm sorry about that baby. It will not happen again."

Chapter 24

NADIA

The BBQ was a hit. There were so many people there, it was crazy. Just imagine having regular social gatherings, Parties, and hangouts. My parents love Jason. Amid everything, my mom pulled me aside and told me that I more than deserved him as he deserved me, and she was so happy to see me smile, a real smile.

"Nadia."

"Yes, mom?"

"Don't forget to keep him happy. That's also very important. You guys are beautiful together. Inside and out.

It's a definite compliment, to say the least. I thought.

I can't wait to have some grandbabies."

"Mom," I said, blushing, "this is still new."

She interrupted, "And? You guys keep doing what's right, and you will always have that 'new' feeling."

I am the last of the bunch and the only one with no children. I mean, why rush when I have all these beautiful children to spoil and, best of all, I can give them back to their rightful owners? When I lost my baby years ago, I asked God not to let me get pregnant again until it was for the right person. So far, he has kept me grounded and didn't disappoint me because it's obvious that Tristan can't get me pregnant.

Jason's parents are wonderful. They made me feel welcomed and like part of the family from the beginning. All of his siblings were there except for one of his brothers who happened to be on a business trip the same weekend. So, I will have to meet him at another time. It's crazy how they all look alike but different, if that makes sense.

Everyone blended well. I think Mel and Jeff even got some business. This night turned out great. I'm so glad we did it this way. Our parents, the ladies, and Jay's boys stayed back to help us clean up once everyone left. There wasn't much to do because we were cleaning as we went, so it wouldn't be too much for us to do at the end of the night. All the food and desserts were gone. Jay, the guys, including our dads, took all the trash out. I washed the dishes, and the ladies helped me tidy up. Our moms sat and got to know each other better. I even saw them exchanging numbers. Look at that. It was after 1:30am. when everyone left. Thank God we did this on a Saturday.

Thinking about that close encounter that Jay and I had was like whoa. He is fine as hell with his clothes on, but NAKED! JESUS! No words can explain it. Let's just say I can enjoy that view at any time. I knew I was wrong for teasing us both, more so Jay, but I just had the sensation of being a little naughty, and boy, oh boy, it almost took us to the next level. I do not regret anything so far. I held his manhood in my hand, not wanting to let it go. In that moment, I wanted to feel him inside me; I wanted and needed him and honestly, I don't know how long I could hold back or resist him anymore, or if I even want to. I'm still trying to figure out how we even controlled ourselves in the shower. Cause I wanted him. I know for a fact that if we didn't get interrupted, that we would have made love in that shower. I was very close to telling him we'll be late to our own party. We've had too many 'almost moments'; we're around each other a lot, so we were doing good, but I don't know how much longer doing good will last. We had made it to the four-month mark. At this point, anything is anything.

We slept in late today; we were tired. I know after the long day we had yesterday, nothing was going to be done today. I don't even want to see the kitchen. I don't even think I want to see food, but I know that's impossible. I got up at about 3 p.m. and took a shower while Jay slept. He was up earlier but went back to sleep. I came out and ordered something for us to eat. The kitchen is one place you weren't going to catch me in today unless I was getting something to drink. I was in the mood for a salad. We are going to have a light lunch and then we can eat better for dinner. I placed the order for PDQ for two chicken salads and side of large fries that Jay and I will share. `

"Hey, baby."

"Hi, Jay." Smiling, I walked over and gave him a warm hug with a gentle kiss.

"You smell good."

"Yeah, that's usually how it is when you take a shower."

He laughed, "You're such a goofball."

"Yeah, that's me."

He replied, "And I love it."

"Did you sleep well?" I asked.

"You know I did; I sleep well whenever you lay beside me."

"Jay, you're the best. I think you're trying to make me fall in love with you, expeditiously."

"Maybe. I have to try and keep up with you because you're doing a phenomenal job."

Man, he just knew the right things to say. Little did he

know I was already falling in love with him. Since we have been together, he has treated me like the queen that I am. He spoils me mentally, emotionally, and spiritually. Yes, he's a God-fearing man and he doesn't hide it. The material things are just a plus, but I would still feel the same way even if he didn't have it to do it. His energy and his words stimulate my mind. He has made love to my mind a lot of times, over and over again. Up next, my body. Yes, lord, my body.

As we sat to eat our food, I thought out loud.

"Wow, I can't believe I haven't been home in a week."

"And?"

"I mean, that's where I live."

"Yeah, by choice." I sat silent for a minute.

"Well, I don't want to overstay my welcome."

"Nadia, if it was up to me, you would be here 24/7. You could never overstay your welcome, baby. This is your home, too. I love your company. I'm okay with going back and forth, but if we're being honest, I don't like being without you for too long. I deal with it because I know you need your space, and it's only right."

"So, are you inviting me to stay, Jay?" I loved being around him as well. It didn't really matter whose house we were at. We just enjoyed each other, and getting along with everyone on both parts was a plus. We didn't have to be doing anything special for us to have a good time.

"In so many words, yes! If you told me right now that you were going to stay here permanently, it would make my day."

"Aww, baby." I couldn't help but reach over and kiss him. He is the best and even though I didn't think he was really interested in me like that, I am so happy he continued to pursue me after the incident in Bora Bora. To think I almost pushed away possibly the best man that ever happened to me.

"So, you love being around my goofy butt, huh?" We laughed. "Get up, let's go work out."

"Really, babe? What happened to relaxing?"

"I need to stay sexy for you Jason."

"Okay, Smiley, but only thirty minutes."

"What, only thirty minutes? Are you scared?" He laughed at me. I tickled him with that last statement. I couldn't help but laugh too.

"Baby, you know nothing about working out scares me."

"Let's go!" My plan worked. I knew that would get him up. We got down once we made it to the gym. We worked on our upper body, and we did some sit-ups. Everything we ate was worked out.

"Hmm, looks like we went over an hour from your thirty minutes," he smirked.

"Thanks, babe. It was a good workout, though."

"You want to play some basketball?"

"Jay, I don't know how to play basketball. No need to embarrass myself."

"Smiley, please, this is me; you won't be embarrassing yourself. I can teach you a thing or two."

"Oh really?"

"Yeah, grab the basketball, let's go." We played around in the backyard for another thirty minutes. He showed me some things. I can say I know how to do a little something, something now, but I still sucked.

"We will come back out and practice another day, and I will show you some more tricks."

"Cool beans, babe. I'm down. You're really good at basketball. What made you choose football?"

"I actually played both, but football gave me the opportunity first, so I took it and ran. I didn't want to turn it down. I got a full scholarship to college off of football. I didn't want to take any chances and end up in a what-if situation. I have no regrets, and everything turned out great. That's what's up, baby. It's always good when you have a story to tell. That's another reason why I came into this field: I can relate to my clients.

"Yes, and that's why they love you."

"I guess so."

We took a shower and decided to leave the house to get something to eat. I built up an appetite with our workout/basketball session. He pulled up to J. Marks. I wanted us to sit down and have a nice dinner. After all, we had a busy weekend and deserve this treat. The atmosphere was quiet. Maybe because it was Sunday, and the rush was already gone. We had a nice time. The vibe was nice. We drank, laughed, and talked about the barbeque.

"I'm so mad you didn't get to meet my brother. The business trip was at the last minute. I spoke to him earlier, and he said he would like to meet up this week or the weekend. I told him that he should let me know once he's sure, and we will plan from there. You will love him. We all have a lot in common. He told me I better not let you slip away when I told him about you."

"Really? This is the brother before you, right?"

"Yeah. We're all close in age except my two older brothers."

"Your mom did an amazing job with you guys. It shows."

"Thanks, that means a lot. We were so happy when my stepdad came along, and she found love again. She deserves it. We don't ever tell people he's our stepdad because he came in and did what a man and a dad is supposed to do."

You could tell Jay loves his mom. You saw the passion in his eyes when he spoke of her and her happiness. After eating, we walked on the beach before heading home.

I said, "Jay."

"Yes, babe."

"I appreciate you. Thank you for not giving up on me."

"Let's go home."

* * *

"Jay, are you tired?"

"Not really, I'm good.

"I want to have a little fun."

"Really?"

"Yes sir."

"Hmmm, what kind of fun?"

"Do you have any cards?"

"Why, I think I do. I have regular cards, Uno cards; what do you want?"

"Either will do; you pick."

"Do you have some room in there for some more liquor?"

"Yep, I sure do." He said with a smile.

"Let's go." We were in the backyard just relaxing.

I grabbed a bottle of Patron, cut up some lime, got a plate, and poured some salt into it.

"Are you ready for some fun?"

With excitement in his voice, he replied, "Yes, I am."

"Okay, where are we going to play? The living room or the bedroom?"

"The living room should be fine." He answered.

I grabbed a couple more shot glasses out of the kitchen. I wanted to pre-prep the shots.

"Which card game are we playing?"

"Let's go with Uno."

Are you sure? I asked.

"Yes. Very sure." He answered.

Jay, listen carefully. The rules are short and simple. We are playing strip uno.He laughed. "Smiley, are you sure?"

"Yes, Jay, we're two grown adults having fun. Plus, it's not like we never saw each other naked." I winked my eyes and blew him a kiss. Little did he know I was looking forward to seeing him naked again and again and again.

I continued, "The loser has to take a shot and take off an article of clothing."

"So, you think you can handle it?" I asked excitedly.

"Hell yeah."

"So, it's double punishment? You have to take your clothes off and take a shot!"

I laughed, "You better make sure not to lose because seeing you take it off definitely won't be a punishment for me. Watch out, I can get competitive sometimes."

He replied, "Say less Smiley, let's go. May the best player win."

I won the first three games. I kept my eyes on him as he took it off. He had fun while taking it off too. Now, he was left with his boxers and socks on. He had taken his shoes off when we came into the house earlier.

I asked, "You're okay over there, baby?"

"Smiley, I'm great." I think I started to get a little distracted by the pleasant view of his body, and his upper body kept calling me. I just wanted to touch it, as I imagined slowly licking some whipped cream off of him while my tongue went up and down his sexy ass abs. I lost. I'm glad I didn't have on a dress. I would have been in the same position as him. I went ahead and slowly unbuttoned my shirt as he watched me take it off. His eyes took in every move.

"Aight, you got me." I took my shot, and we continued. I won the next game. He took one sock off.

"If you want, we can stop."

"Stop! Are you serious? No way. I can still win." He said excitingly.

"I love your confidence, Jay."

"That's right. My confidence helped me get you and it can help me win too."

Lo and behold, I lost the next two games.

He asked, "So, what was that you were saying, baby? You said you wanted to quit." I took my jeans and my bra off. I had less clothes on than him altogether.

"Quit." I replied, "Never! You just have on one more item than I do. Let's play."

He lost. He took his socks off and took his shot like a man. We both were left wearing just our underwear. I felt him looking at me. My nipples were hard, and they were poking out. He looked at me, licked his lips, and took another shot.

"Oh, you took that because you know you're about to lose?"

Smiling, he replied, "No losing over here. I already won. I'll take these boxers off without hesitation right now. I'm feeling good and these shots are getting to me."

He looked delicious. His dick was poking through his Hanes-fitted underwear. I reached over to grab the cards and shuffle them for our final game, and then Jay leaned in and kissed me gently with a little bit of hesitation as if he wasn't sure if I would accept him. We've been at this stage so many times before, so I get it. I wanted him; I knew he wanted me, and this alcohol was a boost. He came in closer, and the kiss became more intense. There's no fighting this anymore. Slowly lying back on the fluffy living room carpet, the kisses went down to my ear, creeping to my neck. I was nervous and anxious like it was my very first time. His lips on my nipples snapped me back to reality. He looked at me as if he wanted confirmation that I was ready. I was, no more resisting. His hands went slowly up and down my side as he took in every curve of my body. He took his hands and rubbed them across my breast. He leaned back and kissed me, a kiss that screamed, "I need you now." I felt his manhood on my thigh. Soft kisses circled my stomach. My moans were turning him on, and my heart was pounding.

"Are you okay, baby?"

"Yes, Jason."

He pulled my underwear to the side and began playing with my womanhood.

"I've been waiting for this moment for a long time, Nadia."

"Me too." I said softly.

Ummm, his hands felt so good. It had been a long time since I had been touched this way. He licked his fingers and went back in using just one finger to penetrate. He began sucking my breast while his finger remained in motion. "Ohh Jason." My legs began to shiver; he pulled off my underwear. "I want to taste you." He began kissing my womanhood; I came what felt like ten times already just by his touch. He knew what he was doing. I'll continue to give myself credit for controlling myself for all these months, hell all these years. I have no idea how I held back so long. He stopped for a second to pick up one of the cups. I felt something cold when he came back. He placed an ice cube and added it into the mix. He licked off every drop while his tongue worked magic around my clit, going in and out.

"Tonight, I'm ready to experience a different part of you, Nadia."

He got up and took his underwear off. His manhood was at attention.

"Let me return the favor, baby. Let me feel that magic stick in my mouth."

"Not yet; tonight is about you."

"No, it's about us Jay." I got on my knees and enjoyed him. After so long, I thought I would be a little rusty, but your girl was on point. My man had no complaints.

He begged, "Baby, stop, I don't want to cum this way." He grabbed the condom and put it on. Coming back down to join me, he laid on top of me, looking into my eyes; he smiled, kissing me; he slowly inserted his magic stick into my womanhood, and finally, our bodies connected. Holding my breath, I felt every inch of him while it throbbed inside of me. This feeling is everything. It felt so good. He held me tight in his arms as he made love to me. The tears rolled from my eyes. All this is mine.

He moaned, "Damnnnn baby. It was worth the wait. He was moaning while I was throwing it back at him.

"Get up, baby." I grabbed a chair from the dining room. "Sit!" I told him. Then I sat on him and took his magic stick for a ride.

"Fuck Nadia! Where have you been all my life?"

"Waiting for you to find me."

"Oh baby, you're gonna make me cum moving like that."

"I want you to cum daddy."

"Not yet." He got up, still holding me, walked over to the wall, and made love to me, standing up, and holding me. He went up and down like he was doing squats. The different feelings that ran through my body scared me. I held on to him tight. We came together. I knew this was the final straw to confirm that I was in love with him. Still leaning against the wall, our eyes connected. I know he felt the same. He smiled, kissed me, and smiled again. I said, "You know, if you didn't have that condom on, I probably would've gotten pregnant tonight the way you made love to me."

Laughing, he asked, "Really? Damn, I wish I knew that I wouldn't have put it on. I wish you told me your pussy was so damn good too."

Blushing, "I don't like to brag, but you haven't seen anything yet."

"Hmmmmm. Is that so?"

"Well, I'm just the messenger, so let me know when you find out."

Smiling, he replied, "I definitely will."

I thought it would have been a little weird for me after we were done making love because that's exactly what we did. He made love to me. Gentle and passionate, it's been so long for me, but truly worth the wait. Our chemistry is different.

Chapter 25

JASON

My relationship with Nadia is nothing short of amazing. Making love to her for the first time was breathtaking. After we finally crossed the line, we made love nonstop every chance we got. We've been together for almost a year, and I'm ready to pop the question. I'm confident she will say yes; I am just trying to figure out how to do it. It has to be special. We don't keep secrets from each other; even though this is a different type of secret, it will still be hard and may require some help. I went ring shopping a few days ago. I didn't see anything that popped out to me, so I will have one made. It will definitely be one of a kind for my one-of-a-kind lady.

"Abby."

"Yes, Mr. McKnight."

"I'm going to be leaving the office early today. I need you to do me a favor, if possible."

"Sure."

"Can you look into a big venue for me? Possibly to hold about two thousand people, but just in case, a little more."

"You're having a big party?" she asked. "What's the occasion?"

"Well, I'm going to ask Nadia to marry me, and I want the world to see. So more like a surprise engagement party."

"What? Yes! That's amazing. You guys are perfect together. She really completes you. I have never seen you this happy, and I've seen you happy."

"I know what you mean. Abby, I even feel different. I feel more than complete. Nadia is the best thing that ever happened to me. I thought I couldn't get better as a person, and she makes me better, and I'm not ashamed to say that, Abby."

"Mr. McKnight, that's right. You better keep her close and never let her go."

"I'm trying. I want to bring up starting a family, but I'm going to hold back because I don't want her to feel pressured, and I want her to be my wife first, so please find some places and let me know ASAP, and then I will check them out."

She replied, "Will do."

"Thanks, Abby. Find you a nice dress and tell your boyfriend to be ready."

"You know we'll be there. One more thing. What date?"

"Just tell them you will need it in about two months or so while I figure out the actual day. I would love for it to be sooner, but I do have to give people time to fly in and prepare."

"Okay, well, I will get the info to you as soon as possible."

"Thanks again. I need all the help I can get. You're the first person I actually told! Now, I have to call my mom."

"I'm honored that you chose to include me."

"You're the best employee anyone can ask for Abby."
She smiled.

"Okay, I'm going to finish up and head out. If you want to

leave early today, you can; just make sure to turn on the voicemail."

I had an appointment to see one of the best jewelers out here. I had to call the guys because they had to help me out. On my way to the jeweler, my phone rang.

"How's my favorite lady doing?"

She replied, "Hey baby, I miss you."

"Miss you more. Are you feeling any better?"

"No, not really." Nadia has been sick for the last two days. She has the flu.

"I told you I would stay home with you."

"No, I'm good. I'm going to go back to bed; I only got up because I had to get some more water."

"You drank all that water I left in the room for you?"

"Yes."

"If you're not a little better by tomorrow, I'm taking you to the doctor even if I have to pick you up and carry you myself! Go get some rest. I'm going to bring some soup and meds when I get home."

"Okay, baby. I love you, and have a great day."

"I love you more Nadia. I will see you soon." Every time I hear her tell me that she loves me, it feels like the first time. I still get that tingling feeling.

I pulled up to the jeweler. I've been here before but under different circumstances. I'm excited! I walked in and looked at the different styles of rings he had available. They're all nice but not exactly what I was looking for, so I described to him what I had in mind, and he drew it out so I could have a visual. It was beautiful. After discussing and making minor adjustments, I put half the money down and will pay it off when I come to pick it up.

I told him, "This ring means a lot to me, so take your time."

I had him do both the engagement and the wedding ring, so that's one less thing I will have to worry about. There's so much that I need to get done, but my mind is just on my baby at home. *I want to call her back, but I'm going to let her rest. Hmmm, who should I call first, my mom or Mike?* I dialed Mom's number before I drove off.

"Hey, Baby."

"Hey, Mom."

"How are you?" She asked.

"I'm good."

"You're not working today?"

"Yeah, I left early; I had some errands to run."

"How's your beautiful lady doing?"

"She has the flu and is home resting. I'm heading to get her some soup right now, but since we're on the subject of Nadia, Mom, I want to ask her to marry me." "What? Jason!" I could hear the excitement in her voice. "I'm so proud of you. That's a big step, and you will be an amazing husband."

"Thanks, mom. Hearing that means a lot. I've been through a lot, and she has brought me peace; I know she's the one, so I am going to go to her parents' house sometime this week to ask for her hand in marriage, the right way. I just left the jeweler if you really want to know how serious I am."

"Baby, just let me know if there's anything you need me to do, she's a lucky lady and you have my support."

"Thanks, mom. Love you. I'll talk to you later."

I have to figure out where to go for some soup. I felt like I was wasting too much time driving. I saw Lagranja, it's a Spanish restaurant, so I decided to stop there. I know I'll get the kind of soup I'm looking for here. I got two different types of soup and ordered some food just in case she built up an appetite.

I called Mike, Eric, and Chris on three-way and filled them in on everything.

"Guys, I feel so bad lying to her."

"Think about the positive outcome that will come out of this "small lie," which technically isn't a lie, more like stretching the truth a bit."

"When you put it that way, it doesn't seem so bad Chris."

"So, we're not going to call it a lie. How about this: you're going to have to stretch the truth a little to make it turn into the beautiful night you envisioned. I have an idea, just include her in it."

"Include her?"

"Yeah, have her go with you to look at the locations, pick out food, etc. That way you would be sure she loves the choices that are made."

I exclaimed, "Eric, You're a genius!"

"Thank you! I've heard that a time or two but for real, you know we got your back."

"Guys, do you think she would say yes?"

They laughed at me like I was Katt Williams telling a joke.

"How can I say this? Both of you are fucked up about each other; what kind of question is that?"

I agree, "You're right."

"A blind man can see that!"

I said, "Okay! Eric, I get your point."

"Just making sure you did."

"I'm pulling up now. Smiley is still sick, so I'm going to go take care of my baby."

"Wait! Are you sure she isn't pregnant?"

"Mike, as much as I wish that was the case, she isn't. We use condoms."

"Still?"

"Yes, still."

"Fuck, Jason. So, you haven't really felt her yet. Ohh, so you think you're fucked up about her now, just wait."

"Listen, we don't have to use condoms, and it's hard holding back from just going headfirst and allowing her to feel all of this, but we're trying to avoid any babies right now. I want it to be at the right time for both of us and as much as I would love to hear *we're pregnant*," I want it to be right."

"Anyway, are you guys still coming over this weekend so I can beat y'all ass in some basketball?"

"We will be there. May the best team win."

I walked into the house and took the soup to the room. She was sound asleep. I touched her forehead; she was hot and sweating, so that's good. I kissed her.

"Baby, get up. You're wet! How long have you been sleeping?"

"Since I got off the phone with you."

"Okay, I brought you some soup. Go take a quick shower so you can eat."

"Thank you, baby," she said, with that smile that could brighten the room even when sick. While she was in the shower, I changed the sheets. It was soaked in the spot she was laying in.

"You look like you're getting better."

"A little."

"I think sweating is helping." I said.

"Jay, I could have changed the sheet."

I gave her the eye. "Smiley, go lay down."

"How was your day?" She asked.

"It was good." *Here's my chance.* "Chris is having a big party, and he asked me to help him plan it and find a location. I know you have an eye for these things; a woman's input is always a plus. Do you want to help me?"

She said, "Sure. How soon do you need to get it done?"

"Asap. I believe he wants to have the event in two months, so we have some time. You need to get better first, then we will worry about that." She stared me in my eyes like she was in a daze.

"I want to kiss you so bad, baby, but I don't want you to get sick."

"I'll take my chances." I kissed her. Nothing explicit. Just a tap on the lips.

"I'm going to take a shower; go eat your soup."

When I got out of the shower, to my surprise she was done eating.

"You were hungry."

"Yeah."

"I'm surprised."

"Me too! I didn't even feel like I had an appetite. I haven't eaten in almost two days."

"Do you want some of my food?"

"No, babe. I'm good." The shower and soup helped. We laid down and watched TV until we fell asleep.

I've been getting strange phone calls these last few days from random numbers. The person would either hang up or stay on the phone. You could hear them breathing but not saying anything and when I tried to call back, it was a made-up number from an app. Once I have some free time, I will get to the bottom of it.

Abby did a great job finding some locations for me to check out. I have an appointment to see one of them later this afternoon. I'm so excited, and the fact that Nadia is going to be a part of it is even better. She's hanging out with Mel and Terri today. So, they will drop her off at my office, and we will go from there. I filled them in already. So far, everything is looking good.

From the outside of this venue, it didn't scream out to me as if I would want to have something here, but I'm not worried yet. There's still hope, and it's only the first one. When we walked in, it was nice. The coordinator greeted us and explained everything while we did a walk-through. We reviewed the prices and how soon the deposit would be given. I told her I would get back to her once I got feedback from Chris.

"What do you think about this one?"

Smiley replied, "Well, it's okay, but it doesn't scream out what you want it for; plus, I don't think it would hold the number of people that Chris is catering for as well."

"Okay. Well, I have a few more lined up."

Nadia had an appointment with a client today. It ran late, so she was going to stay at her house tonight. I disliked these nights the most. I'll be glad when she moves in here completely. To keep my mind off of her, I'll take advantage of this free time to gather everything I need to get done. I needed to go to the supermarket, but it could wait until tomorrow. It's just me. I wanted to hire a personal chef, again that way, we would already have dinner and lunch prepped when we have late nights. I'm thinking about seeing what Mel and Jeff can do. Maybe they can rotate. They don't even have to come here. They can have it ready, and we can pick it up weekly or how ever we agree. I don't know. I'll talk to Nadia and see what she thinks. It's 8:30 and I haven't heard from Nadia yet. I'm going to give her another hour, and then I'm going to check on her. I need to know she made it home safely.

After the proposal, I want us to go on a pre-honeymoon, if I should even call it that. I want it to be memorable. We can do that while I work on how to blow it out of the park for our honeymoon, there is no rush, we still have time. I started web searching, and I decided on Santorini, Greece. We've been to a few places since we began dating, but it's time to step it up. I want to show her a great time. I went ahead, booked the trip and hotel for five days, and set up some tours and activities for our time there. I'm excited and glad that's done.

Walking back from getting something in the kitchen, my phone rang. That may be my baby; I ran to catch the call, but it hung up by the time I made it back. I checked to see, and it wasn't her. The phone rang again.

"Hello." Silence. "Hellooo, listen, if you're not going to say anything, stop calling my phone." I really wanted to say, stop playing on my fucking phone, but I had to stay professional because anyone can call me, and true enough, depending on where you are, there could be bad service. I let it go.

My baby finally called me.

"Hey, Jay. I had such a busy day. How was your day?"

"It was good, yours?"

"It was successful. I'm now walking to my car. I am tired, but their house looks beautiful."

"I must say, job well done. I'll send you the pictures when I get home. I wish I didn't have to do all this driving."

"I'm glad to hear your voice."

"Aww, baby. I'm happy to hear your voice, too." She said.

"I've been thinking about you all day, Smiley."

"Yeah, what were you thinking about?"

"Hmmm, you don't want me to tell you, plus it's so late, and I need you to focus on the road."

"You think I can't focus?"

"Oh, I know you can, but if I tell you what I've been thinking, you may have to pull over until I'm finished."

"Shit! I think I want to pull over and have a little bit of fun. So, are you going to tell me before I jump on this highway?"

"I can video call you, and you could be included."

"Say no more; I'll start unbuttoning my pants right now. It may be just what I need to give me the energy to make it home."

"You know you don't ever have to ask more than once. Are you in a safe area?"

"I will be in a few minutes."

She called me back but as video call.

"Hey, beautiful."

She smiled. "Hey, sexy daddy. I'm ready for you."

She had her phone hooked up to the phone mount, and I had the perfect view. "So, talk to me, baby." She was ready, and I loved her spontaneous adventurousness. She was looking at me. "What did you say you wanted to do to me, Daddy?"

I started talking dirty to her. She placed her hand in her pants while rubbing her breasts. The moans were crazy, and I was mad I wasn't there to assist. I placed my phone where she could still see me, and I joined in on the fun, rubbing my dick and imagining it going inside her.

She said, "Make me cum Jason." I watched as her hand picked up the pace, and her back arched a little more.

"Yes, right there."

"Yes, Jay."

Fuck! She's going to make me cum.

After a few minutes, I asked, "How did you like that?" She laughed.

"Thank you, baby, that's just what I needed to take this drive home. I love you."

"Love you more. I'm happy I can fulfill your needs."

"Baby, please, I'll be fulfilled when I can feel the touch of your manly hands on my body, but I won't be ungrateful. I'll take what I can get; this was fun."

I stayed on the phone with her until she made it home.

"Babe, I'm about to take a hot shower and go to bed. Thank you for keeping me company and making sure I made it home safely."

"You know I won't be able to sleep until I knew you were home." We gave each other air kisses.

"Sweet dreams, Jay."

"Sweet dreams, my smiley face."

Finally, Saturday is here. We're on our way to see two venues. I hope we can make a decision today because time is winding down. I decided that I wanted to do it on our first anniversary. I'll have to find a way to wiggle that in. The look on Nadia's face was everything when we pulled up to the venue. I just knew she loved it.

She said, "The outside of this place is beautiful, Jay. If the inside gives the same feeling, this may be it." She explained her thoughts and ideas while we walked into the building. She said, "Think about it, Jay. People pull up, and Chris can have valet parking; they can stop and take pictures by this beautiful waterfall fountain. Then, this walkway into the building is picture-perfect, too. I'm excited to see the inside." She had me excited with her excitement and I saw her vision.

The coordinator greeted us, "Sorry to keep you waiting. Follow me." He led us into a ballroom. The ceilings are high, the lighting in the room is photo-ready, and the one thing I really liked was the room's design. How can I describe it? It has different levels. You have the flat floor where you can use it for dancing, laying out the food and even having some tables. Then you walk up four steps, and tables are all around, making a U-shape with the railings so you won't fall over. This place is it. I can tell by the look on Nadia's face she was already decorating the room.

I asked, "Do you like this one?"

"You know I do!" The guy smiled.

I said, "Okay, I'm going to get with Chris to give him all the information, find out the date he will need it, and follow up with you next week."

"Also, you can let Chris know it's an open bar." Nadia and I looked at each other.

"Nice to know. You will hear from us soon." We did see the last venue. It was nice, but we already had our minds made up.

On Monday, I called the guy to let him know the date, and we agreed to meet on Friday to give him the deposit. I'm going to stop and get the invitations tomorrow. I had a few people to meet today, so it will be a full day at the office.

"Mr. McKnight, Nadia is on line one."

"That's strange; she doesn't really call me on this line."

"She said she was calling your cell, and you didn't answer."

I looked at my phone. That's weird. My phone didn't ring.

I said, "Okay, transfer her."

"Hey, baby."

"Jay, you had me worried."

"I'm sorry. My phone didn't ring, and not one missed call from you."

She said, "I'm glad you're okay."

"Of course I am, baby." Aww, look at you all worried. I spoke to Chris, and he told me the party's date."

"That's great, when?"

I sat silent for a few minutes because it was going to be the moment of truth. "When Jay?"

I answered, "Our anniversary."

"Really?"

"I told him that it was our special day. He felt bad and said, if need be, he would change the date."

"No! Keep it. We can still celebrate. It's a party; we can dress up and be together. Every day with you is special; we will have many more years to celebrate together alone. What more can I ask for? So, sharing one won't hurt anyone or anything."

"If you're okay with it, so am I. I'll call him back and tell him the date is fine."

"Did you tell Chris how beautiful the place was?"

"I sure did."

"I hope whoever he gets to do the decorations and the setup knows how to bring that place to life."

"Me too."

Chapter 26

NADIA

I was excited once Jason told me the party was on our anniversary. It's not like it was an all-day event. We will be attending at night. So, we had all day for that one-on-one time. I'm just looking at it as a night out with friends. This will be fun.

I'm performing this weekend. I hadn't been there in about a month, so it was time to return to what I loved.

Riri called me yesterday and told me Victoria's Secret has a sale going on. I've been needing to go to the mall anyway. I needed to re-up on some underwear, pajamas, and some other things too.

"Babe, I'm going to the mall tomorrow."

"By yourself?"

"Yep."

"Do you want some company?"

"Hmmm, do I? You want to come?"

"Of course, I want to cum with you!" He laughed; he has such a dirty mind sometimes.

I shook my head and replied, "I'd love for you to come."

I'm so happy that the mall wasn't so packed. The worst thing is having to find parking. Depending on which mall you go to, you can valet park. We went from this store to that store, not wanting anything but just looking around. We stopped at the food court because I wanted to get a strawberry lemonade from Charley's. I couldn't be here and not get some, and Jay had to use the restroom. I found a table to sit at while I waited for him. I pulled my phone out and checked the time; I forgot my watch at home. I thought I heard someone say my name, but I didn't pay it much attention, and then I heard it again. When I looked up, it was Andre. I haven't seen him in maybe two years. He came closer, "Hey, Nadia, I knew it was you." He reached in for a hug. I was hesitant at first. I really wanted to tell him, "You don't deserve to shake my hand," but I reminded myself to be the bigger person, so I gave him a friendly hug. All of the hurt he gave me was gone. I'm happy. He continued, "How are you? You look great."

I replied, "Thanks, Dre. I'm great, and you?"

"I'm doing well, hanging in there, surviving. Nadia, I'm glad I finally got to see you. I know this may not be the place, but I waited a long time for this moment. I want to take this time to apologize sincerely. I know I've tried to apologize before but I was selfish, I really didn't mean to hurt you. I'm not making up any excuses or trying to justify it. I fucked up, and I have to live with that. I loved you, hell, I still love you; I will always love you."

If he said love one more time, luckily, Jason made it back to me right on time. I'm so happy I wasn't here by myself.

Jason said, "Hey baby, sorry I took so long."

"It's okay." Wasting no time, I said, "Babe, this is Andre." Jay had this smirk on his face that told me he already knew who he was. I continued, "Andre, this is my boyfriend, Jason."

Andre said, "Oh, I know who he is; this is Jason McKnight, one of the best football players out there. Sucks that you left the game. You're a lucky man, Jason."

Jason replied, "Yes," pulling me close but keeping eye contact with Andre, "I know, Nadia's the best thing to ever happen to me; thank you for that." Then Jay held my hand and said, "It was nice meeting you, Andre, but we have to go." He kissed me on the cheek.

"Are you okay Smiley?" Jason asked once we left Andre.

"Yeah, why wouldn't I be?"

"I know you haven't seen him in a long time, and I know these encounters can sometimes be awkward or even triggering."

"I thought it would have been weird, but it wasn't. I have you to thank for that, Jay!" I kissed him on his cheek. I looked back, and Andre stood there, watching us walk away. I know it was killing Andre to see me with Jason. He's fine, he has stability, I'm happy, and most of all, he's happy with just me.

Chapter 27

JASON

I was kind of happy that I wasn't too far behind when Andre saw Nadia. I really wanted to tell him, "Thank you so much for fucking up!" But there was no need to. He knew he did. I could tell just by the way he looked at her. He couldn't control it. Seeing her with me was enough damage, and to top it off, the fact that she looks and is happy said it all. When she introduced me, I wished she could have said fiancée better yet, husband. I noticed him on my way back from the bathroom. At first, I wasn't sure who she was talking to, but as I got closer, I remembered seeing a picture of him and knew exactly who he was. I'm happy she didn't have to deal with it on her own.

There are two weeks left until the party. I will pick up the rings and take them to my mom's house tomorrow. I went into the office a little late. As soon as I walked in, I knew something wasn't right.

"Good morning, Abby."

"Good morning, Mr. McKnight."

"Is everything okay Abby?"

"We need to talk. Go get your coffee and I'll be back in your office in ten minutes max." I started to get worried. *Did Nadia find out about the party?* After all this hard work and she finds out now. The knock on my door snapped me out of my thoughts.

"Come in." Abby closed the door behind her. Of all the things I thought she would tell me; this definitely wasn't it.

"Tiffany stopped by this morning around 9."

"She what!"

"Yeah. She said she needed to see you and talk to you. It's important, also, she said she tried to call you, but you ignored her calls." I thought to myself, *she hadn't tried to call me in months the last time I checked.*

"What's crazy is I thought I'd seen her outside this building a time or two but wasn't sure; that's why I never said anything. She looks a mess Mr. McKnight."

"I'm speechless, Abby. There's nothing that she could possibly want or need to talk to me about. We've broken up for almost two years now. The last thing I need is for her to come and try to ruin anything between Nadia and me."

"I know, so you guys please be careful. Pay attention to your surroundings."

"We will, and I need you to do the same. Thanks for letting me know. Thank God I changed the locks once we broke up. She did have a key, which I got back, but she knew where the spare key was, and who's to say she didn't make a copy?"

This is the last thing I need right now. I really wonder what she wants. I've been with Nadia for about a year. I know she knows that I'm with someone and moved on, even if she's unsure of who it is. Wait, I wonder if she's the one who's been playing on my phone lately! Man, I'm not stressing myself. I'll deal with it later.

I found this gold and black blazer to go with the black and gold dress Nadia said she ordered and had to go pick it up. She showed it to me. It was all black with some splash of gold; the cut of this dress was everything: low and sexy.

"Jaaaaaaasssssson, where are you?"

"Leaving the office now. I'm on my way to meet you guys."

"Just checking. I had to make sure you didn't forget about us."

"Jade, come on, give your brother some credit. Have I ever forgotten y'all before? "Welllll", Jade said sarcastically. okay, that was one time, and I had an understandable reason." She laughed. I would do anything for my sisters.

I continued, "I should be there in ten minutes. Where are you?"

"Meet us at the food court."

"Okay. See you soon." They absolutely love Nadia. They wanted to find something to wear for the party, and I wanted to get a backup dress for Nadia. I know how women can be sometimes. I grew up with three of them. Even though they might have three different personalities one thing I notice with woman is when it came down to their wardrobe, they were just about all the same. So, I would rather be safe than sorry. I snuck up on them, eating some churros and ice cream.

"Hey baby, let me get a taste of your ice cream," they turned around, ready to snap. "Jason, I was ready to curse your ass out. I hope those weren't the weak-ass lines you used to get Nadia."

"Janae, we know he had to do better than that because he got her."

"That's true, Jade."

"Umm, I am standing right here." I said.

"You did it to yourself, but you know we love you." I

hugged them. We finally made it into a store, and Janae started looking through some dresses.

"Look at this, Jay," Jade and I turned around.

"Yes, Janae, that dress is everything."

"I have to agree with Jade. I like it. It's tan with a rose gold sequence, long and beautiful."

"This dress will be perfect for her, Jason, and she wouldn't need any accessories other than earrings. Less is more and her hair can be up or down.""This is why I love you ladies; you guys make my life a little easier, even though I know I could have done it without y'all."

"Whatever, Jason. You wouldn't know if you were coming or going if you were in here by yourself. You would probably buy one of everything to save you from stress."

I laughed, "That's what you think of me?"

"Yup!"

"Come on, growing up with you guys helped me figure out women. A lot."

"So, did you figure it out?"

"I think I got a good hold on it. With that being said, I think we should get another dress just in case."

"That's fine, but we know she's going to pick this one." Nadia reminded me of Janea; she's my baby sister, and we have always been close. Mom called us Bonnie and Clyde. We did everything together. We kept no secrets. None of us kept secrets. We're all open and honest with each other, but it's different between Nae and me. She's my best friend. They didn't have Nadia's size in stock, so I had to order it.

"Now, she can pick which one she wants to wear. It's always good to have choices. I'll just get an all-black suit with some rose gold cufflinks. Does mom have anything to wear?"

"Jade, call mom and find out." While she was talking to Mom, I looked around some more.

"She said she has a dress."

"That's good. How about we buy her another one? I'll pay for you guys' dresses as well. Get what you want."

"Whoa. That's music to our ears." They said.

It turned out to be easier than I thought. Everyone's dress was brought from here. One stop shop. I know the sales lady was happy today. She was really helpful to us, so I gave her a $100 tip on the side. I know they probably aren't allowed to get tips, but you can't tell me what to do with my money, especially when it was deserved.

The RSVPs are coming in. As of right now, we have 910 confirmed. Mel referred me to a chef to cater the event. Everything is ready to go. This is going to be one big anniversary/ engagement party.

Tonight is date night with the crew. We're going to meet up and have dinner, Mike suggested karaoke. It's about twelve of us tonight.

"Jay, how about we start having game night? Whatever day we choose, we rotate locations. Whoever's house it's going to be at picks the game. Like the ladies and I had movie nights, and whoever's house it at, we watched what they chose. Wait, we can probably start that back, but as couples." Smiley jumped on the couch with excitement. "What do you think, baby?"

"That's a good idea."

"How about you mention it tonight?"

"Yeah, I think I will." She said ecstatically.

"Just so we have different things we can do as a group."

"I'm going to have Alex drive us tonight. I want to drink tonight, especially if we're doing karaoke; and, I want to enjoy you a little. I don't want my focus to be on driving, just on you."

Dinner was great. We brought some food for Alex; he's a great guy and doesn't complain about anything. Once he dropped us off, Smiley told him to come in and have some fun.

Alex said, "Thank you so much for the invite. I think I might just take you up on that offer. Once I eat this food, I'll be right in."

"Good, but if you want to, you can save that food for later because we will be ordering finger foods and other things in here, and if you want a meal, I got you."

He said, "Okay, thanks Jason, Well, I'll park and come in."

I invited him to come in for dinner with us earlier, but he said he had to go take something to his son.

Karaoke was so much fun. I'm so happy we invited Alex to be a part of this. He can sing. He shut it down. The rest of us were drunken singers. I loved it. We were building memories. Nadia and I sang together. All the ladies sang together, then the guys. We just went in there, took over, and brought the crowd to us.

On our way home, Nadia and I sat in the third row, and I'm so glad we did. Smiley and I have a high sex drive. She's making up for those three years. She didn't waste any time pulling my dick out and giving it all the attention it needed and more.

She whispered, "What's the point of having someone drive us if we're not going to have fun?" Smiley wasn't drunk but I know she was feeling good.

The next chance I get, I'm going to get a window installed to separate the front and the back, or I'm just going to buy a vehicle that has it already. I'm looking forward to more times like this. Alex had the radio on, and he was singing his heart out, which helped to tune us out a little.

"You like that daddy?"

"Oh, Nadia," I whispered while her tongue made circles around the head of my dick. It didn't take long for me to cum, and she licked up all our babies.

There are two days left until the party. The suit and the dress came last night. She loved it. So, we're going with the rose gold dress. My sisters were right. I bought a shirt to match the dress and my cufflinks. I was on my way out when the phone rang.

"Jason speaking."

"Hi, Jason. I miss you. I know you miss me."

"Tiffany? Why are you calling me?"

"I miss you, Jason!"

"Tiffany, you need to stop."

"Oh, you got you a new bitch, so I'm not good enough."

"First off, what you're not going to do is disrespect my woman. I don't give a fuck what you think you're feeling, but you better get your mind right when it comes down to her."

"Fuck you, Jason."

"Yeah, wouldn't you love to? Now it's clear there's no relevance to this conversation, so stay off my line and stay away from my place of business or anything or anyone that has anything to do with me." I hung up before she could say anything else. She called me back three times, and I ignored the calls. I didn't want her to ruin my day.

I woke up extra early this morning. Today is the big day, and I'm starting it off right. I made breakfast. I'm not a cook, but I'm willing to do anything to make my lady feel special. Before I took it up to her, I put on "It's Our Anniversary" by Tony Toni Tone. I made it to the top of the stairs and walked into the room, waiting before I could press play. She was sleeping like a baby, I hate to wake her up especially since we don't sleep late, and she's worse than me with the getting up early thing but today is an exception, it's our anniversary. I pressed play, put it on repeat, and decided to have a little fun. I placed the tray next to the bed and climbed in. I started sucking on her breasts; It was protruding from her shirt. she opened her eyes and smiled.

"Happy anniversary." I whispered. While staring into her beautiful eyes.

"Happy anniversary." I kissed her and my dick wanted her.

I made love to her as my girlfriend; the next time will be as my fiancée and then as my wife. We ate breakfast, and then the bell rang.

"Smiley, can you get that for me?" I stood by the stairs so I could capture her reaction. The delivery guy delivered roses, a fruit basket, and a medium-sized teddy bear with our names and the date engraved in it. She stood by the door for a few minutes after the guy left. Playing it cool, I asked, "Who was it?" She looked at me, crying and laughing, "Jason, this is beautiful. Thank you so much." This is what made me love her more. The little things made her day.

"So, you think that you're the only one that got tricks." She walked into the living room and gave me a box. It was a personalized desk blotter. I loved it. "Hold on, baby, one more." She gave me a bag. Opening it, I felt a tear roll out; it was a 3d crystal photo of us. I got up and hugged her. "I love and appreciate you so much."

We hung in the house all day and even took a nap. I got up and ordered some food. "Jay, I have one more gift for you."

"Are you pregnant?"

Laughing, she replied, "No, silly. I hope you're ready the day I tell you I am."

"Oh, I'm ready. I wish we could stop using condoms; then I can make love to you and make it a reality."

"Soon, baby."

"Soon. Nadia, I want to feel you, baby."

Laughing, she said, "Jay, we're getting off track." She gave me a card, and I opened it. It was an anniversary card with eight tickets to go ATV riding. I was speechless.

"Yeah, so you, the guys, and your brothers can go. I know that's only seven but the eighth one is for Alex. Go have a guys' day out." This, by far, is the best anniversary ever.

We're going to take another nap to prepare for this party later. It starts at 8 p.m., two hours should be good enough. It's 3 p.m. now. I put a movie on and laid next to Nadia.

My phone rang and woke me up. I can't afford to ignore any calls due to the party tonight. Without looking, I answered the phone.

"Hello. Jason!" I looked over; Nadia was still sleeping. I quickly moved.

"What do you want?"

"I'm telling you, Jason, you shouldn't have let me go."

"Ha, first off, I'm sure you don't need me to remind you of the fucked-up shit you did."

"I thought we got past that."

"Oh yeah, I got past it and let your ass go. You can now have any man you want. I'm not in your way."

"But Jason, I want you."

"Listen, Tiffany, I'm sure you do want me. What happened, those other men didn't want you anymore once they realized they didn't have anyone to push your ass back on? Guess what? I don't want you either, and I don't need you. You fucking up was the best thing you could have done for me. I moved on, and I'm happier than I've ever been!"

"Yeah, let's see how long that's going to last."

"What is that supposed to mean?"

"You should have just let me back in, Jason."

"Listen, don't call me again. Remove my number from your brain."

"Give me some dick from time to time, and our secret will remain a secret."

"What fucking secret?" She's starting to piss me off. I walked back into my room and straight out to the balcony.

Laughing, she said, "You know you miss this pussy."

"What fucking secret, Tiffany?"

She laughed some more. She started to sound like a crazy person.

"Jason, we have a baby! A boy."

"Bitch! We have a what?" Now, I'm not one to call women such names, but under these circumstances, it slipped. "You better go call the dude you were fucking with."

"Jason, I know he's yours!"

"You want this so-called baby to be mine. You forgot you didn't want any children from me. Remember! Plus, the last time I fucked you, it was with a condom, and now you want to call me two years later to tell me I have a fucking baby! You lost the little bit of sense you had! Get the fuck off my phone!"

I'm so mad right now on so many different levels. I couldn't control the tears. I called my mom and explained everything that had been going on: the phone calls, her coming to the office, and this very last phone call. I know she never really cared for Tiffany, but she was always supportive of me.

"Mom, this is supposed to be the best day of my life!"

"Baby. It still is. You're about to make a big move tonight!

You're about to ask the love of your life to be your wife. Don't ever let anyone or anything stand in the way of your happiness. You love Nadia, and she loves you. Do what you have to do to make sure no one ruins that. After tonight, you get to the bottom of it, but I'm telling you, as a woman, don't hide it from Nadia. Talk to her Jason, soon!"

"What if she doesn't want to be bothered with me anymore?"

"I highly doubt that, but it's a chance you have to take. It's a baby we're talking about, supposedly."

"I don't even know if there's really a baby, Mom."

"Exactly, Jason."

"But mom, what if there is, and she tells me now!" I heard Nadia in the background sound like she was coming out of the bathroom. I tried to wipe my face before she noticed.

"Hey, baby. I was wondering where you went."

I cleared my throat and tried to avoid eye contact, "I just stepped out here to talk to Mom on the phone."

"Oh, hi, Mom." I couldn't help but smile.

"She said hi back, happy anniversary, and she looks forward to seeing you later."

"Same here. Well, I'll let you guys finish talking. I'm going to grab a snack in the kitchen. Do you want something?"

"Sure, babe. Surprise me."

"Got ya."

"Mom."

"Jason, breathe, it's going to be okay. Put it aside for now, and go enjoy your lady. It's your anniversary. I'll see you tonight."

"Thanks, I love you, mom."

"Love you too."

I just stood there staring with one leg on the railing. *Why now God? Why is this happening to me?* Nadia walked up behind me, hugging me, singing it's our anniversary.

"Baby, turn around; let me see your face." She started back singing, but this time, a line from Keyshia Cole, "I wanna be the one who you believe in, your heart is sent from (sent from heaven)."

"You are, Smiley. You are."

"Baby?" She said while holding my hand.

"Yes?"

"What's wrong?"

"What do you mean what's wrong?"

"Jason, what's wrong?"

I had to give her that, what you talk-in bout Willis' look.

"Baby, I know you." She did know me, and it wasn't working in my favor.

"Really, baby, it's nothing. I'm just a little tired; a call woke me, then I had to call Mom, and I got caught up talking to her."

"I'll take that for now, Jay. Here, I made you a smoothie. Something that can hold us until tonight. We have an hour and a half before we need to start getting ready. We don't have to be there exactly at 8. Let's lay down for a while, even if you don't go to sleep."

I must say, we looked great when we got dressed. I can't believe how perfect this shirt matched Nadia's dress.

"Baby, I'm so happy you bought me this dress." I absolutely love it. She did look amazing. She contemplated how to do her hair but decided to wear loose curls. She looked perfect. She didn't have to try hard at all.

We got to the party at about 8:45. Alex brought us; he was also invited. People were outside taking pictures. We pulled up and I walked around to open the door for Nadia. Her dress was so long she could have worn some fluffy bedroom slippers, and no one would have known the difference. Once we were out, Alex went to park the car. We took some pictures and had a small talk with a few people outside, while we made our way into the building. The decor was amazing. The decorator did her *thang*, money well spent.

"Look at how many people are here, Jay. This is such a great turnout, and they're still coming in."

We got a glass of champagne from one of the caterers walking around. We found our table. I had it set up with our parents, and then the tables next to us had our friends and siblings. I'm so glad everyone was able to make it.

"You guys look beautiful," Nadia's mom said.

"Thanks, Mom." We both said. Then we mingled a little and took some pictures. There were about three photographers who walked around, so no memories were missed. They came earlier before everyone started coming so they could take photos of the inside once it was set up and catch people as they entered.

"Jay, this is amazing."

"You are an awesome friend to help Chris pull this together."

"Stop acting like you didn't help."

"I know I did, but he asked you, and you did what you had to do."

"You're different." She said.

"They are not friends to me; they are family, and I'll give them the clothes off my back if I had to. Really and truly, I should be thanking Chris." I kissed her before she can ask me how and why and then went to get us a drink and some appetizers.

I was going to do it after we ate dinner, but I didn't want

to wait any longer. I found Chris, and we went over the plan. While I was walking back to the table, Chris walked out onto the dance floor. "Here, babe," I gave Smiley the drink and sat down. I sat next to my mom. She slid me the ring while Nadia was focused on Chris.

"Good night, everyone. I hope you're all having a wonderful time. I've been looking forward to this night, and I'm so glad everyone, plus some, came out. You all look amazing. I'm always looking for a reason to bring us together, but honestly, I couldn't have done it by myself. Jason, can you come here for a second?"

I got up and went to meet him. We hugged each other.

"Everyone, Jason is not just my friend but my brother, and I'm so grateful for him. Here, Jason, say something."

"Nah, Chris, I don't have to."

"Come on, Jason, okay, okay. Guys, thank you so much for coming out tonight and showing your support and unconditional love. It wasn't just me that made this night special; we all played a part. So, I know Chris wanted to make a toast, but before he did, I wanted to thank my lady for helping pull together this beautiful night. This is what true teamwork looks like. Baby, I mean Nadia, can you come here, please? It wouldn't be long." She had that look that said I'm going to kick ya ass. I knew she was shy, which I never understood because she was different in front of the crowd. I read her lips, and she told me she would get me for this, and I replied, "I love you."

Watching her step, she carefully made her way to Chris and me.

"So, everyone, this is my Nadia. Like I was saying, she also played a big part in this night coming together, so on behalf of us all, I wanted to say thank you." She started to blush.

I had written her a poem and practiced it every day, so I will know it by heart to recite it tonight. I was trying to figure out how to make my next move.

"Before we continue with our wonderful night, I want to add that today is also our Anniversary. I turned and looked at Nadia and said I was thinking that since we're expressing our gratitude, I want to share something with you, Nadia. Guys, please bear with me. I am the student that's trying to impress the teacher."

They laughed.

Taking a deep breath.

"Nadia:

You are a gift from God that I'll never return; every day that I'm with you,

there is something new that I learn.

You're like a breath of fresh air that I love to inhale; I have known sorrow for so long,

and you showed me that love still prevails.

In detail, let me explain.

From the beginning till the end, you are more than my lover; you are my friend.

You are not only beautiful on the outside, but you also possess the beauty of the spirit.

If I was to lose my sight today

I could still feel, hear, and see it

from the sound of your voice and the whispers of your tone, it sends chills through my spine, my heart you now own.

I have never known real love until I felt your delicate touch, mixed with your patience and your virtues; that is why I love you so much

You are the oxygen in my lungs that enables me to breathe

You are my own personal healer; you are a sigh of relief.

If I were to be on my dying bed, you would bring me back to life; you're filled with so much joy and energy, and you are the generator to my light

now that I have made it this far, I have written this for you.

I take no credit for it because you're just being you.

Happy Anniversary. I love you."

Everyone gave me a standing ovation. I'm pretty impressed that I wrote this; let me go ahead and brush my shoulders off.

"How did I do, baby?"

"Jason, that was beautiful!" She began to cry, "Baby, please don't cry." I hugged her. "Let me get you a chair so you can sit down." I grabbed a chair and put it in front of me. "Here, sit down." Grabbing some tissue, I got on one knee to wipe her face. I purposely put the mic out of her sight but where everyone could still hear.

"Nadia, I didn't mean to make you cry."

"You know I'm a crybaby.

Jay, get up. Why are you on your knees?"

"I just wanted to talk to you quickly before finishing the speech. Every word I wrote is true. You brought things out of me I didn't know existed. You were the missing piece of the puzzle in my life. I am complete now. You are my heart."

"Jay, I love you; I am proud of you. Every word of that poem was amazing." She kissed me. I got up.

"In front of everyone tonight, I'm telling you I love you! I love you today, tomorrow, always." The photographer was taking pictures. Our eyes locked on each other. "Chris, come here with your glass so we can make a toast. Let's toast to life. Let's toast to happiness, let's toast to strength, let's toast to friends, let's toast to family, and most of all, let's toast to love," I gave Chris the mic and walked over to Nadia, and I tripped just like we practiced, Chris ran over, and Nadia leaned in, "Are you okay?" Chris held the mic close to me, and I held the ring up. "Will you marry me?" I didn't know her eyes could stretch that big; her hands covered her mouth. I definitely surprised her. The room was silent; you could hear a mouse run across the room.

"Jayyyyyy, Yes! Yes! Yes!" I put the ring on her finger; "You love to make me cry, huh?"

"Yes! But only good tears. I love you so much, and I promise to always keep that smile on your face, Smiley." We kissed and everyone cheered.

"Congratulations to my brother and sister. Happy anniversary," Chris said. "Now, cheers." The DJ started playing 'Let's Get Married' by Jagged Edge. Everyone got up and started dancing. We got our share of hugs and congratulations. Her eyes were red when we finally sat down, "Let me guess, this was never about Chris, was it?"

"Nope."

"So, everyone knew what was going on?"

"Yep."

"Every single person? Wow! I never had anyone go out of their way to do anything like this for me."

"I'm not everyone. Remember the first time I saw you, and we were on the beach? What did I say?" She laughed, "Yes, you told me I was going to be your wife."

"Glad you remembered.

I'm going to be the first to do many things for you, so sit back and enjoy."

"That poem, though. Let me find out I have some competition."

"Hey, I learned from the best."

"This ring is beautiful too."

"I have one more surprise for you."

"Jay, please, no more surprises."

"Sorry, it's too late. We're going away tomorrow morning. The bags are already packed; we just have to go."

"Where are we going?"

"You will find out at the airport." We ate and enjoyed the night.

"On behalf of my fiancée and I, we would like to thank everyone for coming from near and far. To everyone who helped me pull this together and ensured it didn't fall apart, thank you, and I love you more than words can explain. Please eat and drink as much as you like and enjoy. I walked into this party with a girlfriend, and I am leaving with a fiancée. I can't wait for the next stage." We danced for a little.

"Jay, you want to sneak out?"

"Yeah, I was thinking the same thing. I'm going to call an Uber so Alex doesn't have to leave." "Maybe we should tell him at least." She suggested.

"I'll text him, let's go." Grabbing my hand, she led the way. "Let me get the door." As I opened the door for Nadia, I thought my eyes were playing tricks on me. Maybe I had too much to drink. I stopped right in my tracks. "Jay, what's wrong?" It was Tiffany, dressed to kill. "Babe, what's wrong? Why did you stop?"

"Let me come out of the building." Still holding her hand, I proceeded to walk out. "Goodnight, Jason." You guys are having a party and didn't bother to invite me? She dressed like she was trying to get someone's attention. Makeup and hair done.

"Tiffany! What are you doing here?"

"What do you mean? I came to party." I felt Nadia squeezing my hand. I knew she wasn't happy, and neither was I, but this was just the beginning. This is an invite-only party. I heard Chris and Mike come out asking if everything was okay. Apparently, someone standing outside saw what was going on and told them.

"So, I see you finally got her. I understand how you could fall for her; I would, too. She's beautiful."

"Tiffany, you need to leave."

"Mike, it's cool; I didn't come to start any trouble."

My mom came rushing out.

"It doesn't seem that way. You shouldn't be here." I saw the Uber car pull up.

She smiled, "Hi, Mrs. McKnight. Did Jason tell you guys the great news?" My mom looked at me with concern. "Listen, Tiffany, Jason has moved on and is clearly happy with his life. You should try doing the same." Now, it takes a lot for my sisters to say anything or get involved, and the fact that Janae said something means that they won't let this get too far before they snap.

"Tiffany, I don't have time for you and your childish games. My fiancée and I are on our way out."

"Fiancé, huh, so is that what we're celebrating? How does your fiancée feel about being a stepmother?"

I heard Eboni in the background, "What the fuck is she talking about, Jason?"

Nadia had let go of my hand, "Yes, Jason, what exactly is she talking about?"

"Aww, he didn't tell you we have a son together?" Everything became a blur; I felt like my head was spinning, and my heart was racing. I can't believe she just did that! What the hell am I supposed to say? Jade and Eboni had to be held back from trying to knock Tiffany's ass out!

"Jason! Did you hear me?"

"Yes, baby, let me explain."

"See, that's the thing; there shouldn't be anything to explain." She couldn't hold back the anger.

"I'm leaving."

"I'm coming with you."

"No! You should stay here and figure your life out."

"Baby, please wait!" She got in the car and drove off. Fuck! I'm so pissed off right now. I had to keep it together. I can't let Tiffany get the satisfaction.

"Chris, Eric, Mom, Mike, someone get her out of here before I say or do something I will regret."

"I'll leave. I tried to work something out with you, Jason baby, but you didn't want to listen and play by my rules. I'll be waiting for your call. Smooches."

I had to gather my thoughts. I apologized to everyone and then asked Mike to gather Nadia's and my immediate family and friends, and I explained everything to them.

"She called me hours before we were to come here. I wasn't trying to ruin our anniversary and honestly, I don't believe her. I planned to tell Nadia in the morning about everything while we were going to the airport. I didn't think Tiffany would come here. I don't even know how she knew about tonight."

"Jason, if she was stalking and doing everything you said she was doing, I wouldn't be surprised that she came here or how she heard about it; plus, you are a pretty popular guy."

"That's true, but I still want to apologize for this."

"Forget apologizing to us; you better go home to your fiancée and get things right."

"Thanks, Dad."

Alex went and got the car. "Please, guys stay and have fun. If not for me, for Nadia."

I jumped in the truck. I called Nadia five times, no answer. I hope she went to my house. Just to be on the safe side, I stopped at her house first. I went in and searched the house, and she wasn't there. We pulled up to my house. Alex is spending the night so he can take us to the airport later.

"Thank you so much for everything." I said to Alex.

"Are you guys still going?"

"I hope so. Come in and get some rest. We will see what happens in the morning."

I ran into the house. "Nadia! Nadia!" I looked in our room. She was not in there. What the fuck? I went to the living room, but still, she was nowhere in sight. I started to get worried. Where can she be? Is she okay? I called her again. I heard her phone ringing. I followed the sound; she was lying down in the backyard on the swing, still fully dressed. She loves that swing. We sat there many times and watched the sunset. It looked like she had a drink right out of the bottle! The bottle was laying on the swing and the liquor was dripping out.

"Baby, baby, wake up. Nadia, wake up." I saw the dry tear marks on her face. She looked different; she looked sad. Her pulse felt low. I grabbed her phone and called 911.

Oh god, please. Don't let me lose her. I called Alex so he could open the door for the ambulance. I didn't want to leave her side. I held her hand and said, "I'm so sorry, Nadia, baby, I'm so sorry, please don't leave me." I cried.

The ambulance came, and we were rushed to the hospital, where I had to make the dreadful phone calls.

The End